# LOXLEY

When Harry Loxley, the 11th Duke, is called away to the Western Front, he leaves behind his young wife Bronwyn to run the estate and cope alone with her formidable mother-in-law, Katherine the Dowager. Aware her marriage is already in trouble, Bronwyn finds herself increasingly drawn to the life of Nell, the 5th Duchess of Loxley and guardian of its ancient walls, at a time when the country was engaged in a bloody Civil War. What is Nell's secret, and why is her tortured ghost said to haunt the Hall? Bronwyn's search for answers reveals parallels with her own life that she could never have imagined . . .

Books by Sally Wragg
Published by The House of Ulverscroft:

MAGGIE'S GIRL
PLAYING FOR KEEPS

SALLY WRAGG

---◆---

# LOXLEY

*Complete and Unabridged*

**ULVERSCROFT**
*Leicester*

First published in Great Britain in 2013

First Large Print Edition
published 2014

A catalogue record for this book is available
from the British Library.

ISBN 978–1–4448–2187–1

Published by
F. A. Thorpe (Publishing)
Anstey, Leicestershire

Set by Words & Graphics Ltd.
Anstey, Leicestershire
Printed and bound in Great Britain by
T. J. International Ltd., Padstow, Cornwall

This book is printed on acid-free paper

To Olivia with Love
A fellow Strutty-Bangar

Everyone suddenly burst out singing;
And I was filled with such delight
As prisoned birds must find in freedom,
Winging wildly across the white
                    Siegfried Sassoon
                    April 1919

# 1

'May the Lord add His blessing to the reading of His word . . . '

Sunshine was pouring through the dining room window which was open, allowing access to a large bumblebee from the honeysuckle on the wall of the West Wing which had grown in such profusion this year. Katherine, Dowager Duchess of Loxley, born Lady Katherine Trippett, daughter of Lord Trippett of Milne, lifted an imperious hand and wafted the insect away from the family bible, open on its plinth by the table. Watching her with a hint of amusement in her lively dark eyes, Bronwyn, her daughter-in-law, conjectured that if only she, Bronwyn, could be so easily dispersed, Katherine would be delighted. How her dear mother-in-law hated the liaison between Henry, her precious son, otherwise known as Harry, eleventh Duke of Loxley, and — following his father's death the year before — last in line of a proud and noble family, and Bronwyn, younger child of Owen Colfax, an impoverished, if kindly, country doctor. So much a mismatch as to be beyond the old termagant's understanding.

Bronwyn would never, ever be forgiven for marrying Harry for all too clearly in Katherine's eyes, Harry was clear of any blame.

'And may the Lord bring the world back to its senses!' Thus succinctly casting her disapproval on the state of European affairs, Katherine concluded morning prayers, shutting the Bible with a resounding thump and treating Bronwyn, meanwhile, to a haughty stare. Was she a mind reader too? Her mother-in-law was many things, her mind like a terrier worrying all that passed through it. The comparison was too much. Bronwyn lowered her head, relieved her sense of humour, at least, was still in good shape. Unmindful of its peril, the bee buzzed perilously close to Katherine's head. One of the parlour maids, a new girl, clamped her hand to her mouth and smothered a laugh.

Soames, the butler, inhaled sharply. There'd be trouble downstairs. Straightening her face, Bronwyn shot the girl a warning glance. Harry helped himself to the kedgeree and, amongst the bustle of servants dismissed to their own breakfasts, the family sat down to their meal. Whatever else was wrong with her husband's life — and, as Bronwyn was only just beginning to admit, with his marriage too — it hadn't yet affected his appetite. They'd married because they loved each other. He must love her to have defied his mother! But had things turned out as she'd so innocently assumed when first they'd embarked on this union? Six months was so little time to find out she was already full of regrets.

'Anything in the papers?' Katherine enquired, toying with her toast, beckoning Soames to pour coffee. Mindful that her frame was inclined to spread, she ate sparsely. A large and powerful woman, her luxuriant copper hair with its sprinkling of grey was swept to the top of her head, in accordance with the fashion at the end of the century in which she was still so firmly rooted. Her royal-blue day dress, with its outdated high collar, rustled in anticipation. Katherine was as keen to know the news as Bronwyn.

Harry took the paper from the tray by his plate and unfolded it, frowning over the headlines. 'Asquith declines to assure Germany of our neutrality,' he read out, glancing up and looking troubled, though it could have been no more than he expected. Since a Serb-sponsored terrorist had assassinated the heir to the Austro-Hungarian Empire, too many European powers were looking to feather their own nests, Britain included.

'How can we stay neutral when it's so wrong?' Bronwyn protested, unable to keep her opinion to herself. She stopped, embarrassingly aware she might have committed yet another faux pas.

But her father had always encouraged her to speak her mind! She took heart. Why shouldn't she say what she thought? Pink-cheeked, she pressed on, encouraged by Harry's small, tight smile of approval. 'There will be war anyway. Surely Germany's gone too far?'

'They might think twice if they realise we mean it!' Harry put down the paper and picking up his knife and fork, attacked his breakfast with gusto. 'If it comes to it, we'll give them a bloody nose. It'll be over by Christmas.' He spoke through mouthfuls of food.

'So long?' Katherine murmured dryly.

'It's true then, we will go to war.' Colour flooded Bronwyn's face. But she'd hate it! Harry would go away and they'd never have the chance to sort out their problems! Refusing to think of the danger he'd put himself in, appetite deserting her, she pushed her plate away. Her eyes fastened helplessly on his. 'You'll join up, I take it?'

'He'll have no choice,' Katherine cut in sharply, her voice a curious mixture of pride and a fear even Bronwyn could see she was struggling to keep at bay. Harry was her son and she was proud of him but she worried for him too. Of course he'd fight! He was a Loxley, body and soul for King and Country, but was it only the thoughts of this made him so determined? Why did Bronwyn feel there was something else of which, as yet, she was unaware?

'It may not get so far.' The bright smile she loved him for, illuminated her husband's face. He finished his breakfast, draining his coffee cup before turning to his mother. 'Georgina's expected?' he enquired, deftly turning the conversation. Difficulties. Evasion. It was one way of dealing with Katherine. Sunlight was streaming through the window, catching the gold threads in his hair. He brushed crumbs from his moustache and Bronwyn's heart constricted. If anything should happen to him . . .

'This afternoon hopefully, though I don't expect she'll think to bring little Eddie.'

Katherine's voice held a surprising hint of disapproval. Landing the son of an Earl in her debutante season, albeit the youngest of four, and already starting her family, Georgina, Harry's sister, could do no wrong other than keeping her baby son from his doting grandmamma. Given Bronwyn had yet shown no signs of conceiving, this was another department in which she was deemed to have failed. It was a point of issue with Harry too, to which Katherine's longing only added fuel. Of course both Bronwyn and Harry wanted children. The succession to Loxley at stake, Bronwyn was only too well aware she should quickly become pregnant. It wasn't even for lack of trying. Her nightmare was it was somehow all her fault . . .

Her wistful gaze wandered to the window and the terraced gardens beyond, already baking in the sunshine. If she inclined forwards slightly, she could even see the river Lox and the ruins of the old Hall where Nell, Loxley's colourful fifth Duchess, had first had visions of building this splendidly opulent palace in which they now sat. But how sad the old place had been allowed to fall into such a tumbling state of disrepair, its broken and ivy-clad turrets fingering the sky as if in accusation of their lot. A monument to the Loxley name, as Katherine never tired of reminding her.

'Bronwyn, you're miles away.' Harry spoke gently, sounding amused.

At the sound of his voice, she jumped up and, without thinking, began to side the dishes. At home she'd always helped her mother with chores. Indeed, with Tilly the only servant her father's pay would run to, helping out had been a necessity.

Katherine's sharp intake of breath brought

her sharply to her senses, shattering her complacency. Bronwyn froze, too late realising she'd committed yet another gaffe. At once, Soames glided across the room and, leaving it unclear whether servant or mistress was the more affronted, delicately removed the plates from her nerveless fingers. He stalked away, leaving Bronwyn staring helplessly after him and wishing she was anywhere other than here, at Loxley, where she was always so out of place. Her gaze shifted to Harry only to see his expression as shocked as Katherine's. But why must they look at her so when she'd only sided a few pots!

Anger, slowly simmering, finally burst to the fore.

'I'm beginning to wonder if my mother wasn't right. We should never have married, Harry!' she cried hotly, irretrievably.

Katherine's snort of anger was too much. If she stayed longer she'd only say more and make things a whole lot worse. Throwing her husband a look part anger, part anguish, even then wondering why he didn't rush after her to beg her to stay, she hurried from the room.

★   ★   ★

The Estate Manager's cottage was, as usual at this time in the morning, a bustle of activity.

'Mind! Mind!'

'Of course I don't mind, mother!' With wicked disregard for the tray of eggs her mother was carrying across the kitchen, Ursula Compton seized hold of her, spinning her round to plant a warm kiss on her cheek. 'And how are we this bright and beautiful morning, mother, dear?'

'For goodness sakes child!' Despite herself, Mary's laughter rang through the house, a plump, good-natured woman with a pleasant face. Righting the tray with a surprising dexterity, she found herself thinking on her Tom's warning. Their Ursula was spoilt and needed a firmer hand. But who spoilt her more than her father? was Mary's slant, for which the poor man never had an answer.

'Morning, grandfather!' Like a whirlwind, Ursula ran across the flagged floor to fling her arms round the old man who sat, collarless and in his shirt sleeves, by the corner of the hearth, slurping, with relish, the tea he'd just poured into his saucer.

'It never is,' he grumbled, good-naturedly, turning sightless eyes her way but seeing her all too well, in his mind's eye. 'No need to ask how you are this morning!' he retorted, waspishly.

'Don't encourage her, dad!' Disregarding the cataracts that had taken her father-in-law's sight when their Ursula was only a little girl, Mary shot him a warning glance. Generally the family took no notice of its oldest member's blindness and that was exactly the way he liked it. She put the eggs on the table, fetched the cutlery from the drawer and made a start on laying the table.

'I've no time for breakfast,' Ursula murmured, treating the old man to one last hug before skipping back across the kitchen. She reached for an apple from the bowl on the table.

'You're not leaving without breakfast!' Mary retorted flatly, shooing her away.

'Why, what's up? Art courtin' again?' Ned Compton chuckled, dropping easily into the dialect of his youth when the ninth Duke had first taken him on as a raw young lad. He'd worked his way up to Estate Manager, a job for which his son, Tom, had long ago succeeded him. The Comptons were a canny lot. They'd done well for themselves. He nodded happily, enjoying the opportunity to keep up to mark with his granddaughter's life.

'I might be courting! You'd best ask Freddie . . . ' she returned, eyes twinkling.

'Yon's been sweet on you long enough,' Ned observed. But everyone knew young Fred Hamilton was sweet on their Ursula. It would be a good match too, Fred being the only son and sure to inherit the farm one day. Raith Hamilton was getting on and the union would keep their Ursula close to home. No-one could blame Ned for being pleased.

'Leave her alone, dad,' Mary answered, sharply for her, crossing the kitchen to fetch his cup and refilling it from the teapot she always kept warmed on the stove.

Taking advantage of the diversion, Ursula darted forward and, seizing an apple, ran outside before Mary had a chance to stop her.

'You'll catch it, my girl!' she shouted after her.

Her daughter's laughter floated through the open doorway.

Outside, Tom Compton was deep in conversation with Reuben Fairfax, the estate gamekeeper. Both men looked worried. They were surely talking about the war — all anyone seemed to talk about nowadays! Biting into her apple, Ursula's high spirits sobered, if only momentarily. Things must be bad if these two most unlikely of confidants were passing the time of day. Reuben Fairfax didn't talk to anyone much, least of all to her easy-going father. Mindful her father had seen her, signified by the amiable hand he flapped in her direction, she slowed to a sedate walk, maintaining it until she reached the gate through onto the road where sight of her slim figure, demurely dressed this morning in navy-blue pinafore and plain blouse, would be obscured by the high stone wall skirting the grounds of the cottage.

The scent of wild rose and jasmine drifted from the hedgerow. But why must life be carried on at half a pace! Unmindful of her mother's warning that she was always to walk and as sedately as possible, Ursula's pace quickened. Shortly, she broke into a run and as she ran, stretching out her lithe, young limbs, she struggled with the thought of exactly what her life here on the estate was like. Not as free as she would like it but freer than it might be. She was lucky, she supposed.

She slowed again, tossing the apple core into a blackthorn hedge, startling the black-bird roosting there and then walking on, a little out of breath, up to the brow of the hill, her eager gaze already seeking Freddie who was spending the week stonewalling in the fields below. Behind her the sun was already rising into a cloudless blue sky, shining gold threads over the towers of the New Hall and the fields of corn which were already ripe for harvesting and of which the estate largely comprised. A few sheep, a prize herd of cattle. The new Duke was determined to sort out what had been a tangled state of affairs when he'd inherited it. Tom Compton said the old man had been a maverick who'd run down the estate and Harry Loxley would do well to look to the future. Ursula smiled happily. For the moment, her future was Freddie whom she loved more than life itself, even if she'd die rather than admit it, even to Freddie.

She'd reached the edges of the estate. Sloping fields dotted with sheep, tugging at stubble baked dull gold by the long, lazy summer. Dry as tinder, her father said and needing 'nowt' but a spark to set it alight. Ursula's eyes widened, falling greedily on the familiar figure, stooping low by a gap in one of the limestone walls which criss-crossed the fields like patchwork. With a whoop of delight, she hitched up her skirts and began to run, too quickly gathering speed into a giddy descent in which her laughter reached him long before the rest of her.

At the sound of it, Freddie straightened up, his suntanned face splitting into a wide grin. Lively blue eyes with more than a hint of devilment, a prominent nose broken fighting with the village lads. Not a handsome face but one worth a second glance. Plenty of village lasses had cast more than a longing look in Freddie Hamilton's direction, a fact of which Ursula was only too well aware. He stood braced against her descent, laying willing hands on her waist before swinging her round and pulling her close to drop a kiss on the tip of her nose. Wanting more but not daring, she mused, laughing provokingly up at him.

His grip tightened. 'I'd given you up,' he groaned.

'I couldn't get away.'

Not sure of the kiss nor if she should have given him opportunity, Ursula tilted her head the better to look up at him, guessing at once he was in one of his more troublesome moods.

'Made your mind up to marry me yet?' he teased, meaning it all the same and betrayed by the longing springing into his eyes. Ursula jumped back quickly.

'Stop it this minute!' she commanded him. 'You shouldn't joke. If my mother had the slightest idea . . .'

'I'm not asking your mother!'

'You know what I mean!'

'She'd have me guts for garters and hang 'em on the washing line to dry!'

'She would too,' she answered hotly, colour rising to her cheeks and brightening her eyes.

'I wasn't joking, Ursula.' Freddie's voice lowered and took on a wheedling note. Longing to pull her into his arms again, yet too aware she'd only slap his face, he braved another step towards her. 'If the Kaiser won't budge, I shall join up,' he coaxed, enjoying the flicker of alarm in her eyes his suggestion provoked. 'I shall have to do my bit, Ursy. You'll not let me go so far away and still

13

unanswered?' It was grossly unfair to pressure her so but wasn't everything fair in love and war? Being in love with Ursula Compton, Freddie thought, was surely harder than any trouble this daft business in Europe could bring him.

The war again! Ursula pulled a face. Why must everyone go on about the war so, even Freddie! 'You think I've nothing better to do than hang around waiting?' she retorted, ill-temperedly, irritated he wouldn't drop the subject when she'd so been looking forward to seeing him. Yanking the head from a nearby daisy, she strolled nonchalantly away to sit, deceptively calm, legs dangling on a section of the wall already repaired. In truth, she was troubled by the perplexing problem of why Freddie's world should be expanding whilst hers remained so stubbornly con-stricted. 'It isn't fair,' she muttered crossly. But life wasn't fair, she'd long since realised. Nor was it fair to fall in love, only to have the object of her affection snatched away before she'd made up her mind whether she wanted him or not!

'It'll only last a matter of weeks,' he coaxed, heaving himself up beside her and edging as near as he dared, which wasn't anywhere as near as he wanted.

'Why should you have all the fun?' She frowned, unable to drop the matter. 'I hate

14

being a girl. It's so . . . so inhibiting!' She struggled after the right word. Freddie shook his head, not sure whether to laugh, then catching the look on Ursula's face and quickly deciding against it. Her gaze widened. 'Remember the dancing classes I started in Nottingham last week?' she demanded, her ill humour, in its usual way, vanishing as quickly as it had arisen. 'I never got there. I went to a suffragettes' meeting instead. They reckon women can do anything every bit as good as a man!' There'd been a notice on the door of the church hall she'd passed. In her haste to follow the procession of women inside, she'd happily forgotten all about dancing. Hang dancing classes! As if she'd nothing better to do with her life than learn the quadrille!

'You'll catch it!' Freddie warned, shocked.

'The speaker said women should have the vote and that we all have a duty to make something of our lives!' she answered him.

'Hah!' His scorn stopped her in her tracks. 'Women can't push a plough or mine a seam of coal. Women can't go to war!'

'I would if I could, Freddie,' she retorted indignantly.

'You can't and that's that,' he answered her, flatly.

Freddie thought he'd got her where he wanted her, stuck at home whilst he went to

15

war and had all the fun. Heartlessly, Ursula crushed the flower between her fingers and dropped it to the ground. She'd known Freddie Hamilton forever and loved him for even longer but even she knew she'd nothing to compare him with. It wasn't right she had no experience of life! She jumped nimbly down, standing to gaze thoughtfully up at him. Mayhap it was all talk. The war would never happen. Freddie would stay here all his life, working his farm, settling down and raising a family . . . Would it be with Ursula? That was the question. For the minute, she didn't care one way or the other. He jumped down after her, sidling nearer and, good humour fully restored, she pushed him away before spinning quickly out of his reach. Ignoring his cry of frustration, the yearning in his voice, her laughter trailed after her as she streaked off up the field.

★　★　★

Wretchedly, Bronwyn realised her mother had been right all along. She and Harry had grown so far apart; they'd never be able to work things out! Feeling herself in need of solitude, if only to calm her racing thoughts, she hurried down the stone steps onto the lawns, steeling herself meanwhile not to look back to the house where she knew Harry was watching her through his dressing-room window. She'd upset him but he'd upset her too.

A dusty track dissecting the meadows beyond the house invited her down to the bridge which forded the Lox. The river was prone to flooding in winter-time and, according to Harry, who liked to tell her these things, it was one of the reasons why Nell Loxley had built the New Hall in the first place. The ruins of the old building, a crumbling pile of darkened stone and ivy more suited to her mood, crouched low against the hillside, drawing her nearer, though she'd never meant to walk this far. Tugging herself free from a thorn bush which snagged at her skirt, spurred on by the piping cry of swallows swooping low through the gaping windows with an ease suggesting long practice, she scrambled down the bank and struck out towards it.

Despite the heat of the day, Bronwyn shivered. On winter evenings Harry said the servants loved to scare each other silly with tales of Nell Loxley's ghost still haunting this place. Blatant tomfoolery, no doubt, but no-one could argue, given Nell had survived the turbulence of the Civil War, that she hadn't lived in troubled times. Perhaps her ghost did wander here, demanding sanctuary! Katherine had proved surprisingly reticent on the subject; Bronwyn had to wait for Harry to tell her the local gossip that Loxley's illustrious Fifth Duchess had also been unhappy in love. It left her with a strange feeling of empathy for the woman, so she longed to find out more.

The hot, dank smell of water was overpowering. Passing under the lintel of a tilting doorway, she emerged into a courtyard nature had long since reclaimed. Coarse grasses thrust upwards from under the flagstones. Brambles and ivy dripped from the crumbling walls. What must this place have looked like in its heyday, she wondered, disconcertingly feeling hemmed in, as if the walls were closing in on her, bringing with them the sound of laughter and voices, long since departed this life. She stood, almost mesmerised and staring upwards to the shattered roof through which the sunshine streamed; remembering the first time she'd ever met Harry . . .

★　★　★

Bronwyn hung back, embarrassingly afraid to mount her horse, a fiery little mare she'd taken an instant dislike to.

'She'll settle once we're off,' Robert Colfax murmured complacently. He swung up onto his horse, shooting her a look of amusement touched by exasperation he had such a milk-sop for a sister. The day was cold and dry, the ivy-clad front façade of the New Hall burnished russet and gold in the bright autumnal sunshine. They were ready for the off, the scarlet jackets of the Loxley hunt standing out vividly amongst the usual mixture of servants and onlookers who'd turned up to see them off. Was that why Bronwyn, young and inexperienced as she was, felt so out of place?

A large man with a red face climbed up onto a huge brindle bay nearby, causing her to jump back. She'd never liked horses much but Robbie had insisted that this opportunity was too good to miss. Fresh air, the thrill of the chase. Monty Palliser, son of a local landowner and one of Robbie's circle of friends from Oxford, was a member of the Loxley hunt. He had horses to spare. Naturally he'd suggested Robbie join him, bringing his young sister with him too, if he'd like. At the time, Bronwyn hadn't been able to think of a single reason why she shouldn't go. If her parents had never been able to run to the expense of a horse, they had at least ensured their daughter had lessons enough to handle herself. It would be a change from the round of carefully chaperoned tennis parties and dances, her mother, ever-practical, pointed out. Seeing the prancing beast she was expected to ride had quickly cooled Bronwyn's sense of adventure.

'Hurry up, Bron!' Robbie's horse edged sideways, allowing its rider opportunity to talk to Monty. Shortly the two men were deeply engrossed in conversation. Bronwyn frowned, wondering what had happened to his promise to look out for her.

'Don't worry. You'll be perfectly safe,' a man's voice murmured. A nice voice, exuding calm and reassurance, she decided. She spun round, attaching it quickly to a slim man with a thatch of neatly trimmed blond hair who was standing nearby. She frowned, wondering if she recognised him. But then he smiled and she couldn't help but smile back. It was that sort of a smile and it seemed so churlish not to.

'I'd love to join you but as you can see . . .' He glanced down to his arm, which she saw now was resting in a sling; the result of a fall, he told her. His free hand caught the reins, whilst his head drew close to murmur softly into the horse's ear. A man apparently used to horses Bronwyn discerned, for at once, the wretched beast calmed. If only the same could be said of its rider! Tentatively, Bronwyn lifted her foot into the stirrup and hoisted herself up, perching awkwardly side-saddle before accepting the reins he proffered.

'I'll see you at the Ball later, I hope?' The expression in his eyes held more than a simple invitation. Her interest turned too quickly to disappointment. Unfortunately, attending the Ball had never been part of their agenda and, given she'd never had pretensions to be other than she was, a simple country girl with a smattering of education and an odd yearning she didn't understand for a change in her life, she wouldn't have it any other way.

She was tempted to tell him the truth. 'I'm afraid the Ball's far too grand for me!' she scoffed, keeping her tone light and hiding her discomposure in leaning forwards to stroke her horse's mane. Unlike Robbie who'd had the benefit of college and who'd grown less inhibited by his background, Bronwyn's life remained firmly rooted in the small provincial Midlands town from which they hailed. She read widely, anything she could lay her hands on. She helped her father in the surgery when she could coax him into it. Despite it, marriage to a professional man with a home and children, if she was lucky, was the most she hoped for. Hobnobbing with the members of the hunt, most of them above her socially, had never been her idea of fun.

It appeared he wasn't about to give up so easily. 'Please say you'll come. You'll outshine any woman there,' he pleaded softly. 'The new Duke's easy enough to talk to, if you're worried. You might enjoy yourself more than you think.'

Something in his smile at last jogged her memory. Bronwyn's grip on her reins tightened, a hot tide of anger rising, staining her face. Why, now she remembered! She'd seen a picture of this man opening a new wing to the local cottage hospital, in the paper only last week.

'But you are the Duke!' she retorted, indignantly.

At once he looked shamefaced. 'I'm sorry. That was unfair. But who ... what I am ... you wouldn't believe how it gets in the way! Please ... Change your mind?' His eyes softened so he'd seemed, after all, only a man and an oddly endearing one at that.

The Master of the Hunt was already blowing his horn, sending a steady stream of horses filing out of the stable yard and down onto the meadows and the fields and woods beyond. Cheers, cat-calls, clattering hooves ringing bright sparks against the flagstones. Throwing him a hasty glance, too confused at the moment to answer him one way or the other, she'd steered the little mare away, aware and already regretting, that in all probability, she'd never see him again. But he

22

was a Duke — and what could he possibly see in her! She must have been mistaken, misinterpreted what in anyone else she'd have known for a barely concealed attraction.

Thoughts of the invitation, seemingly so genuinely offered, refused to leave her, fuelling her disappointment; so that when, miraculously unscathed, she returned to the stable yard later that morning, at once she looked round for him, only to realise wretchedly that he was nowhere in sight. Her disappointment, so overwhelming, told her she simply had to see him again. Was that why, later that evening, she'd allowed herself to be swallowed up in a crowd of excited young folk, bent on dancing; Monty's mother in accompaniment and acting as chaperone?

One look in her wardrobe beforehand had nearly put her off the idea. A dress she'd had made for her parents' wedding anniversary had sufficed in the end, the best of a sorry choice Tilly had brightened with fresh ribbons she'd fortuitously bought on her last trip to market.

At the sight of the Duke, almost a dream figure to her now, standing in Loxley's vast entrance hall to greet his guests, Bronwyn, inexplicably overcome with nerves, nearly took flight. Next to him was a formidable-looking woman whom Robert whispered was the Dowager, his mother. There was nothing for it but to sink into a low curtsey.

'Your Grace,' she murmured, vexed to discover her voice was shaking and yet still gratifyingly aware of the way his face lit up. She was undone, consumed by her own emotions and the feeling, like fire, running the length of her veins as he leaned towards her, taking her hand in his one good hand and kissing it gently. Regardless of the crowd around, he moved closer.

'I'm so glad you changed your mind,' he said, his breath fanning her face.

'Was there doubt?' she responded steadily and deciding at once it was no use pretending. She was attracted to him and, wonderfully, it appeared, he was attracted to her. She was torn away, swept along with the crowd into the ballroom which was already thronging and where she refused countless offers to take to the dance floor until, duty done, he sought her out.

Regardless of curious looks, so many tinged by envy, he laid a proprietorial hand on her arm, guiding her through the press of bodies and the too-hot room, into the quiet of the orangery where supper was laid out. Here, they found a dark corner to sit and talk, endlessly, about what, now, she had no idea, only that he'd wanted her opinions on

24

everything. Bronwyn had always had plenty of opinions. The evening flew by.

She'd never met anyone like Harry Loxley. A man who took what he wanted and, this happening to be Bronwyn, literally, he swept her off her feet. It was fortuitous the Dowager, his mother, had no idea how often after that night her son visited the villa next to the surgery where Bronwyn lived with her parents. After that first heady visit, so shocking to her mother, he spent whatever time there he could, always carefully chaperoned by her mother, of course. How passionate he'd been, overriding her father's suspicions and even her mother's quiet reticence. Dorothea Colfax, with her sturdy good common sense, had plenty to say on the matter. 'Bronwyn, you're out of your depth. Think of the life he leads! You haven't a chance of fitting in . . . '

Bronwyn had been altogether too much in love to heed the warning and worse, too easily convinced by Harry that together, they could overcome anything, even his mother. Nevertheless, he was the one who'd borne the brunt of Katherine's wrath and, such a dominating force as she so obviously was, Bronwyn could only imagine it. But Harry was stubborn too and if Katherine Loxley had an Achilles heel, it was her son. He wanted Bronwyn. He'd have no-one else! Finally, even Katherine had to accept the futility of argument, typically then taking charge and sweeping all before her, even Bronwyn. Church service, wedding dress, guests, all fell to her capable hands as if it was what she'd wanted for her precious son, all along.

She might have fooled the county. She hadn't fooled Bronwyn!

By the time the honeymoon was over, Katherine's mood had settled into a furious anger, at odds with her stoical determination to make the best of a bad lot. Harry was married. She'd been left with no alternative but to go along with his plans. A woman at war with her feelings. Bronwyn was sorry for it and worse, left to deal with it on a daily basis, she was even sorrier for herself.

Bronwyn leaned back against an interior wall, staring upwards toward the sunlight streaming through the shattered roof, over-come by an odd smell of lavender, instantly reminding her of home and her mother who loved all things lavender. Common sense had begun to kick in. Surely, life wasn't as bad as she was making out? She loved Harry. Given the differences in their upbringings there was nothing so certain than they'd been bound to meet problems.

'Bronwyn, there you are! What are you doing down here?'

It was Harry, smiling contritely, his face swimming into view, though she was aware his expression also held a lingering resentment over her unforgiveable behaviour at breakfast. Despite all he'd attempted to teach her, she'd proved she could still behave like a provincial middle-class housewife. She returned his smile, relieved at least to see him away from the house and Katherine, the cause of so much of their trouble.

'What's wrong, Bron?' he asked, drawing nearer.

'I needed some fresh air. I'm sorry, Harry, I shouldn't have rushed off.'

He held out his hand and she took it gratefully, her spirits lifting as she followed him out between the piles of broken masonry and into the heat of the mid-morning sun. It warmed her bones, making her feel better at once. Together, they scrambled back up the bank, walking part-way along the bridge before Harry stopped, turning to rest his arms on the fretwork and gaze down to the swirling waters beneath. She lingered beside him, resting her hands against his, feeling the warmth of his skin; her mind, meanwhile, seizing on a problem she knew now they should have discussed long before this.

'I never realised things here would be so difficult, Harry,' she began, hesitantly.

He turned to face her, his eyes full of an encouraging sympathy.

'Mother's not helped. You've no need to tell me, Bron. I have eyes in my head.'

She nodded, unhappily. 'Your mother, the servants, even your friends! I'm out of my depth — you must know that!' She spoke truthfully and he was too honest to deny it.

'Of course things are difficult, darling. Given the circumstances, they could hardly be anything else. And I know I haven't been as supportive as I might. I'm afraid I never realised how much the estate would be a drain on my time.' He straightened up, stroking his moustache and watching her thoughtfully. 'You must have noticed how we struggle? Death duties, overheads . . . Father didn't leave us well off, I'm afraid. He was always too close to Eddie to save money!'

Bronwyn knew George, the tenth Duke and Harry's father, had been amongst Edward VII's charmed inner circle of trusted friends. 'That must have had its difficulties,' she ventured uncertainly into another subject out of her remit. Harry bit his lip.

'Eddie enjoyed life and made sure father did, too. Cards, horses, gambling. Father would have died rather than admit he

28

couldn't keep up. We're still suffering the consequences.'

'But I'd no idea things were so bad,' she murmured, hurt he'd never yet chosen to tell her this when surely, she'd had a right to know? Some of his tension had relaxed.

'Mother will come round to the idea that cuts have to be made. All she cares about is Loxley.' At once, startling her, he seized her hands and pulled her close. 'If only you could fall pregnant, Bron. It would give her something positive to concentrate on. It would make such a difference, you wouldn't believe! I don't suppose . . . there is news yet?'

So that was the problem. Her unforgivable failure in this, her most important role of all. Sadly, she shook her head, wise enough to know the fact of providing an heir had placed too much emphasis on an act that should only have been about love. The knowledge lay, half formed in her mind, like the baby not yet conceived. She couldn't even put it into words.

'Has she been on about it, again?'

'Not exactly . . . '

'You mean she has!'

'She's bound to want the line ensured, Bron! That's what we all want, isn't it?'

She pulled away, stung by his insensitivity. Seemingly uncaring as to how much his words hurt, his gaze shifted back towards his precious Loxley. 'Given the way things are with the world, the succession's more important than ever,' he said.

He was worried about going away to fight and its possible consequences. Bronwyn took a steadying breath, instantly putting her own doubts aside.

'In the circumstances . . . Wouldn't a baby be an added complication?' she asked quietly.

'There's no biological reason you haven't told me about?' he muttered, ignoring her. He might as well have dealt her a blow.

'No! Of course not! Lord, Harry, how should I know?'

'I have to ensure the line, Bron. You surely understand so much?'

She understood nothing, only his indifference to her pain. Did he think their baby nothing to her? 'I'm not a brood-mare!' she snapped, her colour high. Worse, he'd allowed Katherine to think of her in this way too. It was unforgiveable.

They were as far away as ever from solving their problems. Miserably, feeling more alone than she'd ever felt in all her young life, she spun away out of his reach and headed swiftly back towards the house.

★　★　★

30

'I hope you've slept, Harry?' Unable to sleep herself, Katherine had risen early and was already at breakfast. It was the following morning. She cracked the top off her egg, her sharp eyes which missed so little, following her son into the room. Was he ailing? He'd never had much colour and neither had his father. She sighed heavily. Of Bronwyn, there was no sign.

'Well enough, mother.' He crossed to the sideboard and taking the coffee Soames poured, brought it back to the table to sit down opposite. Why reveal the truth he'd lain awake fretting over his marriage? he mused. Weren't things bad enough without telling her this too? He'd half a mind she'd guessed anyway. He threw her an exasperated glance.

'Paper not arrived yet?' he asked.

'The boy's late, your Grace,' Soames interjected, his glance wandering towards the door.

Harry nodded.

'If you would, there's a good man.'

Grateful for time alone with her son, Katherine waited for the door to close.

'Will it come to war?' she asked.

He nodded unhappily. 'There's no other course, I'm afraid.'

'Be careful,' she murmured quietly, shocking him, if only in the fact she expressed the

31

thought. Her hand dropped to his, resting so carelessly on the table. Warmth. Comfort. He was curiously touched. Even if he'd always known she loved him, too much if the truth were known, they'd never been a demonstrative family.

'Have you ever known me be anything else?' His tone was light, brimming with as much confidence as he could muster. At that moment, Bronwyn burst into the room, the morning's papers crushed in her hand.

'Have you seen the papers?' she demanded.

He took them from her, scanning the headline and then aware only of a great relief flooding upwards to illuminate his face. His gaze lifted, locking onto that of his wife's, any differences they might have fading into insignificance at this: what should have been the worse news of all if only now, unforgivably, he didn't see it as a chance of escape.

Already breaking her heart over it, Katherine read over his shoulder, her lips moving silently, as if in prayer. 'We choose the Path of Honour! Great Britain is at War . . .'

# 2

'I expect you've an early start tomorrow, Tom?' Katherine Loxley's voice was laced with unhappiness. Tomorrow was market day and, for lack of a good cowman, her son's herd of prize Friesians were set for slaughter. She turned, calling to the two gun dogs bounding, tongues lolling, across the front lawn.

'It's a crying shame, your Grace!' Tom answered, giving heated voice to his feelings — Katherine's too, if few would guess it — and only Tom because he'd known her longer than most. He stooped, fondling the ears of the first dog and giving her time to compose herself. She'd enough on without this, poor lass. Yesterday, the Loxley and Harringtons, Harry at their head, had marched out from their training camp high in the Derbyshire Peaks, towards the troop train stationed at Basely, destined for the docks and the ferry to the Front. No wonder she'd found it so hard to settle and that as soon as breakfast was over, she'd donned her coat and walking shoes and gone outside. Tom, who had seen her striding across the lawn, thought she'd

33

looked as if she'd all the troubles of the world on her capable shoulders. He straightened up and sighed. It was October, the time of harvest, of putting the year to bed and dwelling pleasurably on thoughts of the year to come. A time of year, more normally, he loved. So why did he feel so apprehensive now?

'We'll get through, your Grace,' he ventured cautiously, squashing his natural inclination to put a comforting arm around her shoulders. And yet, she was a mother, like any other and with as much cause for sorrow too, splendid as had been the sight of the marching men, brass buttons winking in the sunshine, snapping smartly to attention as their route took them past the Hall. A fit and fighting force on their way to the Front, transformed from the rabble of gardeners, estate workers and farming men of which they were largely comprised. And if it hadn't been for young Eddie, the gardener's lad, cycling home from the camp, where he'd gone in hope of catching a glimpse of his father, they'd have passed through and none been the wiser. As it was, the news had spread like wildfire. Doors flung wide as mothers, wives and children cascaded out to run helter skelter, towards the snaking procession. Even Bronwyn, Harry's wife, had dashed out, her hair unpinned, to stand shoulder to shoulder with laundry lass, housemaid and cook. Tom's gaze slanted towards Katherine, aware even then this woman had managed to stay aloof, battening down her emotions enough to remain indoors and watch events from an upstairs window.

The Schlieffen plan had failed. The German advance on Paris scattered at Marne to flight and entrenchment above the River Aisne and the twenty-five-mile stretch along the Chemin des Danes Ridge. Speculation was rife that both sides were scrambling north to the sea and control of the ports. What mother wouldn't be afraid, even this one, much as she strove to deny it?

The thought put into perspective Tom's present and more pressing preoccupation with the fate of Harry Loxley's herd. 'Shall I get on, then, your Grace?' he asked, quietly. Katherine Loxley nodded, her attention momentarily diverted by the sight of the motor which had appeared from the direction of the stables and Bronwyn, who'd ordered it for a visit to her parents, emerging down the front steps ready dressed for the journey.

As her daughter-in-law approached, Katherine allowed her gaze to fall speculatively to her waistline and remembering now, belatedly, the heated voices she'd heard from her son's quarters during his last leave home. Delicacy had forbidden she raise the subject though she wasn't normally so reticent. It didn't alter her opinion — if Harry was unhappy, Bronwyn was at fault. Brought up to sacrifice, appeasement, the bending of her will to the common good, Katherine could no more understand its lack in another than she could have sprouted wings and flown.

Bronwyn stooped to fuss one of the dogs which whined and snuffled at her hand.

She looked unhappy and was it any wonder, Tom thought.

'It's a nice day for a drive, miss, and it'll give you a chance to pass the herd as you go by,' he began, doing his best to sound cheerful and guessing, too late, he'd chosen the wrong subject and only somehow managed to make things worse.

The young woman's general air of unhappiness deepened.

'There's nothing other than they must be sold? But it's such a shame!' she retorted, echoing his own sentiments but in a manner which made him love her for it. Bronwyn Loxley knew as well as any how much the herd meant to her husband and how hard he'd worked to build it up. He'd be devastated and so, it appeared, was she. Tom tipped his cap to the back of his head and wished he could offer her some crumb of comfort.

'Every able-bodied man joined up, there's no-one else to look after them, miss . . . ' he ventured. 'If the men hadn't been allowed down from the hills to help with the harvest, the crop would have gone along with 'em too. We're in a pickle and there's no denying it.'

Bronwyn's gaze shifted to Katherine. 'There's no staff to be spared from the house, I take it?' she asked quietly and giving air to the one question Tom had longed himself to ask and hadn't dared.

Katherine's brows arched. 'We're stretched enough as it is,' she answered flatly. Her tone brooked no argument. Despite it, Tom took courage from the example set by this young slip of a lass by his side.

'Mayhap . . . We could take on an extra woman or two from the village?' he suggested tentatively and putting forward a solution he should have proffered long before now. 'There's no point taking women on only to lay them off again. Besides . . . ' Unexpectedly and distinctly un-Katherine like, her voice softened. 'Women tackling men's work would be tantamount to tempting fate, don't you agree? The war will be over before we know it. We've only to muddle through . . . '

Tom shot her a curious glance. The war

was making fools of them all, even Katherine it appeared, giving expression to the sort of claptrap he'd never heard from her before. His natural protest died, snuffed out by the reality that his employer's personality held a deep vein of pigheadedness and this was precisely the situation to bring out its worst. Katherine decreed the war would soon be over, so over it would be! He sighed, recognising it needed a stronger man than himself to tell her the truth.

'Harry will be so upset!' Bronwyn spoke heatedly, drawing a snort of derision from Katherine, telling her she'd strayed onto territory that was none of her business. To Katherine's mind, she should remain strong, maintaining a stiff upper lip at all times. Even though Bronwyn was now Duchess and Katherine in all effects moved sideways, the reality was of course, nothing had changed. Katherine ruled Loxley and everything she said went.

'He'll be alright, miss,' Tom murmured, misunderstanding the young woman's troubled gaze and touching her arm gently.

Calling to the dogs, Katherine climbed the steps to the house. Bronwyn Loxley smiled gratefully, surprised to find her eyes filling with tears. Tom Compton was a kind man and one she sensed wished her well. Life had been so hard, so much at odds of late; she took comfort from it. 'They'll all be alright, Tom,' she responded and giving air to words she might, with effort, even come to believe herself.

'Back before we know it — that's the ticket! Enjoy your ride, your Grace.' Tom touched his cap respectfully, a timely reminder if she needed it, that she, Bronwyn was Duchess of Loxley and must get used to the idea. Even if it was too late to save Harry's precious herd! Heavy-hearted, she climbed into the waiting car.

★ ★ ★

'Fetch another bag of flour from the store, Tilly, there's a good lass. My hands are all floured up.' Sifting the remaining flour from the kiln jar over the dough, Dorothea Colfax began to knead the day's bread, feeling some of the morning's tensions flow out through her capable fingers. No wonder Andrew had harnessed the pony and trap and gone out early on his rounds! No wonder she was left rushing from one task to another, giving her so little chance to think! Andrew was right. Keeping busy was best. Busy kept the mind from fretting over what was happening. The world gone mad. Everyone at each other's throats. Robert's regiment awaiting orders to go to the Front . . .

Her glance strayed fretfully to the morning's papers spread out on the table.

Not bothering to hide her displeasure, Tilly Rowbotham put down the bottle of Scrubb's ammonia with which she'd been cleaning the windows, climbed down from the chair and, chuntering quietly to herself, headed for the pantry. She'd washed and dried the best crockery, beaten the carpets and fettled the master's surgery, leaving it shining as brightly as the proverbial new pin. The old woman's tongue clicked in disapproval. Ordered about like any young chit of a girl when she'd been with Andrew Colfax, man and boy and his father before him too! Something in her mistress's face on her return, however, stilled her tongue so she placed the bag of flour on the table meekly enough.

At that moment, the back door opened and Bronwyn walked in. Her unprecedented gloom lifting, Dorothea flew round the table and threw her arms around her. 'Oh, darling, but it is wonderful to see you,' she murmured, letting go reluctantly and standing back to gaze at her in undisguised admiration. Her daughter was wearing a lilac silk coat, unbuttoned to reveal an ivory shirt of rich Venetian satin, looking as if she'd stepped straight from the pages of one of the Society magazines

Tilly had taken to reading of late. My but she did look a picture!

'There's nothing wrong, is there?' she demanded and noticing now how pale the child looked. Surely she wasn't sickening for something? And that waist was no more than a hand's span either or her name wasn't Dorothea Colfax . . .

'The Battalion's left for the Front!' Bronwyn replied quietly and immediately explaining all. 'Yesterday. Out of the blue. No-one had any idea. I guessed you'd want to know.'

Dorothea re-embraced her. 'Take your things off, darling, and sit down. We'll have a drink of tea,' she murmured, her voice laced with sympathy and also a hint of frustration. Tea and sympathy. There was little else she could offer.

'That'll be three cups we're wanting then?' Pique forgotten, beaming, Tilly lifted the kettle onto the hob, aware if anyone could lift her mistress's mood this morning, Bronwyn could.

★ ★ ★

'It was bound to happen sometime,' Dorothea mused, taking her daughter's cup to refill it. The two women had retired to the parlour with the tea tray, away from Tilly's constant interjections and her too-obvious delight in Bronwyn's wonderful marriage. That her mistress wasn't of a like mind went without saying. 'Despite such bad news, it is still wonderful to see you,' she went on, her homely features falling as she recollected all she'd read in the morning's papers concerning the progress of the war and which she'd been trying so desperately hard to forget. 'Your brother won't be long following either, I'm afraid.'

'Oh, goodness, and here's me going on about Harry when there's Robert too!' Bronwyn's cup rattled in its saucer. Her thoughts had been so centred on Harry she'd hardly given poor Robert a thought. But her mother must be feeling every bit as bad!

'He's safe, if only temporarily,' Dorothea reassured her, which was the most, the older woman reflected, anyone could hope for in these troubled times. She sat back, considering her daughter speculatively. Bad as it was Harry going, she was sure there was something else troubling the lass.

Aware of both the look and her mother's reasoning powers, Bronwyn frowned. She'd made a promise to herself before she'd set off. She had to talk to someone and who else if not her mother? 'Harry couldn't have gone at a worse time. Things between us are . . . difficult . . . ' she admitted, unsure quite how else to describe the unbridgeable differences which had emerged between herself and her new husband, engineered, she suspected, by their respective upbringings. 'Even now, when he's been away so much,' she continued wretchedly. 'I'm beginning to think . . . hard as I try . . . Oh mother! I'm sick of bridge and riding to hounds and as for the house parties . . . Don't they care there's a war on?'

'Goodness, it doesn't sound like it!' Dorothea exclaimed, sounding shocked. Bronwyn sipped her tea, taking time to consider the improbabilities of life at Loxley and the unpalatable fact that there was nothing Katherine wouldn't criticise her for. 'Remember your position!' her mother-in-law had hissed, on more than one occasion. What the old termagant had thought of yesterday's behaviour when the men had gone hardly needed stating. She wasn't the only one either. Bronwyn's unhappy gaze rose to her mother's, seeing again Harry's affronted expression at the embarrassing spectacle of his wife rushing from the house in such a dishevelled state. But of course she'd cared nothing for her appearance! What else could she have done but downed tools and rushed straight out? 'I wish I'd listened to you, mother,' she muttered. 'You always said marriage would be a mistake . . . '

'Take no notice of anything I said!' Dorothea urged warmly. 'The fact is, darling, you are married. You have to make things work! Harry's a good man.'

'One of the best!' Bronwyn agreed, if too quickly for her mother's liking. Unable to sit still, the young woman sprang up, crossing the room to pick up the framed photograph of her parents, taken at the start of their marriage and which had residence on the dresser. Impossibly young, idealistic, so touchingly her parents. Andrew Colfax stood behind his new wife, his hand resting awkwardly on her shoulder, his blissful happiness at their union still shining through his tentative smile.

Nothing had changed after all. Her dear father hated having his picture taken. He loved his wife beyond anything, his children a close second. Was it wrong to want the same for her marriage, too? Struggling to keep her feelings under control, she replaced the frame, her mind centring on Harry and their last meaningful conversation before he'd returned to the camp . . . His manner all that evening had been distant and, no doubt, that was why the ridiculous question she'd asked him had first entered her head. 'If you could go back in time, knowing what you know now, would you still have married me?' she'd demanded, giving the thought instant expression.

They'd finished dinner and retired to the drawing room. Katherine, unaccountably tactful, or perhaps sensing an atmosphere she'd wanted no part of, had already retired to bed.

'Why of course!' he'd blustered, too obviously discomfited. 'What an idea. Of course I'd have . . . married you!' There'd been only the slightest hesitation and if she hadn't been so upset at the time at thoughts of his imminent departure and the ever-widening gap between them and of which she'd become so increasingly aware, she might never have noticed. As it was, he might as well have struck her.

'Harry, I'm sorry! I know you want children . . . '

'Bron, please don't. Not now. It's no-one's fault.' His voice was tired and flat, a man with too much on his mind to worry over domestic issues. And if only, even then, he'd put his arms around her and held her close. Nothing they said would ever solve it. Only Bronwyn becoming pregnant would make things right.

'I wish we could have children!' she burst out.

Dorothea put down her cup. So she'd been right in her assumptions. But how odd it was that, only the other evening, she and Andrew had discussed how wonderful it would be to have grandchildren. Until of course, the truth had dawned. Any child of Bronwyn's would eventually inherit the Loxley Estate. The thought had been a sobering one, quietening them both, even Andrew. A Colfax heir to half of Derbyshire took some swallowing and that was the truth.

'Succession's all, isn't it, amongst these people?' She frowned.

'It's all they care about!' Bronwyn agreed quickly, wondering then if she was being unfair. 'What am I going to do?' she implored.

'Nothing,' Dorothea counselled. 'Do nothing for the moment. These things take time. You're both so young, darling. You've all the time in the world.'

'But we haven't!' her daughter wailed, the full impact of Harry's departure engulfing her afresh. She had to face the fact. There was a distinct possibility that Harry might not be coming back and already it might be far too late. The thought struggled for expression, lacking only the words to fit her fears. At that moment, the door burst open and kept up-to-date of the guest's arrival by Tilly, his

46

face wreathed in smiles, Andrew Colfax burst into the room. Spinning round, her face cracking uncontrollably, Bronwyn rushed into his arms and burst into tears.

★　★　★

Tom Compton's mind was still lingering uncomfortably on Harry Loxley's ill-fated herd and the notion, fast growing, that in the way she'd stood up to Katherine, there was more to the new Duchess than anyone had yet given her credit for. Such a slip of a lass, too! He finished the last of his toast, washing it down with a swallow of tea. There'd been no time for breakfast so he'd popped back now for a bite to eat. He was tired and overworked and this morning's business had done nothing to improve his temper.

At the opposite end of the table, Ned sat polishing the brasses: a mid-week job, entrenched enough in his routine to withstand even the excitement of yesterday and the men leaving for the Front. The old man's hand slowed. A fine body of men, by all accounts, but he was old enough to know it for the tomfoolery it so obviously was.

'The lass has a point,' Tom murmured.

'Taking on women! I've never heard such rubbish . . . The men'll be back before we know it and then there'll be trouble!' Ned speeded up, finding solace in the sound of his brush against a fender he could only sense was polished enough to see his face in.

Wearily, Tom climbed to his feet.

'According to the papers, both sides are digging in.'

'Hah! Stuff and nonsense!'

'Now look . . . He'll be on all morning!' Mary stood wiping her hands on her apron.

'Goodness, Tom. Isn't there trouble enough? And where've you been, young lady!' she scolded, barely pausing for breath as Ursula strolled in from outside, the bunch of wild roses she'd just picked from the hedgerow trailing in her hand. After all the trouble of yesterday, Mary's temper took no rousing. 'I thought I asked you for a hand to salt the beans? Well? Where have you been?'

'Edna wanted help rolling bandages!' Ursula returned defiantly. Edna Greening was both village postmistress and local representative of the Red Cross and at least it had made her feel she was doing something to help the war effort.

'And did tha' get many done or was tha' just tittle-tattling, like?' A broad grin split Ned Compton's weathered face.

'Enough to wrap an army in, grandpa!' she returned, happily. Skirting cautiously past her mother, she filled a jar at the sink and dumped in the flowers before carrying them back across the kitchen to hold them up towards the old man so he should smell their sweetness. 'I shall press one for Freddie and send it once I know where he is. I wish you could have seen them,' she murmured, not meaning the flowers and her mind winging swiftly back to yesterday and the men's departure. And Freddie in his new uniform, the handsomest of all! Why hadn't she done like the rest and run out into the road instead of skidding to a halt by the bridge where, unaccountably overcome with shyness, she'd only stood to watch the procession? Freddie's frantic gaze had found hers, steadying at once; the look passing between them, so full of love and yearning, the ache it engendered in her likewise had been worse than a physical pain. And then they'd gone, the whole caboodle of them, the sound of their boots, clattering away into the distance, leaving her to trail home, forlorn and alone. How wretched she'd been feeling since, like the sun had gone in and a storm was brewing! She put the flowers down on the table, her ready smile disappearing.

'Here, give your old dad a kiss.' Aware of one of his daughter's more mercurial mood swings and correctly guessing its cause, Tom

Compton crossed the kitchen and folded her into his arms. Over her head his gaze, seeking his wife's, pleaded that she should let the child be. The premonition was too strong on him this morning. What should a child know of war! Anyone who thought it something that would be put to bed in the few short weeks to Christmas was in for a sorry disillusionment. Dropping a light kiss on the top of her dear head, he released her, reaching for his cap hanging on the back of the door before returning outside.

'Go up and get changed, lass,' Mary murmured, not unkindly, shaking her head but whether over husband or daughter, she had no idea.

★　★　★

Upstairs, in the neat little white washed room that was her bedroom, Ursula knelt on the window seat to watch her father dragging a sack of feed onto the cart. His back bowed with the strain. He straightened, catching hold of the reins of the horse waiting patiently by and, crooning softly to her, led her out through the gate. Beyond the hedge, the hills loomed, burnished white gold and still bearing the marks of what had been a searingly hot summer, fading into this curiously intense and brooding autumn, where already, the nights were drawing in. Was this why she was so restless, her mind so full of Freddie, she couldn't stop thinking about him from one minute to the next? He was gone. He couldn't expect her to sit here pining, as if all she cared for was rolling bandages and gathering flowers.

Disregarding her mother waiting downstairs, she traced the letters of Freddie's name in the glass, rubbing it out when she'd finished with a little pout of dissatisfaction. Since when did what Freddie Hamilton wanted count for anything? Weren't her needs important too? Her expression sobered. Women were wanted for all kinds of work now there was a war.

Farming, transport, even in the factories, producing the machinery of war! She twisted round, dropping her feet back to the floor, her mind returning as ever to Freddie and the fact if it had been up to him, he'd have married her before he left . . .

It was a soft velvet night with a high harvest moon, keeping her wide awake without the need of Freddie below, throwing pebbles up at her bedroom window. She jumped out of bed, gliding swiftly to the window to yank up the sash and thrust out her head, shocked to see him grinning up at her when he was meant to be up in the hills with the rest of the men.

'Freddie Hamilton!' she hissed hotly. 'You'll catch it!'

'Ursula . . . darling . . . have a heart!'

'Don't you darling me!' she retorted loudly but not loud enough, she hoped, to wake her mother. He stood back, bathed in moonlight and too obviously aware of how splendid he looked in his uniform and with which he'd been issued at long and wonderful last. His voice, floating up to her, was full of urgency.

'Ursy, I have to see you,' he wheedled.

If her mother had any idea! But Mary Compton was fast asleep, her snores clearly audible. Impulsive as ever, Ursula withdrew her head, stopping only to throw on the first clothes to hand before creeping downstairs, praising the fact, meanwhile, not two days since, her grandpa had oiled the bolts on the door.

Outside, wonderfully, Freddie's arms folded around her, pulling her close.

'You'll catch it, Freddie Hamilton,' she scolded, pushing him away almost instinctively. 'You'll be put on a charge. Drummed out of the army before you've a chance to pick up a rifle!' she warned and glancing nervously back towards the door. It was too late. Again he imprisoned her within the circle of his arms.

This time, she didn't struggle, but stood impotently, staring up at him.

'Marry me, Ursula?' His voice came rasping, sawing away at the gloom, his arms drawing her ever closer until she could feel the rough thread of his uniform against her cheek. 'Say you'll marry me! You'd never be so cruel as to let me go the way things are?'

He'd asked to marry her so many times but never this way, with this curious mixture of fear and hunger. 'Freddie, I can't . . . ' she anguished and yet, all the while, thinking, why couldn't she! Plenty of couples were doing exactly that and wasn't it the most exciting thing?

'You mean you won't?' he demanded, crossly. His arms dropped and he flung away, leaving her staring, longingly, after him. But he was never giving up without a fight? What an odd mood he was in! Already the army had changed him, made him harder and older, a Freddie out of control and she, who so much liked to be boss between them, wasn't sure that she liked him this way.

'Don't go like this!' she called after him and uncaring now who should hear her.

He crashed to a halt and trembling, swung back towards her, that same soft longing on his face. 'Why, how else should I go?'

'You know I like you!' she whispered softly

but knowing, instinctively, liking wasn't what he wanted. He wanted more, something he ought not to have, or at least until she was sure. She longed to run back into his arms. Something, some vestige of sanity saved her, thereby saving them both. 'After . . . when this is over,' she urged, reaching up to kiss him before springing back and turning reluctantly away into the darkness and towards the house. She didn't look back — she couldn't, unsure now what it was she'd promised him. It felt as if they were bound to each other for life.

How could she have guessed, the very next time she saw him, he'd be off to the Front! And if she had known it, would it have made the slightest difference? How confused she felt. She'd no idea what she wanted, only that, now the war had started, invading their lives whether they liked it or not, she had to do something to help.

Her mother's voice calling up the stairs, increasing in tempo, invaded her consciousness. She'd be for it if she didn't get a move on. Stilling her clamouring thoughts, she threw on an old skirt and blouse and ran downstairs.

How peaceful it was to lean against the leather upholstery of this splendid little motor, the wind ruffling her hair as, behind the hills, the autumn sun set in a blaze of reds and purples.

She might have married into the Loxleys. They didn't own her.

Seeing her parents had done Bronwyn good, giving her strength and reminding her, whatever anyone else might think, she was her own person and a match for any Loxley, even Katherine! 'You enjoy your work, Lizzie?' she enquired, turning towards her driver, a vivacious young woman, daughter to Alf Walker, Loxley's more usual chauffeur and one of the first to join up.

'It's a question of having too, Miss — I mean your Grace . . . ' The girl blushed shyly. 'Though I was that made up when dad suggested I keep things ticking over until he gets back. At least it takes my mind off Bill.'

'Your young man?' Bronwyn hazarded.

They were going uphill. Lizzie's capable hands clamped to the wheel as if she was willing the machine forwards. 'William Clarkson, your Grace,' she returned. 'He's with the Loxley and Harringtons so dad says he'll keep an eye on him. He was Steward's Room footman. Mr. Harry . . . his Grace . . . says the job will still be there, waiting for him, when he gets back. We're going to get married then, miss . . . Oh, so long as nothing happens!' This last emerged in a long, drawn-out moan.

Knowing exactly how she felt, Bronwyn shot her a sympathetic glance. A girl near enough her own age who only wanted her young man back in one piece. One of a number of capable young women left similarly positioned and with so much to offer the war effort. It gave her food for thought.

'It'll be over before we know it!' she encouraged, then remembering her father's words on the subject and suddenly not so sure.

'It'll last longer than the papers suggest,' Andrew Colfax had mused, lifting her chin with one finger and smiling in that reassuring way that had always made her world seem so much safer. 'Keep busy, darling. It's bound to help. What else can we do?'

He was right, too. There was no use dwelling on a thing over which they had no control. They'd reached Loxley land, skimming past the outlying estate workers' cottages and towards the old Hall, Nell Loxley's domain. And what would Loxley's illustrious ancestor think of the lily-livered way she'd handled her position here so far, Bronwyn wondered bleakly. In the fields nearest Tom Compton's cottage, the doomed herd cropped pasture she guessed should have been ploughed long before now. Already there was an air of shabbiness about the place, a feeling of neglect and things left too long. The biggest part of the work force gone, Katherine behaving as if everything should carry on just as it was, it was no wonder Mother Nature had so quickly retrieved her own. And no wonder Tom Compton looked so tired! Loxley's Estate Manager stood at the top of the road, talking to a man with thick, dark hair over a scowling face and who was leaning heavily on a walking stick. Reuben Fairfax, the gamekeeper.

'Stop, Lizzie!' she demanded impulsively. 'I need a word with Tom. I'll walk the rest of the way.' Seeing Tom reminded her of Harry's Friesians, the cause of the present friction. She'd come to a decision. She couldn't stand back and see them slaughtered and never lift a finger to help. She scrambled out, waiting for the car to depart before making her way up to the two men. At her approach, Reuben swung round, his eyes like two storm pools. He was obviously and disconcertingly displeased to see her. But he must be bitter his disability prevented his enlisting when every other able-bodied man on the estate had already left for the war!

'I'll get off, Tom,' he muttered, first touching his cap to her but in a way suggesting he resented it. Brushing past her, he hurried away, fast as his limp would allow and down towards the Old Hall and Dead End Wood and his dwelling in the cottage, whose lights Bronwyn could see from her bedroom window.

'Take no mind, miss. It's only his way,' Tom Compton said, watching after him and with a resigned smile on his face. His gaze swung back towards her and she saw now the shadows lining his large, handsome face. She was sorry to be burdening him further. Katherine's acceptance or not, with Harry away, it was time she took some responsibility. The thought dispersed some of the uneasiness she'd been feeling since her husband's departure. If she was incapable of providing him with an heir, there was at least something she could do. As her father had rightly pointed out, there was a profit to be made on a good herd of milkers.

'Tom, I'll not stand back and see these beautiful beasts slaughtered for want of help to care for them!' she muttered fiercely and then almost laughing out loud at the man's startled response. Her voice steadied, gathering strength. 'I want you to ask round and see if any of the village women will help out. And if there's no-one, try the outlying districts. There must be willing hands somewhere! You can manage a few days more until we arrange something, surely? It's a crying shame we can't deploy some of the indoor staff . . . ' It was the nearest she could come to criticising Katherine. Tom Compton sucked in his breath.

'But her Ladyship . . . '

'I'll smooth things over with her Ladyship!' she responded and mentally crossing her fingers. So what it would cost money they could ill afford. Baldly put, they were saving money on the men away. Her face filled with determination. Despite what Katherine said, this war wouldn't be over quickly. Milk would be needed and better they provide their own and sell the surplus on.

'Rather you than me, your Grace!' Tom commented uneasily.

A look passed between them surmounting Tom's dismay and her anxiety. She wasn't as alone as she'd thought. Taking encouragement from it, feeling much as if she were off to war herself, she threw him a grateful look before walking away and down towards the house.

★   ★   ★

The last of the sun sank down over the margins of sky and sea, spinning a widening triangle of red gold rays over the deepening blue. It would be dark by the time they reached Le Havre. Freddie Hamilton could smell cattle or, maybe, he was just homesick for he guessed it was a long time since this rusty old bucket had seen sight or sound of cows. His rough workman's hands clamped more firmly round the barrel of his rifle. Unlikely soldier that he was, he could at least manage to look like one.

'Gi' o'er, lad. We'll be there soon enough.' Alf Walker settled his back more easily against the side of the boat, a calm and competent countryman more suited to the horses amongst which he'd grown up than as a private in His Majesty's army. His pleasant gaze shifted round his fellow men. Lizzie's lad Bill great gormless lump that he was but a good lad at heart. Thomas Marsh, estate worker, Anthony Davis, footman now batman to master Harry. Arthur Haines, night porter. What a company they looked and not a real soldier amongst 'em! They'd suffered square bashing enough to forge an army of soldiers.

'I'd be shuttin' the greenhouse up, normally, this time of night,' Frannie Mower, second gardener, murmured wistfully.

Alf shot him a warning glance, motioning with his head to little Stanley Pickering, Loxley's boot-boy and youngest of the company, perplexed anew at how he'd managed to hoodwink the recruiting officer he was all of eighteen when he was hardly yet breeched.

The poor lad was as pale as ditch water and swearing blind it was only a lack of sea legs. As if to prove the point, suddenly he groaned and lurched up to dangle his head over the side of the boat and from which direction, shortly, retching could be heard.

His predicament raised affectionate laughter. Grinning along with the rest of them, Freddie propped his rifle against his haversack, turning to rest his hands on the rails to gaze towards the vast expanse of water beyond. As if the sky had turned upside-down and sprung to a vivid and restless life oddly reflective of his thoughts.

A soft sigh escaped him. What would be expected of him? What if he flunked it, or worse, turned out to be a coward? He'd never be able to look Ursula in the face again.

'Everything alright, Private?'

The voice scattering his thoughts was more suited to the elegance of Loxley's dining room than here, in this battered wagon. The glowing stub of his cigar revealed Harry Loxley, his lean pale features, strained and tense.

Blasted toffs! Freddie could only think what strange bedfellows the war was making. 'I was only thinking, sir,' he muttered, biting back on a sharp retort and wondering then what the man would say if he told him what he really felt. He wanted to go home. He wanted to see Ursula, right now, this minute! Dear Lord, it wasn't fair of her to keep him dangling on a length of string like this . . .

'Any girl in particular?' Harry persisted, sensing a hostility he couldn't as yet understand. The fact he couldn't troubled him when he'd lived with these men all his life. Opposite ends of the social scale they might be, they were men just the same and women ran rings round them. He leaned over, dropping the butt of his cigar into the sea, his smile fading, caught by the breeze and carried away, far into the gloom. Would he ever make things right with Bronwyn? Had marrying her and in such haste been the biggest mistake of his life? It was too late to do anything about it now. They were married, welded together for life and he'd never give his mother the satisfaction of thinking she'd been right all along!

'We'll be alright, sir?' Freddie's voice, tinged as it was with apprehension, broke through his defences, striking a common chord. Harry nodded, his hand dropping into his greatcoat pocket and folding around the orders from HQ.

His men. His responsibility. Of course things would be alright. Disembark Le Havre, transport 0600 hours from station to the infantry base depot at Etaples and the 2$^{nd}$ Battalion. He stared towards the churning foam-flecked sea and wished the company were already at . . . where was it? An odd-sounding name. His tired mind fumbled towards it, wondering what its achievement would bring. Ah, that was it! Urgent reinforcements, of which they were the biggest part, to the little Belgium town of Ypres.

# 3

## Christmas 1914

'If it ain't a pretty VAD nurse! Going far, darlin'?'

'Piccadilly Circus . . . If you don't mind!' Ursula answered haughtily, giving the young bus conductor a disapproving stare before scrabbling, pink-cheeked, in her bag for the money for her fare. It was her precious afternoon off and why shouldn't she hop onto one of the Omnibus Company's distinctive red and blue buses and go where the fancy took her? Piccadilly Circus, Buckingham Palace, even the Tower itself. She was spoilt for choice, dizzy with excitement, settling on Piccadilly as nearest and drawn by the lure of the shops, even if, with the afternoon drawing in, the frontages were shaded against possible attacks from the zeppelins she'd read so much about.

London unfolded before her wide-eyed gaze. Mindful of her dignity, of the thrillingly undisguised approval of the conductor, she composed herself to appear more the young lady she meant to be. It was Christmas and her first ever spent away from home, at the

Royal Harold Hospital in Kensington, where she was enrolled for three months of basic nursing training. First Aid, home nursing and hygiene and any spare time to be taken with bed making and patient temperatures, all under the eagle eye of Sister Sinclair who was in charge of the ward. What Ursula really wanted was to join the dashing company of women who drove the fleet of Red Cross Ambulances across the streets of London and which were already a common sight. Hands on experience of the war! Talk was, once the Medical Corps had cleared the proposal, women would even be allowed across the channel, a happening which couldn't come soon enough for Ursula and who meant, given luck, to be one of the first.

How she blessed Edna Greening, the post-mistress, for putting the idea in her head in the first place, for it had been at Edna's shabby little shop where the plan had first been mooted. Dear Edna, who'd gone to school with Ursula's mother and, knowing her so well, had suggested laughingly that Ursula would be better getting her father onside first. At this wise advice and as if she'd been scalded, Ursula had dropped the box she'd been filling with comforts for the troops and rushed straight home, cornering her doting parent in the garden where she'd found him digging potatoes and where, fired with determination, she'd forced him to hear her out. If it had been marriage to Freddie over which she'd been so impassioned he'd have given his blessing at once. The unfairness of it had lent weight to her tongue. The poor man had never stood a chance.

'I should be doing something for the war effort, father. All kinds of women are discovering skills no-one's yet given them credit for! And London! Think how wonderful that would be. I'm old enough . . . Father, you know I'm old enough! You won't stop me?' She pouted, doing what she'd done from her first stumbling steps, which was to coax him round to her point of view by whatever means it took.

She'd wanted this more than she'd ever wanted anything in her life. What luck Edna's niece already worked at the Harold and had written of the need for fresh recruits, living under constraints enough to satisfy even Mary Compton's strict rules regarding the safety of her precious daughter. Glancing out of the window at the streets below, Ursula glossed over the unpleasantness of overcoming her mother's protests, even with her father on side. Her grandpa hadn't helped either and who'd been equally determined she wasn't to go. But go she did, eventually, however much unpleasantness it had taken.

'My, but you're a sight for sore eyes!' The conductor had returned and stood watching her speculatively. Ursula's temper rose.

'Do you want something?' she demanded, trying to frown and failing. He was too handsome, she was too happy and the day was altogether too exciting. Never mind he had a look of Freddie about him and whose last letter nestled in her bag. Taller than Freddie, leaner and hungrier and watching her like a fox after the chicken run. She'd met enough of his sort on the wards. 'Why aren't you joined up?' she asked abruptly.

Instantly, the young man's air of good humour vanished.

'Bus driver's reserved,' he retorted defensively.

'Conductor isn't,' she answered scornfully. 'Women conductors are two a penny!' Ursula had seen them and the posters declaring able-bodied young men should take themselves off to the Front. Her patriotism, ever present in these troubled times, leapt to the fore. What was wrong with this young man that he wasn't fighting too?

'Who says I don't drive?' he muttered huffily before moving off to take the fare from a woman at the front of the bus. Shortly, he was back, his gaze clouded and troubled.

67

There was more to him than first appeared. He was upset she could see. He leaned back against an empty seat, tipping his cap to the back of his head with his thumb and nodding his head towards the driver. 'Me and Jim are doing the driving in shifts. Ain't so many buses needed on a Sunday. Besides . . . Things ain't always what they seem.'

It still didn't explain why he hadn't joined up. He scowled, spoiling his face which had become sharp and fox-like. Not so much like Freddie then. This man she sensed wouldn't be anywhere near as amenable as Freddie who adored her with a satisfying, if worrying, devotion. And it was true things weren't always what they appeared. Ursula's shoulders lifted, suddenly tiring of the talk and of him, too. 'It's none of my business,' she concluded, still determined to have the last word. The bus had rounded Regent Street, coming to a halt by Shaftesbury's famous statue of Eros. She jumped up, brushing past him and running nimbly downstairs to leap the last two steps and onto the pavement, unaccountably pleased when he followed her, grabbing hold of the pole as the bus moved off and, leaning out precariously, shouted after her.

'I finish at four. I'll take you out to tea, if you like?'

'You'll do no such thing!' she yelled back. She walked on briskly, unable to help a smile tugging the corners of her mouth upwards.

'Lucky man whoever he is!' he returned and his good humour apparently restored. 'You know where I am if you change your mind.'

Change her mind? But how could she? That would be disloyal to Freddie, who was risking life and limb to save them from the barbaric Hun! The young man's voice trailed after her, fading into the darkening skies. Men all over, so full of themselves and never knowing when to give up, not even Freddie.

Thoughts of Freddie and what he'd written to her in his last letter home momentarily sobered her. So full of himself, so brimming with pride in doing his bit and all his plans for their future when the war was over. Where, in all his outpouring was any room given to Ursula's plans? As if it had never crossed his mind she might have any plans and, if she had, they should only accede to his because, after all, she was only a woman.

The bus disappeared from view. An hour's shopping lay ahead. When she lay at night listening to the echo of guns from across the channel, Ursula wondered how she could deny Freddie Hamilton anything . . .

It was Christmas morning and it seemed to Bronwyn, the bell from the tower over the stables rang with an added solemnity. How beautiful everywhere looked with its sprinkling of snow, dusting the trees and the grey slated roofs of the stables and the hunting tower, rising sharply behind. The sky above it was full and heavy. There'd be more snow later. She was out for a walk, calling round at the stables for the dogs, to discover Lizzie lounging against the bonnet of the Rolls, absorbed in a letter, no doubt from her young man for something had made the young woman forget the pail of hot soapy water, with which to wash the car, cooling rapidly nearby.

'Any news?' Bronwyn called. Her heart skipped a beat. Any snippet from the Front would be welcome though she hardly liked to ask.

'It's a letter from Bill, your Grace!' Lizzie returned, glancing up and her ready smile a measure of the relief she'd felt yesterday when the village postman had first placed the missive into her hands. 'I've been so worried. It's so long since we'd heard . . . '

'Everyone alright?' Bronwyn demanded, giving up pretence of detachment and hurrying over. Lizzie nodded.

'There's been a standoff with the Germans. Their trenches are so close together, Bill says they can just about touch each other! He's bored, he says but at least now he's time to write . . . ' The young woman blushed prettily, it being on the tip of her tongue to tell her Grace, who was far too pale for Lizzie's liking, the rest of what Bill had said too, and surely meant for Lizzie's eyes alone. What wouldn't he give to feel her in his arms again!

'Any . . . mention of the Duke?' Bronwyn asked, guiltily remembering and instantly rejecting, Katherine's warnings concerning her over-familiarity with the servants. Her need to know overrode everything, even what Lizzie might think. She couldn't bear to admit, two hastily scribbled postcards, in a hand she'd scarcely recognised for Harry's, was all she'd received so far. But how wonderful to receive a letter spilling thoughts and feelings, no matter in how uneducated a hand!

'There was something . . . ' Lizzie turned over the page, her voice bubbling with pride and yet still wanting to help this young woman for whom she was so unaccountably sorry. Her dad always said the gentry didn't have it easy and here was the living proof of it. What a thing, her Grace knowing less than Lizzie. 'I've managed a pretty decent sort of a trench,' she read. 'His Grace says he'll make a soldier of me yet. He's alright, Harry and mixes in with the men, not like some of the officers . . . ' She glanced up quickly, blushing at the over-familiarity but finding only relief on her mistress's face. She did so like her, such a kind and genuine lady and if only she could tell her something to really put a smile on her face.

Bronwyn relaxed. Harry was alive, at least when this letter was written, and getting on well with his men, which was something to tell Katherine who was as worried as Bronwyn if she'd only unbend enough to admit it.

'Thank you, Lizzie. I appreciate it,' she said.

'Beautiful flowers, your Grace?' Lizzie returned, wanting to delay her and her gaze falling to the Christmas roses Bronwyn carried, the point of the walk if she had but known it. Bronwyn however was in no mood to be delayed.

'Aren't they,' she agreed. She smiled goodbye and calling to the two dogs, lolling on their bed of straw inside the stable, turned away, the dogs bounding joyfully in front as she set off briskly towards the meadows which linked the New Hall with the ruins of the old. It was a fine morning for a walk and shortly, she'd built up a head of steam, raising her spirits enough to call to the two women, rough country folk, employed from the nearby village of Harrington to care for Harry's precious herd of Friesians. Milking done, they were marshalling the beasts into pasture land and returned Bronwyn's greeting cheerfully. What a ruckus there'd been with Katherine before Bronwyn had got her way and the cattle had been saved. Harry at least would be grateful. But why hadn't he written? she wondered. The question crackled up accusingly from the frozen ground beneath her feet. She loved him. She missed him; weighed down this Christmas morning by the feeling he no longer cared. Out of sight, out of mind, she supposed. What other inference could she put upon the fact, in all this time, he'd never found two minutes to write.

The briskness of her pace had brought her to the river which, swollen with the previous day's rainfall, gushed up beneath the gaping windows of the ruin. As if in answer, a churning emotion rose up, assuaging the feeling of doom which had been growing upon her of late. If Katherine had the slightest idea what Bronwyn was doing here, she'd think her crazy, and all the bad things she'd ever imagined about her daughter-in-law, every bit true.

Ducking inside the lintel into what had

once been the courtyard, she glanced down ruefully at the flowers she'd carried so carefully all this way. Who wouldn't think this morning's outing crazy? It was her tribute to Nell whose birthday it was today, a fact she'd discovered only by chance a few days ago when, happening to be first in the breakfast room and standing to glance down idly at the family bible open on its plinth, Nell's name had jumped out at her, her date of birth and marriage to a man named Hyssop. It also noted the birth of her son, yet another George and at a time when the country was embroiled in civil war. Given the way she'd refused to answer any of the questions she'd tried to put to her about it, Katherine evidently thought as little of her illustrious ancestor as she thought of her son's new wife, Bronwyn mused.

The dogs lay panting at her feet, watching her with a puzzled air as she stood, feeling vaguely foolish and not even sure, now she was here, where she should leave her little offering. She spun round, taking in the broken stairwell, the heaps of stone and rubble and the remains of the crumbling walls marking out long-forgotten rooms. How could she leave her flowers here? Was she really so unhappy with Harry that she must fill her life with foolish fancies no-one else could possibly understand?

Her indecision proved her undoing. Turning too quickly, the toe of her boot caught in an upraised flagstone and she stumbled, startling the dogs who leapt up barking. Vainly, her free hand flapped, horribly finding only thin air. Even then she might have righted herself if only one of the dogs hadn't bolted recklessly under her feet, sending her toppling backwards and tumbling sickeningly to the floor.

She lay, momentarily winded, cursing softly before gathering herself enough to pull herself up into a sitting position, excruciatingly aware of the pain tearing across her ankle. The dogs lolled, tails wagging, their apologetic gaze enquiring what came next. 'Don't ask me!' she snapped, wiping away tears of vexation and appalled she could think of nothing better than to sit and cry. Her predicament had become only too clear. No-one knew she was here. She hadn't even told Lizzie though Lizzie conceivably might, after some long time, notice she was missing. But as far as Katherine Loxley was concerned, if her daughter-in-law never came home again it would be far too soon.

Wincing with every movement, Bronwyn inched backwards until she came to rest against the nearest pile of broken masonry, discovering herself exhausted with even this small effort. All at once, a strange scent of lavender, so at odds with the snow dusting the tops of this ancient monument, drifted down from the top of the stairwell. Her eyes sprang open. The dogs backed, barking furiously, before they fled, yelping from the place, deserting her in her hour of need. Curiously, Bronwyn felt only a soothing calm, as if all her worries had floated away to join the flakes of snow drifting, windblown, from a sky threatening more. She'd always loved lavender, the scent of which brought her only happy memories. The flower-strewn garden at home and her mother stooping over her bed to kiss her good-night. But the scent of lavender and in the middle of winter? The first faint ringing of alarm sounded, grew, shattering her complacency.

'Hello? Who's there? Any one in need help?'

A man's figure stood, framed in the broken doorway, his brooding eyes fastening in perplexion on Bronwyn before he limped across to take her arm and coax her upright. She dropped her flowers, putting her injured foot gingerly to the floor and wincing. 'Think you can walk?' Reuben Fairfax demanded, sounding incredulous.

'I'm not sure,' Bronwyn returned, inwardly cursing why her rescuer had to be this man of all men. Better him than no-one came a whispering reply, as if someone stood behind her, a party to her innermost thoughts. Her nerves were overstretched. Nevertheless, she glanced nervously over her shoulder before a sharp pain, stabbing upwards from her ankle, wrenched her mind too quickly back to the present. Reuben knelt, exploring the injured area with a surprising gentleness.

'It's only a sprain but we must get you home,' he said.

She was in no position to argue. Gingerly bearing the weight on her injured foot, Reuben's arm around her waist, she allowed herself to be led back through the ruins and outside, heading towards the bridge. Their progress was painfully slow and, all the while, Bronwyn was aware of what a ridiculously odd-looking couple they must make.

'A case of the blind leading the blind I believe!' Reuben muttered dryly and as if reading her thoughts. His voice held an odd hint of humour. Bronwyn's natural retort died on her lips, silenced by a pain she was determined not to show in front of this man who made her feel so uncomfortable.

'You must leave me. Go for help!' she panted, unable to hide her distress any longer. Her fingers dug into his arm.

'You must try to go on.'

'I cannot.'

'There's nothing else for it then!' he returned angrily. Suiting his words, he threw down his stick and before she could stop him, in one swift movement, swept her up into his arms. He righted himself, shifting her more comfortably into his shoulder. Startled, she looked up into his face, seeing only pain there, mirroring her own. 'Put your arms around my neck,' he commanded, staring stonily ahead.

'I'll do no such thing!'

'Then you must have us both over,' he growled before taking a first, stumbling step forwards.

There was no alternative. Reluctantly, Bronwyn did as she was told. Her head nestled against his chest. That he was in pain she knew. That he was doing his best to hide it from her, she also knew. Tight-lipped, he staggered on, grunting with effort every time his bad leg hit the ground. Bronwyn, meanwhile, only wished the ground would open up and swallow her, the morning's whole crazy enterprise revealing itself to her now, for exactly what it was. A horrible nonsense from a foolish woman with too much time on her hands!

They made slow progress but at last, as the stray flakes of snow thickened and filled the sky, dusting Reuben's hair and eyelashes, the New Hall, at first so tantalizingly in the distance, gradually and mercifully loomed large. Shortly, he was stumbling through the gates and along the terraced walk to the front steps and finally, thankfully up to the front doors which happily flung wide at their approach, allowing Soames and the little maid, who'd seen their approach through the drawing room window, to hurry, horrified, from the house.

'Leave her be!' Reuben roared, when they would have relieved him of his burden, instead clinging onto her for dear life, up the steps and inside to dump her, unceremoniously, on one of the gilded chairs that resided either side of the stone fireplace, now hung with a mistletoe Katherine, in an uncommon spirit of the season, had fetched from the woods that morning.

'Whatever's happened?' She hurried downstairs to stand in the midst of a melee, compounded by the dogs who, tails thumping, had miraculously reappeared somewhere in the garden and followed the procession inside. 'Silence!' their owner retorted sharply, her startled gaze sweeping all before her as Bronwyn falteringly began to explain, if unsurprisingly holding back on the reason for her walk. Not making sense of it, not troubling to hide her exasperation, Katherine raised an impatient hand. 'Soames, call Peters. We must get this seen to.' Peters was the family doctor. Her tone was cold, holding a perplexing anger Bronwyn couldn't begin to understand. She'd fallen. She'd hurt herself. Must she be castigated for it too? Soames hurried away to the telephone. Christmas or not, Bronwyn wished the day heartily over, wished now too late, she'd never heard of Loxley Hall or of Harry Loxley either!

'A good job I was there!' Reuben thundered, ignored, treating like with like and red-faced though whether from fury or his efforts, Bronwyn had no idea. Expecting an outraged response from Katherine, her eyes widened in shock when none appeared forthcoming. Oddly, her mother-in-law's stance modified, exactly as if someone had pulled a pin from her body, letting out, thereby, all her customary hot air.

'Go down to the kitchens,' she muttered, if begrudgingly, remarkably civilly, 'Cook will make you a drink . . . a meal should you require . . .'

'I've things to do!' Reuben snapped, flapping his hand irritably as if he would have flapped Katherine away too, if only he could. She'd surely never stand so much and from the gamekeeper to boot but to Bronwyn's further amazement, it appeared she would. She bowed her head, reining in on an anger Bronwyn guessed must still be simmering inside. Reuben's gaze shifted towards Bronwyn and of which she was instantly aware, softening surprisingly before, turning on his heels, he limped away. Bronwyn scarcely knew what to make of it all. Ankle throbbing, near to tears, she was left alone to await the advent of the doctor as Katherine hurried away upstairs.

'My dear Bronwyn . . . I know how difficult things have been between us of late and believe me, I wish I could put things right. I love you. I miss you. Only thoughts of you keep me from insanity . . . '

Candlelight cast grotesque shadows over the Officer's dugout. Harry's hand balled into a fist. It was all true enough but it wasn't what he wanted to say most of all. Why couldn't he tell her the rest of it! *I wish we hadn't married. Being out here has made me realise, it was grossly unfair chaining your life to mine!* He'd never been good with words. He'd never been good at anything much, he realised now. Always too keen to maintain the peace and go along with wrongs he should have stood out against. Damn it but there'd be changes when he got home. If ever he got home . . .

What a way to spend Christmas! How many letters he'd tried to write and now this one apparently going the same way. Exasperated, he threw down his pen and ripped it up, scattering the pieces to the floor. Whatever needed saying, now evidently wasn't the time. He needed fresh air and normality or whatever passed for normality out here. Buttoning up his coat, he made his way outside and along the roughly fashioned tunnel towards the front trench. Four days front line, four days reserve, then four days rest. It was a routine of sorts. The men were battle-weary and sleep-deprived, surviving the harshest of winters which had brought with it an insidious cold he'd never experienced before in his life. At least, yesterday's snowfall had hidden the worst of the mud and other, terrible things, horrors Harry pushed to the furthest corners of his mind lest they should rise up and drive him mad. He wondered if the other men felt like this too or if they merely dealt with it better. The only way to survive, he'd quickly learned, was to shut it out, concentrating instead, as much as possible, on the everyday.

Today was Christmas Day and they'd eaten bully beef and cold Christmas pudding in its honour. He looked about him, smiling grimly. Despite the cold, some of the men lay sprawled, reading or dozing or merely staring vacantly into space, thinking God knew what. Some sat hunched up, under rudely fashioned shelters made of sandbags, writing letters or smoking cigarettes from Queen Mary's gift box which had been issued earlier that morning. Dirty faces wreathed in smoke and cheerful this Christmas morning when, for once, there was no shell fire. Muted conversation drifted towards him, snatches of normality, families and children, Christmases past, what must feel like other lives to them now. A few short yards away, a small group huddled for warmth around a brazier, fashioning grenades from jam jar tops and filling them with anything to hand. Rivets, hobnails, small bits of metal. Several weeks' warfare had taught the men more than any training. Learn quickly and stay alive. Some hadn't. Some letters Harry had simply had to write. He died bravely, the supreme sacrifice; his last thoughts were of you . . . God help the poor blighters if they ever learned the truth! He stopped and lit a cigarette, cupping his hands around the flame. The defeat of the German defensive in Flanders had ended with both sides entrenched along four hundred miles of continuous front. Losses had been heavy on both sides.

'Look lively, lads!' a voice rippled out. 'His lordship's here.'

The men grinned, happily welcoming him into their ranks. If Harry had achieved nothing else, he'd become part of these men, learning from their good-natured acceptance of the unacceptable, their way of going about things was, surprisingly, much the same as his own. Alf Walker cupped one large mittened hand to his ear. 'Our mates over yonder have laid on entertainment!' he said, grinning. Conversation ceased, laughter breaking out as, astonishingly, the sound of men's voices floated out over no-man's-land, rough and ready and coming from the direction of the German trenches.

'Silent night! They're singing Silent Night!' Little Stanley Pickering shouted, hopping up onto a support and raising his head to peer over across the expanse of glittering white. 'Get down! Damn little fool!'

'No, wait!' Freddie Hamilton muttered, quickly joining him. His head bobbed up then just as quickly ducked down again, sliding back to face his mates, his face split wide with amusement. 'They've only put a banner up, wishing us a Merry Christmas! They've got a Christmas trees an' all!'

'And Merry Christmas to you lot, too!' Alf shouted, a lone voice, followed by an explosion into laughter.

'Sing it back to 'em,' Stanley cried.

A crack-brained suggestion but someone took it up, Alf or Bill Clarkson, Alf's would be son-in-law. Everyone joined in. A rousing rendition of Silent Night followed, two sets of voices floating up and over trenches, tangles of wire, voices intermingling over the strange place called no-man's-land. Freddie's head bobbed up again, this time remaining where it was. His voice filled with wonder.

'There's a couple of Germans in front of the wire . . .'

An attack . . . ? A trick all along. Can't trust the damn Bosch. Hands reached for rifles, bodies tensed, faces filling with consternation as recklessly, gone mad, surely, Freddie sprang up and over the top of the trench, craning his neck to shout back down to his comrades. 'They're beckoning us over . . .'

'Don't be a fool, man. It's a trap, bound to be. It would be the last thing we'd do.'

'I'm going over anyway . . .'

'You'll do no such thing private!' Harry barked, alarmed, too late.

Deaf to the order, Freddie took a tentative step forward and then another before coming to an uncertain halt and not sure now what to do next. He swallowed, feeling his mouth dry as sawdust. The Germans across the snow had swelled in number, several men weaving between the tangles of wire to stand in front of their trenches and near enough now for him to see their faces. One waved cautiously, looking as gut scared as he imagined he looked too. Dare he? Why shouldn't he! It didn't seem to matter that for days, both sides had been hurling shells at each other, doing their level best to wipe each other out.

'Young fool!' growled a voice. Harry Loxley stood by his side, fingering the gun in his holster and wondering how to get the pair of them safely back into their own trench. Two of the Germans in front of the wire had already broken away and were walking towards them. 'See?' Freddie whispered. 'They only want to make friends.'

Something in Harry snapped, lifting a heart so long beaten down and filling it with a wild and crazy hope. Why shouldn't they meet up and make friends? It was only as senseless as anything else happening around here.

Both parties came to a tentative, fear-filled halt, face to face, somewhere central to the two lines. Two young soldiers, an officer and a private, pretty much like themselves, Harry thought, shocked to find himself staring directly into the face of the officer, a man roughly his age, his cap tipped to the back of his head, his blond hair, what he could see of it, cropped above a pleasant, ordinary face.

'Merry Christmas,' he murmured dryly, in perfect English. He held out his hand and, unable to think of a reason why not, Harry took it. Something seemed to snap, and there was a tangible wave of relief as across the length of the line, as far as the eye could see, men threw down their rifles and, climbing up and over their trenches, began to stumble forwards. Grey and khaki coated figures, laughing, shaking hands, falling into each other's arms and wishing each other the best. Someone had a football, giving rein to an impromptu game. Relief swept over him, a bubble of laughter rising up inside when he saw the German take from his greatcoat pocket a hip flask and two glasses, bidding him take one whilst he filled it.

'What shall we drink to?' he demanded and wondering, recklessly, if he dared to suggest 'To King and country!' The thought of such a toast and to such a man brought the smile rocketing to his face. He'd think him mad and so he was, mad with relief as if he could say anything to him, his enemy for so long. He raised his glass, unsure now it came to it, what to suggest.

'To the fatherland and freedom?' the other echoed softly, forestalling him.

Harry's hand froze. His expression was uncomprehending. But freedom was what they were fighting for! 'You invaded Belgium, surely?' The words burst from him, he hoped not in anger.

'And what choice had we?' came the reply.

'My friend, what choice has any of us?' The words floated away into the air, over the heads of the men swapping small tokens with their enemies, buttons, cigarettes, pictures of their families. Oddly understanding what he meant, Harry nodded. None of them wanted to be here, British and German alike, reduced to automatons, machines mindlessly obeying orders, no matter how cruel and senseless. What else was there to drink to? The end of the war and surviving in one piece? The only thing he could possibly drink to . . .

'To us, my friend,' he whispered softly, raising his glass.


## January 1915

Bronwyn threw down the morning's paper which was full of the sinking of the *Formidable* by a German submarine off the south Devon coast. The enemy was battering at the door, giving strength to rumours that an invasion was imminent.

'Harry will never get leave,' she moaned disconsolately.

Katherine beckoned Soames for coffee, annoyed at such defeatism, and in front of the servants. 'They have a job to do,' she answered sharply and satisfied to see her words strike home. Bronwyn blushed and leaned back awkwardly as, unasked and unwanted, Soames moved to pour more coffee into her cup. Childishly, she pushed it away, taking satisfaction he'd taken note of the gesture. Pompous man. If only he weren't too old to go to the front! It was an unworthy thought and, instantly, she was ashamed of it. 'I just wish Harry would write.' She sighed. Or at least answer one of her letters, if only to enquire if she missed him given he so patently didn't miss her!

Katherine put down her cup. The aroma of coffee filled the breakfast room, pushing out against the wet, drab world outside. January had brought with it a thaw which dripped off the trees, swelling the river, turning the meadows into a sodden mass. It was no morning for a walk though Bronwyn had already decided a walk was just what she needed. Her ankle was so much better. Peters had called yesterday, declaring the patient fit to resume normal duties — if only she knew what these duties were.

'I must see Reuben and thank him. After all, if he hadn't happened to find me, goodness alone knows how long I'd have been out there.' For all eternity as far as this woman was concerned. Trying to stare her out, she failed miserably but not before she'd seen the odd expression which had crossed her mother-in-law's face at mention of her gamekeeper. Why, Bronwyn wondered, when she allowed the man such familiarity and despite so patently disliking him?

Katherine sat crumbling toast onto her plate, staring at her frowningly. 'I'll send a message. He must come to the house,' she answered, more sharply than she'd intended and sorry for it when she saw the girl flinch.

'I'll go myself and take the dogs,' Bronwyn retorted, by now past caring what this incorrigible woman thought. Her rebellion at least gave her satisfaction, a small success to set against the rest. 'What happened to his leg?' she asked and wondering now why she'd not thought to ask before.

Katherine looked away, a faint colour rising to her cheeks.

'Some childhood thing,' she muttered, her indifference palpable yet too studied to be believed. She knew and wouldn't say and Bronwyn was suddenly too tired to care. Breakfast was over. Mutinously obstinate, she fetched her hat and coat, calling to the two dogs, lying sprawled in front of the sitting room fire.

She was pleased to get outside and feel the slap of damp, cold air against her face, walking on, tentatively at first but gaining in confidence once she realised her ankle was holding up and causing her only a mild discomfort. It was a relief to leave the house behind and centre her thoughts away from Harry and onto the enigma that was Reuben Fairfax. The man was abrasive, ill-mannered and over-bearing and yet something else too, sitting uneasily with the perception Bronwyn had so naturally formed of him. He had cared enough about her to carry her so far and in such pain; the wonder was he hadn't done himself a permanent injury. And if he had, she knew instinctively, he'd have made sure she never learned of it.

Skirting past the Old Hall, reminding her uncomfortably of her accident and the nonsensical idea she'd formed that Nell Loxley's spirit had somehow tried to comfort her, she left the path and made her way down towards the edge of the trees and the thickness of wood which stretched to the perimeter of the estate and on towards the village. Only once before had she come this far, with Harry, in the first days of their marriage when he'd been so keen to show her the extent of his inheritance. With hindsight, she thought now, even if it had been too late by then, he'd been trying to warn her exactly what she was letting herself in for. But she'd never have changed her mind even if she had known — at least she hoped that was true. Unable to answer this last, she joined one of the myriad of paths interspersing the trees, trusting on instinct as much as judgement, to arrive at the clearing in the glade she remembered, at the bottom of which stood the gamekeeper's cottage.

It was a quiet and brooding place and she wondered how Reuben stuck it here alone for its solitude was enough to drive anyone mad. There were the pens where he kept his birds and, stacked up by the fence perimeter, a pile of neatly chopped firewood. An air of order arranged out of chaos. A few hens scratched round, taking no heed as she walked down the path towards the door. 'Anyone there?' she called, prodding the door which, surprisingly, swung open. Nervously, she stepped inside into the kitchen. Table, chair, a simple stove. Of Reuben, there was still no sign and she wondered if he was upstairs, calling out to him and deciding, receiving no answer, he must be elsewhere on the estate. A low fire burned in the grate. A meal for one was set at the table, knife, fork, and mug, everything neat and in order.

She stood, looking round her and wondering how long she could afford to wait, when her attention was caught by a wooden carving, lying carelessly on a low stool by the fire and by it, the woodcutter's knife which had transformed it. It was none of her business but she simply couldn't resist. Swiftly, she crossed the room to pick it up and take it over to the window, the better to view it. It was, she saw now, a bird of prey, fashioned out of a block of wood, its wings outstretched and the whole imbued with such life she wondered how Reuben, for Reuben it must be, had managed to capture it. Why, she could almost feel its heartbeat quickening under her fingers. Bronwyn knew very little about art and yet knew instinctively that this was the creation of a man of talent. If only she could take it and show it to her father, who had an interest and knowledge! But how odd to think of Reuben sitting here alone by his fire and creating a thing of such very great beauty . . . What a conundrum the man was. Bronwyn smiled.

'What the blazes are you doing here?'

Reuben's voice, so shockingly close behind her, shattered her composure. Heart crashing, Bronwyn whipped round to discover him towering over her, a wild thing leaping from her worst nightmare, his face red and twisted with anger . . .

# 4

'I'm sorry. I've frightened you. Please don't be frightened.' Reuben stooped to pick up the wooden carving which, startled by his unexpected appearance, Bronwyn had let clatter to the floor. A wintry sunshine crept through the cottage door, falling on his face and softening his features, the harshness of which, seconds before, had so unnerved her.

'I shouldn't be here. I'm sorry. I had no business prying into your things,' she murmured, wishing now she'd had the sense to wait outside. Miraculously, his anger had disappeared. 'Please . . . sit down. There's more upstairs. I'll fetch them if you like.'

Astonishingly, moments later, Bronwyn discovered herself seated by a freshly-stoked fire, wondering over the delightfully fashioned creatures Reuben hastened to fetch from his room. Badgers, foxes, bright otters, button-eyed, reminding her of walks with her father when she was a child. He sat watching her face, gauging her response as she gave each her undivided attention, imagining him meanwhile, alone in this tiny cottage, deep in the wood, absorbed in his work, amazed he was capable of such craftsmanship and more, had unbent enough to show her when she sensed he'd kept them to himself until now.

'Reuben . . . they're beautiful,' she stumbled, lost for words.

'You like them?'

'Why shouldn't I?' She hesitated, wanting to ask more but lacking the confidence. Seizing her courage, she plunged in. 'Why do you insist on keeping people at bay?' she began awkwardly.

His frown was unnerving.

'Can you blame me? I feel awkward round people . . . '

'Is it because of your leg?' she intuited and unable to think of anything else. Her curiosity was roused. Why was he so reticent? Why did he appear to dislike people so? 'What happened, Reuben? I do wish you'd tell me!'

'Something . . . nothing. It was a childish prank, that was all,' he muttered, refusing to be drawn. He stood up, leaning with one hand on the mantlepiece to stare down into the fire which crackled and burst into life. She'd broached a subject he was uncomfortable with, so much was clear. Outside a blackbird sang, soft and mellifluous, seeming to release some inner tension. He looked up and, surprisingly, smiled. 'I dealt with it,' he murmured thoughtfully. 'I suppose . . . it affected me in so many ways. Some would say for the worse. How do you think I feel, every other able-bodied man on the estate away fighting for his country whilst I'm stuck here?'

It wasn't his fault, even if he believed it so. 'Reuben you do what you can!' she soothed him. She looked down at the carvings tumbled in her lap, aware she held so much more than their sum. 'I'm sorry,' she muttered, feeling the need to apologise even if, for the moment, she wasn't sure for what.


April 1915

'Dear God, don't look at me like that, man . . . it wasn't my fault. I told you to get down! No . . . NO!'

Bronwyn jerked awake, her every sense flooding into consciousness at sight of her husband, sitting up in bed, his eyes wide and staring and seeing only God knew what. Moonlight sifted through the curtains, falling on his hands which pulled and twisted at the bed covers, his lips framing words she shut from her mind. Fearful of waking him too quickly, she sat up, reaching for his hands and holding them gently until their trembling ceased and his breathing returned to normal, so he was Harry again and not this stranger who'd returned so unexpectedly, exhausted and bruised from the Front. He was due back in the morning. Was that the reason for his nightmares, or did it go deeper? He must be dreading his return. He turned towards her, blank incomprehension shifting to understanding and then, wretchedly, embarrassment.

'It was a bad dream that was all. I didn't mean to wake you. Go back to sleep.'

'I wish you'd talk to me, Harry,' she prompted gently, guided by her instinct that only by getting him to open up about his experiences would she be able to help. Despite the propaganda in the papers, anyone with sense could guess how bad things were for the men at the Front from the casualty lists emerging from Neuve Chapelle. Her grip tightened; she was hurt he lacked the confidence to talk to her. 'Please, Harry . . . '

'Bronwyn you've no idea!'

'I won't, if you don't tell me,' she pointed out reasonably, and miserably aware she'd only succeeded in making him angry. Exasperated, she released him, drawing up her legs and folding her hands around her knees. And when there was so much she wanted to say to him! She was desperate to bridge the chasm yawning between them. The interest she was taking round the estate, everything she'd done to keep the work flowing smoothly. It was mundane but comprised her life whilst he was away.

It might do him good to put his mind to normal life for once.

'I want to help,' she persisted doggedly. But how, when even sight of the precious herd she'd fought Katherine so hard to save, had failed to move him? Katherine, sensing some of what Bronwyn was going through, and no doubt meaning well, had said let him be. War was man's work and Harry would come round when he was good and ready. Bronwyn, she pointed out, would do well to get on with her own life.

Still resenting the implied criticism, Bronwyn frowned into the gloom, her gaze falling on Harry's uniform which hung on the back of the bedroom door, freshly laundered and ready for his return. Her marriage was in trouble and one of them had to sort it out. 'Darling, you must know how much I've longed to see you,' she murmured. 'At least I know now you're safe. You must write and tell me everything, no matter how bad you might think it. I'm here, I'm always here! I can't bear to think of you going back to all that horror when we haven't even had a chance to talk . . . ' Words, crowding for expression, tumbled from her lips. Her husband! They should comfort each other, be all in all to each other, no matter how bad times were.

Some of her distress must have reached him. At last he put his arms around her, stilling her outpouring with his lips before easing them down into the bed and where she lay, hardly daring to breathe, head pressed against his chest, whilst he stroked her hair, his gaze turned to the window and the first of a pale dawn chasing shadows from their bed.

★  ★  ★

'Are you alright, your Grace?' Lizzie gazed at her young mistress, wondering anxiously if she'd heard a word she'd just said. The two women were standing by the glasshouses at the top of the kitchen garden. Bronwyn had been on her way to begin the watering, planning on planting more seed potatoes too if she'd time, a task she'd taken to herself, despite Katherine's grumblings it wasn't seemly she should involve herself with such menial work. It was three weeks now since Harry had returned to the Front and yet, when Bronwyn stood here, the spring sunshine dappling on the trees beyond, feeling Loxley in all its quiet glory, she could almost believe the war was nothing but make-believe.

If only that were true! 'Lizzie . . . how was your young man? I expect you had a lot to talk about?' she asked quietly. Bill Clarkson had been given leave at the same time as Harry, his commanding officer. The two men had travelled to and from the Front together.

'Well . . . I suppose we did! I was that surprised to see him, miss!' Lizzie quickly agreed, her face bright with the happy recollection of Bill turning up out of the blue, covered in mud and full of the journey back home with the Duke.

'Just him and me!' he'd told her, letting go of her at last and looking suddenly serious. 'I couldn't stop myself talking and a good job too, 'cos his lordship didn't have much to say for himself.' Harry Loxley was finding the war hard, she'd learned, and was cut up about one of the gardener's lads, who'd been killed by a sniper following artillery fire. The guns had stopped, suddenly and unexpectedly after hours of shelling and, innocently wondering what was happening, the poor lad had raised his head over the top of the trench. Things done thoughtlessly. It happened all the time. They forgot where they were, Bill said, that was the problem.

Lizzie wasn't about to tell this nice young woman as much. 'Lawks yes, miss! We never stopped talking!' she agreed, even now

100

blushing at the thought of the question Bill had popped, not entirely unexpectedly, his eyes full of the love he'd never lost from the first moment he'd ever clapped eyes on her. Big, placid William Clarkson, a man of passion! And why not, when he'd known her answer even before it was out of her mouth. Lizzie laughed happily. 'Once he'd seen the right side of the tub and scrubbed up, he was as grand as anything, miss! Lord, I've never seen such mud. Funny wasn't it though, only his Grace and my Bill getting leave? They'll be alright. Just you see!'

She ground to a halt, embarrassed she'd said too much.

But it was wonderful, for once, to be treated as just another person, Bronwyn mused and thinking then, she'd forgotten just how good that felt. She smiled tiredly, wishing her own life was as uncomplicated and that Harry had never stopped talking to her.

'I was saying about Miss Georgina, miss,' Lizzie prompted, her face fired with the resolution which had seen her hurrying over from the stables. 'It's too bad! I really haven't time to go gallivanting round London after dress fittings, even for Miss Georgina, especially not with Tom needing extra hands.'

Georgina, Bronwyn's sister-in-law, was lacking a chauffeur, a shortcoming over which, on her last weekly visit, she'd been only too keen to enlist her mother's help.

Bronwyn's patience was on the point of snapping. Katherine knew their situation as well as any. With the corn yet to be sown and the army commandeering every horse on the estate, her high-handed mother-in-law couldn't have found a worse time to loan out a precious member of staff. The recollection fired the young woman into action as nothing else.

'I'll sort it out, Lizzie,' she muttered defiantly, even if knowing it would take more than mere words to halt the steam train labelled Katherine Loxley. Smiling grimly, she headed off inside.

★   ★   ★

Soames was depositing Katherine's coffee-cup on a little inlaid table by the side of her chair as Bronwyn burst into the morning room. 'What's all this about, Lizzie?' she retorted hotly, cannoning to a halt and suddenly all too aware of her plain stuff dress, sleeves rolled ready for her day's work in the garden. How out of place she was amongst the gleaming silver and the vases of freshly cut flowers Katherine insisted on despite, or was that because of, the country at war.

She stood, feeling foolish, watching the

sunlight streaming through the window, highlighting the grey threads in Katherine's still luxuriant hair, her face, mask-like, devoid of emotion, whatever life put in its way, even Bronwyn.

'That will be all, Soames,' her mother-in-law murmured calmly, taking her cup and waiting for the elderly butler to retire before returning her attention to Bronwyn. 'I haven't the faintest idea what you're talking about,' she went on, smoothly.

'Lizzie Walker!' Bronwyn retorted sharply, thoughts of Harry driving her on and filling her with a courage she scarcely knew she possessed. 'We can't manage without her. If Georgina must visit her dressmaker, I'm afraid she'll have to find other means to get there.'

'It's hardly your business, surely?' Katherine's brows arched in surprise to find herself so confronted and in her own morning room to boot.

Inexperienced as she was, Bronwyn was beginning to understand her position as Duchess on this estate must give her some kind of leverage. 'Whilst Harry's away, anything to do with the estate is my affair. Katherine this is important!' she implored.

'You imagine I don't know?' came the calm response.

Katherine sat back, sipping her coffee and

cursing the impulse which had seen her agree to something she realised now, mayhap had been misguided. But Georgina had looked so tired of late and was it any wonder, her husband away at the Front and Eddie, the scamp, running her off her feet. What mother could have had the heart to tell her no? Certainly not Katherine, who doted on her only daughter.

Georgina was still her father's daughter and had too much of the family's wayward streak, she reflected, accepting it because it was so and she'd always believed in facing facts.

'You involve yourself too much!' she went on, haughtily.

'Someone has to!' Bronwyn retorted, stung beyond caution.

'Tom Compton . . . '

'Tom Compton's rushed off his feet!'

Katherine's intake of breath was audible. 'Estate affairs fall under the direction of the Estate Manager!' she pointed out, quickly recovering. 'If you're really so stuck for occupation, child, why not join me on the hospital committee or in the ladies' sewing circle? There are plenty of worthwhile occupations around if you're really looking for something to do . . . '

Mortified, Bronwyn shook her head. 'I'm perfectly occupied thank you and even so

. . . I'd rather it was nursing or munitions work.' This was a sore point and had already been discussed. As if there'd ever been any doubt a Duchess of Loxley could involve herself in something so mundane! They were wandering from the point, picking old wounds when an alternative was needed.

Bronwyn breathed in deeply, waiting for her heart to resume a slower beat before continuing. 'If Georgina could only be persuaded to wait a week until the planting's finished, I'm sure Lizzie would be better able to leave her duties here,' she went on, fixedly. So small a delay couldn't possibly make a difference. A compromise, even if Katherine Loxley never compromised! The silence deepened, pregnant with thought. Somehow, the answer mattered far more than it ought. Bronwyn stood, shifting from one foot to another and feeling, as Katherine so obviously intended, like a child in the wrong, awaiting correction. To her surprise, suddenly, the older woman smiled.

Katherine Loxley had even surprised herself. Something in the raw emotion flickering across Bronwyn's face had struck a chord, reminding her, oddly, of herself as a girl. More like a raggle taggle gypsy bursting in, demanding she should do this or that! The chit had courage; she had to give her that.

And if Georgina could be persuaded to wait a week, it would give her mother time to sort out her own affairs and accompany her.

Putting down her cup, she stood up, dismissing the matter from her mind. 'What a fuss, child! Why should I mind whether Georgina goes this week or the next? Goodness, do whatever you want!'

'Lord, the scones!' Throwing down the sheets she'd just fetched in onto the kitchen table, Mary Compton flew across the room and yanked open the oven door. Smoke poured out as, across the channel if she had but known it, a curiously peaceful cloud of yellow-green gas drifted along the Ypres Salient towards the Allied lines.

'Now what's to do!' Ned cried, rudely awoken from his mid-morning nap.

'I asked you to keep an eye on these scones, that's what. Now look!' Mary grumbled, hurrying back to the table to tip the burned scones out onto the rack. What she'd actually said, now she stopped to think, was that she was going to fetch the washing in and she'd be back shortly. Still, he must have known the scones were all but done — there was nothing wrong with his sense of smell!

'You'd look well depending on my eyes,' Ned snapped, wondering what had got into Mary nowadays. He got up, feeling his way along the mantle-piece to locate his Wood-bines before returning to his chair to light up, throwing the spent match into the empty fireplace with a grunt of satisfaction.

'Sorry,' she muttered, begrudgingly contrite and accepting now she'd been hasty. She threw him an anxious glance. What a morning they'd had. And what a bad mood she was in! She sat down at the table, taking from her apron pocket the letter they'd received that morning from their Ursula, in France, where amazingly she'd gone to drive one of the ambulances ferrying wounded soldiers from the troop trains to the hospital in Saint-Omer where she was based. No wonder the wretched girl had given them no inkling of her plans until it was too late. And what was wrong with a nice nursing job in England, never mind those nasty Zeppelins! Even Mary knew Zeppelins an unlikely hazard.

'You'll read the print off that,' Ned frowned, alive to the rustle of paper and worse, Mary's sigh over it.

'I should think Tom'll be satisfied now.' Her voice was filled with a sudden anger, giving explanation, if one was needed, for the atmosphere at breakfast that morning.

'The lad's worried too!' Ned snapped, feeling bound to spring to his son's defence.

'The lad shouldn't have let her go in the

first place!' she snapped, inconsolable at the thought of the danger their wayward young daughter had so wantonly placed herself in. She thought her heart would burst with worry and it was all Tom's fault!

'They'll non let a slip of a lass like our Ursula near sight of the front,' Ned consoled her, worried himself and willing to blame Tom too, even if he'd die before admitting it. 'She's hardly in the thick of it. I don't know why you're makin' such a fuss.'

'Dear God let's pray she isn't,' she muttered miserably.

'Got a brew on, lass? We're parched!' Tom's burly frame appeared at the door. He was followed into the room by Reuben Fairfax. Ignoring his wife's flash of disapproval, he bid the man sit at the table. It would have taken a less sensitive man than Tom Compton to have missed the atmosphere Ursula's letter had caused that morning, or where the blame was to be laid. They must know he was out of his mind with worry, too. But there, their Ursula had always done what she wanted and Tom didn't see why he should be the only one to blame. 'And a bite to eat?' he insisted with a forced joviality. He rubbed his hands together.

'You'll have a slice of cake, Reuben?' Mary proffered, belatedly remembering her manners. Biting back on her temper, she fetched the cake from the pantry and mashed the tea, keeping up a busy chatter, meanwhile, in respect of the gamekeeper's natural and, some would say, insurmountable reserve.

'Wonderful cake, my love,' Tom muttered, uneasily.

Mary clicked her tongue, cross he thought he could get round her so easily. Lips clamped tight shut, she folded up the last of the washing already dry and taking the basket outside to hang up the rest was surprised to see Bronwyn's slim figure at the gate. It was a morning for interruptions it appeared, unexpected as was their visitor. 'We don't often see you this way, your Grace,' she called, wiping her hands on her apron and bobbing a quick curtsy. Even Mary had noticed how much interest the new Duchess was taking about the estate. Something to keep her mind off her husband who was away fighting and much good would it do her, poor lass. 'I'll fetch Tom,' she began, already turning away.

'No, please, wait!' Bronwyn returned, waiting patiently for this pleasant-faced woman to hurry up the path towards her. After the run-in with Katherine, she'd needed to stretch her legs. 'I've been meaning to ask, Mrs. Compton . . . Mary . . . I understand you're handy with a needle?'

'Aye, some say so,' Mary agreed and

wondering where the conversation was headed.

'I wondered would you do some sewing for me?'

'A dress you mean?'

'Not a dress exactly . . . actually . . . a pair of trousers!' Bronwyn answered, laughing at Mary's expression. 'A pair serviceable enough for work. There's so much needs doing around the place and I've nothing suitable to wear. Do you think you could manage it?'

It seemed Mary could. Swallowing surprise and only a small measure of disapproval, she nodded, happily. If trousers were what her Ladyship wanted, then trousers she should have and never mind what folk might think. Bye, but she'd like to see Katherine Loxley's face with her precious son's wife in a pair of men's trousers! The same thought crossed both women's minds at once. Their amused glances were instinctive and infectious.

'I have to go into Nottingham this week,' Mary confided happily. 'I'll buy some material. A nice length of calico should do it. You'll call round for a fitting?'

'That would be wonderful, Mary!'

But what a nice lass. Mary beamed her approval. 'If there's anything else I can do, your Grace?' At that moment, Ned, whose hearing was as sharp as a tack, appeared at the door, face pointed towards them.

'There is just one thing,' Bronwyn murmured, catching sight of him. 'Now I'm here, I'd rather like a word with Ned.' The request was impulsive, the matter something she'd been mulling over and never acted upon. If any one had knowledge of Loxley's history, surely this man would, the oldest employee on the estate? Katherine's obvious dislike of Nell was beginning to rile her and no-one could argue she didn't need a diversion.

'Do I know anything of Nell Loxley?' Ned mused, inside moments later and running a gnarled hand through non-existent hair. 'I know I'm old, lass but I dunna think I'm that ancient.'

'Oh, I'm sorry! That's not what . . . ' Bronwyn stopped, confused and blushing heavily.

'Give over, dad! Take no notice, your Grace,' Mary smiled, 'he's only pulling your leg. There's no-one knows more about your family's ancestors than dad!'

They stood in the comfy little kitchen, in which an odd smell of burning lingered, the spring sunshine streaming through the doorway, reminding Bronwyn too achingly of home. She nodded happily to Tom, surprised to see Reuben with him. The gamekeeper

111

shifted uneasily and looked away.

'What did you want to know exactly?' Ned asked.

'Anything!' Feeling suddenly foolish, Bronwyn frowned. Her gaze focused on Ned, of a mind now to take this friendly old man into her confidence. 'There's some mystery attached to her but everywhere I ask, even Katherine . . . the Dowager . . . I only draw a blank.'

'An' it's tickled your fancy, like, your Grace?'

'Something like that.' She smiled.

Ned chuckled. 'You're right, of course. Every family has its black sheep. No wonder no-one wants to tell you!' The old man's head bobbed rapidly. 'By all accounts, Nell Loxley was headstrong, the apple of her father's eye, despite he never had the son he always craved for. He died unexpectedly, poor man, leaving Nell to come into her inheritance too young and marry into a family of local landowners by name of Hyssop. Married below herself or so it was said . . . '

This hardly accounted for Katherine's antagonism. Bronwyn's perplexion deepened. With unnerving accuracy, Ned's clouded eyes found hers.

'They were troubled times. The Royalists raised the Standard in Nottingham, pitting family against family. Rufus Hyssop came

firmly down on the side of the Parliamentarians, taking Nell with him, though most said
she must have had leanings that way for the
lass always had her own mind. Talk about
causing an upset! And no wonder yon blue
blood up at t'hall wouldn't gie' a farthing for
her, neither!'

'Father!' Mary interjected, shocked to hear
Katherine referred to in such disparaging terms.

'A Parliamentarian?' Bronwyn returned and
genuinely shocked. Ned's words had revealed
all. No wonder so a staunch a Royalist as
Katherine refused to have poor Nell's name
mentioned in the house. And no wonder Nell
was said to haunt the old hall! Her eyes were
round with wonder. 'I never realised . . . '

'Why should you, lass? You can see now
why Katherine ordered her picture be taken
down; the wonder being it was ever put up in
the first place. I took it up to the timber yard
myself shortly after her Grace was wed. It's
stored in one of the sheds.'

As soon as she heard this, Bronwyn knew
she simply had to see it. To see Nell at last
when she'd thought about her so much,
would be wonderful!

Ned caught her thoughts. 'I'll take you up
there, if you've a mind to it. You've only to
give me the nod, lass . . . '

'Ned that would be wonderful,' she enthused.

'I'll be off then!' Reuben's voice cut into the conversation.

He got up quickly and pulled on his cap.

'I'll walk back with you,' Bronwyn said, disregarding his scowl of disapproval.

To have refused would have been unbearably rude, even for Reuben. A muscle twitched in the gamekeeper's cheek, his ruddy colour deepening as he waited, with a thinly veiled impatience, for thank you and goodbye to be said, touching his cap to Mary before reluctantly following Bronwyn outside onto the road.

He'd been remarkably evasive of late, Bronwyn mused, darting him an uneasy glance. Heading off in the opposite direction whenever he'd seen her; not being places he was supposed to be when he sensed Bronwyn might be there too. He wasn't the same man who'd opened up to her in the cottage those long weeks since and, piqued by it, she wished their relationship back to its previous footing.

'I've been talking to my father,' she murmured, walking on at a steady pace.

He limped into step beside her. 'Hast tha' now!' he replied, in broad Derbyshire though she felt it affected and that he was mocking her in some way.

'He suggested you might like to show your

work to a friend of his from Nottingham, a gallery owner. Father will take them if you'd like,' she continued, refusing to be so easily put off. It had done her father good to have something else to think about other than worrying over their Robert who'd received his posting to the Front. Reuben halted in his tracks, staring down at her as if she'd told him something distasteful.

'I'll thank you to keep out of my affairs,' he growled.

'Of course, only if you want,' she amended hastily, too late.

'Ah, well, I dunna then!' His smile never reached his eyes, which flashed furiously. 'Loxley by name, Loxley by nature! Didn't take you long, did it!'

Bronwyn stopped, confused. Reuben's lip curled upwards.

'Loxleys! I wouldn't gie' yer tuppence for 'em. Trampling all over folk!'

What had she said to make him sound so bitter? Bronwyn's temper, already tried by Katherine, broke surface. Why did everyone allow this man to behave exactly as he liked, even Katherine?

'You wouldn't talk to me so if Harry were here!' she snapped.

His brows rose. 'Harry isn't here.'

'You've no need to tell me!' She cannoned

to a halt, suddenly too choked up to speak. They were at the fork in the road, leading down to Reuben's cottage. They stood awkwardly, an odd look on the gamekeeper's face. In anyone else, she might have guessed it as sympathy. His hand brushed her arm, his words, when they came, surprising her.

'Bear up, lass. Harry was ever careless a'things.'

How gently he'd spoken, as if to a child. But what did he mean? How was Harry careless? What excuse could there be for his behaviour, or hers come to that? Oh dear God, Harry! What was this war doing to them all?

Embarrassed perhaps, as she'd prompted him into a kindness he'd never intended, Reuben limped quickly away. He wasn't a man who showed his feelings easily but, strip away the thin veneer, underneath was a maelstrom of emotion she sensed, wondering again what had occasioned it. She stood watching him thoughtfully until he'd disappeared into the trees, before walking slowly back towards the house.

★   ★   ★

The early evening sun was already dipping low into a slate-blue sky as the group of

116

VADs, on red alert for the troop train carrying the injured from Ypres, lounged with a growing and ill-concealed impatience against the motorised field ambulances which were lined up in a row outside the prettily painted station at Saint-Omer, their distinctive crosses prominent.

Fighting had been fierce; the Allies pushed back almost to the Belgium town itself which was now a burnt-out shell, its ancient buildings afire and tumbling down into the streets. Hell on earth, a Tommy said, brought into the hospital late yesterday and who was Ursula to argue, she wondered, already preparing herself for the worst. If only a half of what they'd heard was true, they were about to be rushed off their feet.

'The train's late,' she muttered for the umpteenth time, to her companion, a girl called Dodi Macintyre. She was a farmer's daughter from Surrey with thick auburn hair, which to the despair of the matron under whose control the girls were, continually escaped the confines of her cap.

'Missing Freddie, are we?' she enquired, innocently and grinning, knowing full well about Ursula's on-off relationship with Freddie.

'Sort of . . . ' Ursula agreed. She peered fretfully down the track, remembering what she'd said to Freddie on this very platform

the last time they'd been together. He'd managed to get a twenty-four-hour pass. Battle-
worn, weary, needing her and not afraid to
show it. How easy and how wrong it would
have been to give in to him. One of them had
to be sensible and unusually, it was her . . .

'Freddie, you know I like you . . .'

'Like?' he snapped, instantly affronted.

'We can't be together. I've no idea how I
feel. I'd end up making you miserable.'

'There's someone else?' he muttered fiercely,
trying and failing to take her into his arms.
She shook her head, annoyed with him for
putting her under so much pressure. 'There's
no-one . . .'

'I've never wanted anyone else, Ursy,' he
wheedled, refusing to give in.

He was exasperating, stubborn and intrac-
table and that really hadn't been the time.
'But that's what I'm saying, don't you see!
How can you know? We should both be free
. . . free to love where we please . . . At least
until we're both grown up enough to know
our own minds!' She'd looked up, pleading
for understanding . . .

Ruefully Ursula acknowledged, she'd been
too rushed off her feet to give even Freddie
much thought of late. So long as he wasn't on
the train for which they were waiting, she
didn't even want to think about him. Taking a

118

last pull on her cigarette, she dropped it to the floor, grinding it out under the heel of her shoe.

'Good job matron doesn't know you've taken up smoking,' Dodi warned. Matron and her mother both! Ursula grinned. The two girls were firm friends, having completed basic training together and volunteering for the ambulances at the same time; delighted when their applications had been successful, though it had been a Godsend they hadn't realised what they were letting themselves in for. A cattle boat across the channel to the depths of the French countryside and a hospital in a hastily converted medieval abbey where everyone involved, surgeons, physicians, sisters and orderlies alike, were British and female, giving lie to the belief war wasn't women's work. War was as much women's work as men's or who else would have been left to pick up the pieces? Ursula's heart went out to the men, even now, winging their way towards them. Where was the blasted train!

'They should be here by now,' Dodi pointed out and worried too.

'Ought someone to nip back and see Matron?' The girl from the vehicle behind had joined them, a long face under a neat cap with startled, anxious eyes. If they were lucky, the men would have received a rough-and-ready first aid at one of the Regimental Aid Posts along the Front line, enough, hopefully, to see them through to the hospital. But any delay could be the difference between life and death. The girls were on edge, eager to get going as soon as possible.

Murmurings of agreement rose as, at that moment, a horse-drawn army wagon rounded the corner at the bottom of the road, advanced at a rattling pace and pulled up sharply. A dishevelled Tommy jumped quickly out and hurried towards them. 'The train can't get through, the line's bust!' he said, wiping a grimy hand across his face. 'There's been an explosion.'

A cry of disbelief arose from the women who quickly gathered round.

'Those poor men! Now what'll we do?'

'They'll get through when they can or try for somewhere else. I've been sent to tell you. There's no use waiting. There's nothing you can do.' His shoulders lifted in resignation. It was war. Things happened. It left no other option than to accept the inevitable. He climbed back up onto his wagon, not hiding his irritation when Ursula stepped out in front of the horse, barring his way.

'Where was the explosion?' she demanded urgently.

The man frowned, tipping his cap to the back of his head.

'Somewhere before Poperinge. Hardly out of Ypres.'

She frowned in vexation. A trainload of injured Tommies, without food and water and even basic medical attention, didn't bear thinking about, notwithstanding the Army would do its best. But could the Army spare men enough to get the train running again? Injured men were expendable. She stepped back, watching with a worried frown as the soldier, clicking his tongue to the horse, manoeuvred the cart around and drove away.

'If they can't get to us . . . then we'll have to get to them!' The thought, expressed aloud, was an instinctive one. Some of those men would die if they didn't receive medical attention soon. They had to do something!

'Ursula! We can't!' Dodi was shocked. They all knew women weren't allowed anywhere near the Front.

'Why not?' another girl chipped in. Young voices rose, each proffering an opinion. 'We can't just leave them . . . why shouldn't we . . . drummed out of the service that's why . . . Matron'll have a fit . . .'

'By the time Matron finds out we'll be on the way back!' Ursula retorted, unable to help the thrill of excitement bubbling up inside her. Adventure at last. Exactly why she and Dodi had been so keen to get over here! A grimly determined look, the despair of her mother if only she'd been there to see it, settled on her face. So what that the light was fading and none there knew the way to Ypres. The petrol ration had been issued that morning. Given what had happened, it was fortuitous to say the least. 'All we need is to follow the railway line,' she muttered, thinking furiously. A plan and no-one could think of one better. Happily, bristling with determination, she swung herself up into the driving seat of her cab as the rest of the girls hurried back to their ambulances.

'We won't half get a tanking when this gets out,' Dodi warned, nevertheless turning the starting handle and jumping aboard.

Ursula and Dodi at its head, the convoy set off, shortly passing the few straggling farmhouses on the outskirts of town and the walls of the abbey, mellow-stoned in the setting sun. Wherever possible they kept to the roads, maintaining a view of the main Flanders line, a manoeuvre more difficult than Ursula would have imagined. Time and again, she lost sight of it and had to back the vehicles up, ignoring the temptation meanwhile to ask directions of the occasional army vehicle they passed lest they be stopped and turned back. She couldn't risk it.

'We're lost, admit it!' Dodi muttered, at

last. They'd been travelling for a good half an hour, into increasingly impenetrable terrain.

'We are not!' Ursula argued illogically, but her confidence draining by the moment. Worryingly, the road ahead was empty when she would have expected some kind of movement. Army wagons, supplies, men passing to and from the Front, even ambulances.

The foolhardiness of their escapade was only now beginning to sink in. Heaven forbid if, in the meantime, the army had repaired the line and the train was already underway. Their paths would cross. They'd miss each other. She'd be drummed out of the service, and serve her right!

She'd missed a turning, her instincts warning her they'd wandered off course, away from Ypres, which she imagined roughly approximated to where the rim of the skyline was an unnatural fiery red, banishing the dark above. Very lights exploded, like starbursts, the intermittent thunder of artillery becoming ominously louder as they progressed. They were near the front line but where exactly? How much further and what if they'd already gone further than they ought?

Sticking her head out of the window, she negotiated the rutted track they'd wandered onto, thankful when it broadened out into a passably decent country lane. A huge explosion brightened the sky, dying quickly, as over the top of it there came the unmistakeable throb of an engine, growing steadily louder into a dull and persistent beat. Ursula peered anxiously through the gathering gloom, shocked to see the dim shape of a vehicle, rounding the bottom of the road and advancing rapidly. Unusually high, it was a thing solid and heavy, the shades on its front lights throwing unnatural shadows onto the road in front. At her side, Dodi tensed. Was she thinking what Ursula was thinking too? They'd driven too far. They were in enemy lines and this vehicle was a newfangled invention designed by the Boche, intent on blowing them to smithereens! She gripped the steering wheel, staring in disbelief. She was hallucinating. She must be hallucinating! But it couldn't be, they'd come so far, they'd somehow circumnavigated the channel too!

Puthering an oily black smoke, mud-spattered, shelled, hanging together by luck and fervent prayers from such unlikely lips, at the sight of the so unexpected line of allied ambulances the driver of the London Piccadilly bus uttered a howl of relief, slammed on his brakes and jumped out of his cab.

'Am I pleased to see you!' he breathed,

heartfelt, as Ursula scrambled out. 'The ambulance train's derailed. I've a bus full of wounded Tommies here.'

The young woman gasped. The sudden burst of a Very light illuminated the man's face, a face she recognised instantly, sending her spinning back crazily to a winter's afternoon and a bus conductor hell-bent on taking her out to tea. She'd ignored him then. There was no way she could ignore him now.

'You!' she cried.

Sam Tennant's face broke into the fox-like smile she remembered, sending her senses spinning. 'Of all people!' he cried. 'The girl of my dreams . . . Darling, wonderful, gorgeous creature. I've been looking everywhere for you!'

# 5

Sam Tennant looked done in, unsurprisingly, after the night they'd just endured.

He stood, twisting his cap in his hands, watching Ursula expectantly.

'Our meeting again was fate. Don't you agree?' he demanded.

'I don't believe in fate.' She turned away to empty a pail of dirty water into the road. They'd just scrubbed the ambulance out, their final task after carrying the last casualty from the derailed troop train into the hospital, a boy too young to have any truck with soldiering; his life, what remained of it, already in ruins. It broke her heart. There'd been no room for the stretcher, other than in the corridor, to wait for attention from the next sleep-deprived doctor who could find a moment to spare.

Matron had caught her on their way out.

'My office, Miss Compton. Half an hour,' the Scot had retorted, poking her head out of her office, glaring at Ursula, immediately assumed the ring leader of the escapade, which was about the size of it, Ursula had to admit.

It wasn't an interview she was looking forward to.

'I'll see you later . . . ' Dodi emerged from the back of the ambulance, her gaze falling curiously on Sam before she jumped down, walking briskly towards the monastery building, so quiet from the outside, giving no hint of the turmoil within the night's work had brought. Ypres was a nasty business and only liable to get worse.

'I haven't time for this now,' Ursula muttered, wiping a tired hand across her forehead, leaving a smudge of oil which the young man ached to brush away.

'If you only knew how many London hospitals I've been in, looking for you,' he complained.

'Sam, I'm sorry, I really am busy.' Despite her words, something in his expression made her linger. It was odd they'd bumped into each other again, and under such bizarre circumstances neither could have imagined. It did feel as if it was meant. Ursula had always believed in omens. Sam nodded towards the dilapidated, mud-coloured London bus, parked incongruously at the end of the driveway. Twice he'd been back to the wrecked train, putting himself in danger to get men out.

'I'll have some explaining to do when I get back. The army don't care for initiative.'

'The Army and Matron both.' She grinned.

'Only there was something . . . Ursula . . . Is there anyone else in your life?' he blurted out. She should have been surprised at the question but nothing surprised her anymore. It was no business of his anyway.

'Someone who cares for you?' he persisted.

'There is someone . . . Someone who loves me,' she agreed uncomfortably.

'And you love him?'

'No . . . Yes! Oh, yes, I suppose . . . ' She sounded confused and, given her tangled relationship with Freddie, was it any wonder. 'We grew up together,' she went on, trying to explain. 'Living on a country estate, we've neither of us any experience of life.'

'You can't be sure how you feel?' Sam jumped in so quickly; Ursula frowned. It was wrong to discuss Freddie with this man, even if what he'd just said just about summed up the situation. She didn't know how she felt about Freddie and Freddie, much as he protested, couldn't possibly know how he felt about her. She still wasn't sure if living at Loxley was what she wanted for the rest of her life. Freddie, in love with the farming he'd grown up with, wanted nothing else.

What a mess it was. She turned, hooking the pail onto the side of the ambulance, then stood, leaning back against the bonnet. After some of the things she'd just seen, she was fast coming to the opinion this was no time for relationships of any kind.

'It's bad, this, Sam,' she muttered, looking towards the hospital.

'It changes things, I agree.' Even Sam's light-hearted manner had deserted him. 'Life's for living, Ursula,' he whispered softly. 'I do want to see you again.'

She hovered, unable to leave, yet neither wanting to stay. It had been a long shift and before the hot bath and bed she longed for, there was the interview with Matron to face.

'I have things to sort out . . . '

'With this other man?'

She nodded, frowning, not sure why she so hated the thought Freddie might think she was being unfair. 'I could only ever be your friend, Sam. Don't get the wrong idea.'

'What else did you think I meant?' His grin was back, the one she remembered that did her so much good. Her spirits lifted.

'Friendship it is then!' she returned, unsure whether she believed him and suddenly too tired to care.

As she hurried away, Sam stood watching her. Friendship in no way described what he was after. He'd made inroads and it would have to be enough — for now. Ramming his cap on his head, whistling happily, he strolled down the drive and swung himself up on his bus.

★   ★   ★

'It's lilac, isn't it . . . ?' Bronwyn closed her eyes and inhaled the warm scent of the little flowers nestling below the shed window, lifting her spirits when she'd been thinking of Harry and praying he was thinking of her too. She'd called for Ned after breakfast, the pair of them taking the short walk to the timber yard and the first of the wooden sheds at the back of the woods, where Nell Loxley's portrait was stored.

The old man leaned with his hands on the workbench, lifting sightless eyes to the open window, pleased to get out from under Mary's feet and even more pleased this nice young lass should have a need of him. May had been a wash-out but the east wind, so favouring the Boche and their cowardly use of gas, had changed at last.

'I planted the lavender back end of last summer,' he volunteered, forgetting now what had prompted the fancy and only remembering the pleasure of the afternoon's work. 'There's nowt wrong with your sense of smell, lass.'

Bronwyn was afraid to tell him that walking over here, she'd imagined Nell's footsteps shadowing hers, haunting her, just as the servants' gossip had it; she haunted the Old

130

Hall too. But how fanciful she'd become of late! She was overwrought. Worry over Harry was doing strange things to her mind.

'I've always enjoyed the scent of a nice flower,' Ned mused, sensing her awkwardness and, if not understanding it, doing his best to dispel it. 'It's good to think someone else appreciates it, too. Now, where was I?' He felt his way along the bench to the pile of canvasses stacked beyond it, disturbing dust and a large spider which scuttled away to safety. Finally, he arrived at one canvas, wrapped in a sackcloth covering and bigger than the rest. 'It's a while since this has seen the light,' he muttered, lifting it up and onto the bench and fumbling to untie the string, before angling it eagerly towards her.

Bronwyn was captivated. A haunting face stared out at her from the canvas, the face of someone, instinctively, she felt she knew, an old friend she'd not seen in a very long time, but there, waiting to reactivate their friend-ship whenever life allowed. A young woman roughly her own age, a mass of thick red hair piled to the top of her well-shaped head, dressed in a flame-coloured satin gown with full slashed sleeves and a low, straight neck-line, offset by the pearls glistening around her slender neck. Large, green eyes stared back provokingly. Something had amused her and, for a moment, she considered what that might have been. She was beautiful. A young woman as full of life then, in her time, as Bronwyn was now. 'She's holding a nosegay, Ned . . . I'm sure it's lavender!' A wave of excitement washed over her, one filled with omens and portents and all the preposterous things she knew, in her heart, too fanciful by far. It was lavender though. A tiny bunch of delicate, lilac-headed flowers, so perplexing when the powerful scent always made her think of Nell.

'Happen she liked lavender, too?' Ned suggested.

'It's such a beautiful painting to be shut away. It's a crying shame, Ned.'

'And you'd care to tell her Ladyship that?' He chuckled in delight. The heady perfume was all around them now, clinging and over-powering, so much so, even though Bronwyn was aware it was crazy, she couldn't help but glance nervously towards the door. So what if Katherine had forbidden all talk of the vibrant young woman who'd so unforgivably fallen for the charms of a man eschewing the King's cause! It didn't mean to say this portrait shouldn't have a new home.

'I'm taking it with me, Ned,' she said, making her mind up. It would hang in her rooms to be enjoyed at her leisure. She took the canvas and began to rewrap it. Katherine never visited her rooms. Who was to know?

'Are you alright, lass?' Ned asked, instinctively aware there was more to this business than the young woman was letting on. 'But of course you're worried.' He sighed. They were all worried and there was no getting away from it.

'You know the Loxleys are still stationed at Ypres?' Bronwyn returned quietly, the hateful fact momentarily stilling her busy fingers. Harry was alive, so much she knew from yesterday's letter and the lack of his name in the casualty lists, which she scanned eagerly, every morning, the moment the papers arrived. He'd taken her plea to heart, his communications nowadays arriving in a constant flow. Passionate letters full of outrage of all he saw.

'Artillery is the way forward but we never have enough,' he wrote. 'We never have enough of anything! The Boche have released their largest gas attack yet, forcing us back but this time, at least, we were alert to the danger. Fighting has been fierce, our losses heavy. Do you mind me telling you this, my darling? It helps me to write and imagine you reading it . . . ' The unexpected endearment had brought tears springing to Bronwyn's eyes and, so unexpectedly, memories of the first time he'd told her he loved her, so long ago it seemed a lifetime to her now. It had been spring and she remembered so vividly the bright meadow of buttercups and daisies, a waving, scented sea of colour and into which they'd carried the picnic things. Her mother, acting as chaperone, had tactfully walked some way in front. Harry had stopped, put the basket to the floor to lay his hands gently on her shoulders, his eyes warm with the emotion he struggled to hide.

'I've never known anyone like you, Bron!' he'd murmured, daring her to deny it. 'I love you. Please . . . say you love me too?'

'Harry, I love you!' she'd returned, without hesitation because she'd known it from the first time she'd ever seen him. Remembering now, all their present problems — Katherine, her parents, the Loxley inheritance — somehow fell into place. They could surmount anything so long as their love remained strong.

'Ned, how do you think the war's going?' she asked quietly.

The old man lifted his hat from his head with his thumb, scratching his bald pate. 'The Western Front's a stalemate, the same as Gallipoli,' he deliberated and repeating what he'd already said to Tom, that morning, at breakfast. Aye, and got a wigging for it from Mary too, who'd sat at the table sewing gas masks for the troops, ear wigging shamelessly

134

and determined to banish all such defeatist talk from the house. But things got out, above and beyond the papers or what the men said to smooth things over on their brief leave home. He nodded unhappily. 'Casualties are bad on either side and something needs to be done to change it. Appalling as is the *Lusitania*'s loss, at least it's stirred up anti-German feeling. Mayhap it'll bring America in on our side. Let's hope, lass.'

'And you think that will help — America on our side?'

'I reckon it'll win us the war.'

Bronwyn's gaze grew troubled. 'I wish the men would come home, Ned!'

'Aye, lass, so do a lot of folk.'

Sensing her need to be away and reassuring her Tom would be over later to see him home safe, he let her go, standing at the door to watch her off. A nice lass but out of her depth, he mused, wishing her well.

★   ★   ★

Luck was with her. Katherine had taken the dogs for their morning's walk. Struggling with the weight of Nell's picture, Bronwyn passed through the great hall unnoticed, carrying on upstairs to her rooms, where she laid it thankfully on the coffee table, leaving the decision where best to hang it until she got back from her mother's, a visit she'd been promising herself all week. Her mother's good common sense, her father's quiet humour, even Tilly's constant nagging were just what she needed right now. The outing would do her good and Lizzie too, who'd been too quiet for Bronwyn's liking of late.

Finding Nell's picture was wonderful! Light-hearted for once, a sea of calm in a storm of turbulence, she ran back downstairs and outside, making her way quickly up to the stables to fix up a time with Lizzie. The deluge called May might have set the crops back; at least there was no need to worry over the harvest, a blessing considering their short-handedness. They were ready for summer more than ever this year.

'Alright, Lizzie?' she called.

The young woman was sweeping the yard out, the evidence of her hard work all around her in the harness, polished until it gleamed, and the stalls, if unoccupied, clean enough to eat a dinner in. She'd been busy, so much was clear.

'I'm fine, your Grace,' she returned and yet, alarmingly, looking anything but her usual bubbling, good-natured self. Head averted, she finished up.

'Is something wrong?' Bronwyn enquired,

feeling duty-bound to ask and guilty now that she'd sensed something was wrong and done nothing about it. She must be missing her young man and she wasn't the only one, she mused. Lizzie put down her brush, struggling to contain the tears which were so obviously threatening.

'I . . . I can't rightly say what's wrong, miss,' she stammered.

'You do know you can tell me anything, Lizzie? I can't help if I don't know what it is,' Bronwyn prompted, gently and thoroughly concerned by now.

Looking at her mistress, Lizzie felt suddenly desperate and alone and at a time when alone was the last thing she needed to be. If only Bill was here, it would be so much easier, the most wonderful thing in the world! To her dismay, the tears she'd tried so hard to check brimmed over and trickled unchecked down her cheeks. She needed to talk to someone and who better than Bronwyn? She'd have to know sometime. 'I've fallen for a baby, miss!' she blurted out and with her words, the enormity of her plight hitting her anew. She stood trembling, waiting to hear what a dreadful shame she'd brought on her employers, that she must pack her bags and leave this minute. At thoughts of this calamity, her shoulders heaved. Miraculously, she felt only comforting arms around her.

'So that's it! But goodness, it's not the worst thing that's ever happened!' Bronwyn soothed, doing her level best to disguise how disturbed she felt at this news. But she was only human, after all, and she couldn't help but think it. After all a baby would have meant to her and Harry, life was so unfair! 'Is it Bill's?' she probed.

'Of course it's Bill's, miss!' Lizzie returned, still with wits enough to be affronted Bronwyn could possibly think the child belonged to anyone other than Bill, whom she loved more than life itself! 'If only he hadn't kept on so!' she wailed, accepting the proffered hanky and doing her best to mop up her tears. 'He dreaded going back. I thought I'd never see him again . . . ' And she'd only wanted to comfort him, neither of them imagining a baby would be the result.

They hadn't thought and that was the problem.

'I want us to bring this baby up together,' she muttered, rubbing a hand over her eyes. 'But how can we, miss, when he's so far away?'

'We'll sort something out, don't worry,' Bronwyn interjected, thoughts of Katherine's response to events already bringing the shivers racing down her spine.

She'd have to be told. There was no way round it.

'Whatever will her Ladyship say? She'll turn me out . . .'

'Turn you out, child?' came a quiet voice behind. Both girls jumped, turning to find Katherine watching them speculatively. How much had she heard? That she'd heard something was obvious. The dogs, barking amiably, bounded across to Bronwyn to snuffle cold, wet noses against her hand. Their owner shook her head, her emotions anyone's guess.

'Got yourself into trouble, I expect?' she enquired, almost conversationally.

'Oh your Grace, I'm so sorry!' Lizzie wailed, bursting into tears all over again. Katherine snorted. 'Goodness, girl! Pull yourself together. You're hardly the first it's ever happened to!' To Bronwyn's surprise, though her voice was stern, her expression held a surprising sympathy. She threw her a curious look.

'More importantly, what ought we to do?' she interjected, feeling the situation moving beyond her control and wanting to retrieve it.

'What ought we to do?' Katherine's brows rose in cool astonishment. 'That's pretty obvious I should say! You must write to Harry. The man must be sent home, now, at once and be made to put things right . . .'

139

⋆　⋆　⋆

'I am glad to see you, Freddie,' Ursula murmured and, with a rush of relief, discovered her words were true. Freddie's smile at this endearment was his first since he'd arrived, so unexpectedly, tired and unshaven, two hours before. After he'd volunteered for a raiding party, above and beyond the call of duty, Harry Loxley had given him a twenty-four-hour pass, long enough to hitch a lift with a supplies wagon into Saint-Omer to see Ursula, if not long enough to get home to see his family, who must be out of their minds with worry, Ursula conceded. Alarmed at how much weight he'd lost, she'd taken him to the canteen for a decent meal before sneaking him into the girls' dormitories for a badly needed bath. She'd had to be careful. Matron would hang them out to dry if she found out they'd had a man in their rooms.

'I've been in such trouble, Freddie,' she complained, uncomfortably reminded of how much by thoughts of the abrasive, eagle-eyed woman who ran the hospital like a regimental sergeant-major. Absentmindedly, she pulled a leaf from a nearby shrub, twisting it between her fingers. Tired of the girls' common room and too many inquisitive eyes watching their every move, they'd gone for a walk in the grounds. Shrouded shapes of trees and shrubs, the lake glistening in the valley below, reflecting a large yellow moon in an ink-black sky, once she'd have thought romantic. The distant crump of the guns was a distraction they'd both grown used to, hardly noticing tonight the slow boom, as opposed to the rapid bursts betokening a long night and a heavy list of casualties. It was something to be thankful for.

Glad to unburden herself, she filled him in on recent events, ignoring his start of displeasure at her mention of Sam Tennant. 'I met him in London whilst I was training,' she explained and exasperated she had too. Just when she was beginning to wonder if she'd imagined her crazy encounter with Sam, the night the troop train met with disaster, and he'd sent her a hastily scrawled note. His unit, a branch of the Service Corps, was dodging gunfire and shells transporting troops along the Ypres Salient and shoring up defences too severely stretched for comfort. 'I'll see you as soon as I can,' he wrote, together with a lot else she'd no intention of telling Freddie and that she wished he'd kept to himself. It was hardly fair when she'd given him so little encouragement.

'Matron was furious about us tearing off to meet the troop train. She nearly sent me home. I don't know why she didn't.' She frowned. Instead, she'd been grounded and put on fatigues for four weeks. Laundry duties and gruelling days spent scrubbing floors and cleaning the latrines. She supposed it served her right.

'Don't disobey orders again, Miss Compton!' Matron had retorted angrily, her fierce gaze sweeping Ursula from head to toe. But then, oddly, the thin lips had lifted, scaring Ursula more than anything that had gone before. 'You'd make a good member of the team here, young lady, if only you'd learn how to conform,' she'd added, quietly.

'She says I'm hot-headed,' Ursula muttered, shame-faced.

'Hot-headed figures!' Suddenly Freddie grinned, the old Freddie again and so unexpectedly, Ursula's heart banged against its ribcage. He reached for her hand, frowning crossly when she pulled it away. Her gaze drawn to the unnatural glow in the sky to the west, she walked on quickly, arriving at the low railings separating the once isolated monastery from the rest of the world. The sound of the guns intensified.

'How can anyone be the same after this?' she exclaimed, swinging back towards him. She couldn't possibly be the same thoughtless girl Freddie imagined he loved!

Ripples skimmed across the surface of the water, followed by the soft plop of a fish rising, scattering moonlight and glittering stars winking from lamp-lit windows.

'You won't know me. I won't know you!' she whispered, not understanding why the thought was so unbearable.

'Of course I'd know you. I'd know you anywhere!' Freddie's voice came low and husky, swallowed by the crump of guns. He groaned. He'd determined to say so much, and was angry now to find himself so tongue-tied. He couldn't tell her all he'd thought! He stood, running his hand through his hair, looking so young and uncertain; all Ursula's resolutions crumbled.

'What's wrong?' she asked quietly.

'I've been thinking about what you said last time,' he said, sighing and conceding to himself he'd hardly thought about anything else other than all the rubbish Ursula had spouted on his last leave. As if it was right they should set each other free! His eyes glittered dangerously. Give a thing its freedom and it was bound to return. He was desperate and he'd tried everything else. 'It took me a while to realise you were right, that's all. I'm sorry, Ursula. I haven't been fair,' he muttered, glad of the covering darkness, the better to hide his face.

Peering up at him uncertainly, Ursula wondered now why she didn't feel the surge of elation she'd expected now that he'd so willingly fallen in with her plans. 'Are you sure you're alright?' she demanded crossly.

Freddie nodded uneasily, all too aware that he usually told Ursula everything. But how could he tell her what he was thinking now? It made him feel so weak, so much not what he ought to be. 'I always thought I'd die in bed surrounded by my family,' he blurted out anyway and lies turning perplexingly to truth as usually happened five minutes into any conversation with Ursula. He plunged his hands into his pockets, staring moodily out over the water. 'I always meant to have a large family and a happy home life, spending my life looking after the farm. How idiotic it seems now . . . '

His hurt was bruising. Suddenly he wasn't Freddie. She wasn't Ursula. They were just two young people, trying to make sense of senseless things. 'Freddie, you'll go home one day . . . ' she urged. 'You'll have a huge family!'

'Don't be too certain, Ursy . . . '

Wordlessly, he stared into her upturned face so against all her better judgement, she found herself longing he'd put his arms around her and hold her close. But she didn't love him! Only once . . . Oh dear God, only once, in another life, she'd thought she had . . .

⋆ ⋆ ⋆

From her vantage point at the window of the Mews flat over the stables, Lizzie Walker stood watching the morning's sunshine fall over the turrets of the Old Hall, bathing it in molten gold. She was pondering on the letter from his Grace that Bronwyn had received, days since, saying he meant to nominate Bill for a two-day training course in Bermondsley. Something to do with a new artillery gun and Lizzie could bless the army for it and Harry Loxley, too! Bronwyn said no doubt Harry meant to tag a twenty-four-hour leave on it too, which would be time enough for Bill to get himself up here to marry Lizzie. Lizzie wasn't to worry: baby or not, given the turmoil called the Western front, it was no wonder they'd heard nothing since.

But what if Bill didn't want to marry her? What if . . . oh heaven forbid, if only she could stop herself thinking it . . . What if something had happened? You only had to read the papers to see how many families were being torn apart . . .

Unreasonably angry at Bill for leaving her scope to even imagine such terror, she pushed the thought away. Worry wasn't good for a woman in her condition. Oh and she did so want to have this baby and for it to be alright, no matter what else. The thought focused her as nothing else. Letting the water from the sink, she wrung out the clothes she'd washed and, humming softly to herself, dumped them in the washing basket to run downstairs and outside where she began to peg them on the line she'd earlier slung between two trees. It was a good drying day. A good day for so many things! Stooping to pull a blouse from the tangle of clothes and as if already the baby was weighing heavy, she straightened up slowly, feeling her back. So absorbed was she, she hardly registered the hands so tenderly closing around her waist.

'My God, Lizzie if only you knew how much I've missed you,' said the one voice she longed, above all, to hear.

The blouse slipped from her fingers. 'Bill! Oh my Bill! I thought you'd never get here!' she cried, swinging round to throw her arms around him. Joy exploded into her heart, bringing with it a wild and terrible longing. 'The baby, Bill! I didn't know what to do, I've been that worried . . . '

Kisses covered her face, stilling her lips.

'Hush my love. I'm here now.'

'Please tell me you don't mind?'

The wide lopey smile she so loved and had begun to think she'd never see again, illuminated Bill's craggy features.

'It was the best news I've ever had . . . The most wonderful news!'

'I can't believe you're here . . .'

'What and your dad threatened to scalp me?'

'He never did!'

He hugged her to him, lifting her feet from the ground and swinging her round. 'I'm back, Lizzie Walker! Come to make an honest woman of you! Did you imagine I should need telling twice?'

★  ★  ★

'Are you sure, Miss?' Pink-cheeked, Lizzie gazed down happily at the wedding dress she'd just slipped over her head. It was Bronwyn's and made of the finest satin England could provide. Mary had sat up late into the night to make the necessary alterations. There was no time to lose; Bill was due in Bermondsley early the next morning. The church was booked for the afternoon.

'Of course I'm sure.' Happy for her, but most of all happy for the chance for everyone to forget the war awhile, Bronwyn smiled. The dress had only been gathering dust in her wardrobe. It should be put to good use.

'I wish you'd keep still, this hem's still not right,' Mary grumbled, through a mouthful of pins. Easing her knees, she shifted her weight from one side to the other, meanwhile darting an amused glance to Bronwyn. Who would have thought to see her Ladyship taking tea in her kitchen as if it were the most natural thing in the world! 'More tea, your Grace?' she enquired happily.

'You carry on, Mary. I'll brew fresh,' Bronwyn returned, joining in with proceedings with evident enjoyment and jumping up to set the kettle on the stove. Of Mary's start of surprise, she took not the slightest notice. In the old days at home, making tea was a task she'd undertaken willingly enough. How wonderful to make herself useful, putting her position to practical use for once. Easing the situation with the vicar, sending Bill's uniform to the laundry, making arrangements with Cook for the wedding breakfast which, if sparse, should at least be as handsome as Loxley hospitality could provide, Katherine's approval or not. That her mother-in-law had prevaricated at the use of the dining-room for the meal, insisting instead on the servants' hall downstairs, had been an issue liable to end in argument until, red-faced, Lizzie stumbled out it was very kind of her Grace but she really would prefer the servants' hall, indeed it would be awkward and out of place upstairs in the dining room and she wouldn't enjoy it one bit.

The servants' hall it was. It was Lizzie's day and Bronwyn was determined she was to have exactly what she wanted. The morning fled, taken up with making arrangements for the meal, the dress and the flowers for which Reuben had been dispatched to the village to Ada Bennett's, a woman with an eye for a neat floral arrangement. The church was at that very moment undergoing decoration by several village ladies who'd volunteered, so willingly, to help out.

Everyone loved a wedding.

Reuben returned, hovering awkwardly at the door, a bouquet of roses and gypsophilia dwarfed in his hands. 'Here they are,' he muttered, thrusting them towards Bronwyn who'd gone to answer his knock. He hadn't had to help out; he could easily have pleaded pressure of work. Underneath that gruff exterior, there beat a heart after all!

Seemingly oblivious to all that was going off inside — Lizzie's fidgets, Mary's howls of frustration and Ned, who'd wandered downstairs demanding his collar be starched — his gaze raked her face. 'You're pale. Are you alright?' he asked.

'I'm fine, Reuben. You will be going to the

wedding?' she mused, burying her nose in the bouquet and admiring its warm fragrance, her eyes twinkling with thoughts of Reuben's wicked heart.

'And what should I want with a bit of a wedding?' he demanded.

'But I should have thought . . . For Bill's sake, surely?'

'Aye, for Bill, poor lad, for all I'll be out of place.'

'You've never wanted to marry?' she asked curiously and wondering now why he never had. Much as he tried to hide it, behind his scowling exterior, in a rugged kind of way, no-one could deny that Reuben was a handsome man. The sort of man to take a woman's eye and wonder why some woman hadn't set their cap at him.

'Me, marry?' His face expressed astonishment.

'There must have been someone, Reuben?'

'Don't mock.'

'I wasn't mocking.'

'You'd recommend it then, the married state?' He genuinely wanted to know. The fact cooled her rising irritation.

'Of course I do!' she answered and aware she sounded more convinced than she felt. The thought brought the first niggle of discontent into the morning's procedures. 'Reuben, that's really none of your business!'

'You'd be amazed how much of my business it is!' he countered, surprising her. As usual, boundaries had no distinction for Reuben and it was too late to ask what he meant by it. Touching his cap, he was already hurrying away. The day was rushing by. Time was of the essence. Leaving Lizzie exclaiming over her flowers, Mary in a flap over the last bit of sewing she swore she would never get done and Tom and Ned underfoot and ill at ease in their Sunday best, she hurried back up to the hall, satisfying herself as to the progress of the wedding breakfast before flying upstairs to change.

★   ★   ★

'I'd given you up!' Katherine retorted, waiting with a thinly veiled impatience as Bronwyn ran back downstairs, fastening a pin into her hat which was plain and unadorned and chosen to match her dress. If only the same could be said of Katherine's sweeping edifice, its explosion of ostrich feathers waving preposterously above her head. Weren't they meant to remember whose day this was and blend into the background, Bronwyn wondered, even if, valuing her life, she'd never dare to express the thought. Meekly enough, she followed her mother-in-law outside to the landau which Soames, acting in his role of temporary chauffeur, had brought round to the front of the house. The horse, a bay too old for active service and borrowed from Raith Hamilton for the occasion, turned its head, winking sleepily. Bronwyn climbed in, sitting in resigned silence as Katherine proceeded to lecture her on the pitfalls of allowing servants familiarity.

'You must remember to keep your distance,' she admonished and obviously alluding to the inordinate length of time Bronwyn had spent at Mary's of late. She leant forwards, tapping Soames sharply on the shoulder with her reticule, as indication they should make a move. 'You're quiet, child,' she intoned, as if Bronwyn had a chance of getting a word in edgeways. Before she could form an answer, the older woman was off again, regaling her this time with an account of Georgina's recent doings. Wanly, Bronwyn smiled. If only they could move beyond this awkwardness with which neither could conceivably be happy.

It was unbearably hot and a relief when they'd completed the short journey to the church to step inside its cool interior and take their places in the Loxley seat. They were only just in time. The first faint strains of the wedding march struck up as Bill, pale-faced and anxious, jumped to his feet to stand, fingering the collar of his uniform and glancing nervously over his shoulder, his face breaking into a wide grin of relief as a radiant Lizzie appeared on Tom's arm and began the short walk towards him. Tom, who was giving the bride away in the absence of her father, beamed broadly. Mary wiped her eyes.

Bronwyn sat, quietly entranced and, as events unfolded before her, mused on how many weddings there must have been within these ancient walls. She dreamed the ghosts of old Loxlians rose up, watching on in benign approval of all they saw. Life went on, joy in sorrow. How wonderful to sit watching the light pouring through the magnificent stained glass west window, spilling on Lizzie and Bill, so happy and in love.

It was over, the happy congregation bursting outside into the bright sunshine, where the happy couple, clasping hands as if they'd never let go, were instantly submerged by well-wishers and where Katherine seized on the opportunity to harangue the vicar on church matters over which she constantly interfered. Waiting for a moment to offer congratulations, Bronwyn hovered uncertainly by her side, finding inexplicably that she felt nothing other than a draining tiredness. Preparations for the wedding had taken more out of her than she'd realised, she thought, passing a weary hand over her forehead and alarmed at how hot it was. How glad she'd be when the day was finally over and she could escape to her rooms!

'Bronwyn are you quite well?' Katherine demanded, pausing to draw breath.

Not sure if she was, Bronwyn nodded obediently. She stood, breathing in deeply and doing her best to pay attention to the conversation which quickly resumed. Alarmingly, black spots were dancing in front of her eyes, bringing the ground tilting oddly beneath her feet. She swayed, overcome by a fit of nausea and, for want of anywhere else, put a steadying hand on Katherine's arm. Oblivious to her mother-in-law's gasp of surprise, her fingers dug in.

Strong arms caught her as she fell senseless and in a faint, sweeping her up and carrying her tenderly back towards the church and inside. 'I knew there was something!' Gently, Reuben eased her down onto the chair which stood in the porch, kneeling to rub her hands and watching her keenly. 'Focus on my face,' he ordered.

'Whatever's the matter, child!' Katherine cried, hurrying in after him.

'I should think that's obvious woman, even to you!' he retorted, springing up, his gaze swinging back to Bronwyn, who started and coloured up.

She couldn't be. It was impossible! It was

impossible, wasn't it . . . ?

Her gaze widened in startled surprise, locking on Katherine's, her hand instinctively moving to her midriff, momentarily lost for words as a wild and surging hope sprang into her heart. It couldn't be true! How could it? The one thing she'd so wanted to give Harry in the world . . . ?

'You're pregnant . . . ' Katherine whispered, ignoring Reuben's snort of contempt and then again, 'You're pregnant!' she thundered, not even waiting for Bronwyn to deny it but moving quickly towards her, enveloping her in ostrich feathers, brocade and the overpowering scent of eau-du-cologne. When she withdrew, it was the light of triumph illuminating her handsome face. 'You must write and tell Harry . . . Now, at once! But how perfectly splendid, my dear!'

She'd done something right at last and she hadn't even known it. 'How can I be pregnant?' Bronwyn's voice filled with incomprehension as, shocked as any one of them, she struggled with the hysterical desire to shout it from the church rooftop. Katherine's voice, trembling with passion, resounded around the crumbling walls, stirring the bones of Loxley ancestors from their ancient, dusty rest.

'Oh my darling, clever girl! We have an heir to Loxley at last!'

# 6

Seated on the bench overlooking the terrace,
Bronwyn was aware she was still in shock at
Harry's miraculous appearance with the morning's milk, sending the house into uproar and
Katherine into transports of delight. He'd been
hospitalized with a fever and sent home by
the army to recuperate.

'Harry, you are pleased about the baby?'
she demanded, turning towards him and
wondering, when she found it so hard to
accept herself, if he was coping any better
than she.

'It's tremendous news, Bron!' he replied,
his smile causing her to remember why it was
she'd fallen in love with him. At the same
time, she was aware that he was itching to get
back to his men and he wasn't even bothering
to disguise it. He didn't seem to realise, or
worse, care how that made her feel.

'It seemed so awful writing with such news.
I've been so longing to see you . . . '

'I'm here now . . . '

She relaxed, reaching for his hand. 'I
wonder what kind of parents we'll make.'

'Wonderful parents!' he enthused. 'Bron,

you do look well. You're in good health?'

'Even your mother says I'm blooming!' she replied, keen to reassure him. She felt so contented even Katherine Loxley's smothering response to the fact that, at last, she was to become a grandmother, failed to cause ripples in the millpond of her happiness. News altering her relationship with her mother-in-law as nothing else and as she hoped, finally, it would benefit her relationship with her husband. At last she'd done something right, atoned in the only way possible for marrying him in the first place.

Harry cast his wife a wary look, wondering the while if she'd guessed how worried he was that she'd imagine he only cared she was pregnant because of the succession. That didn't begin to describe his feelings and he was frustrated he couldn't find words to tell her. Too buttoned up, he expected, year upon year of doing things the Loxley way. He could only hope Bronwyn would guess his feelings. He was ashamed of himself.

'Poor little blighter! What a responsibility he'll face,' he muttered.

'He might be she,' she reminded him, cautiously. Whilst allowing for the small matter of the Loxley inheritance, so long as everything was alright, Bronwyn didn't care whether they had a girl or a boy. She had hoped Harry felt the same way too.

Reality returned in the shape of duty, stifling their growing warmth.

'A boy would be better though, don't you agree?' he went on, almost despite himself. Inwardly, Bronwyn cringed. Loxley, always Loxley! Oh she knew it was important but . . . Irritated, she turned her head away, not understanding why it had to take precedence over everything, even the baby . . .

★ ★ ★

The night Harry left, so pale and tense even Katherine could see the effort it cost him, Bronwyn's sleep was disturbed by what was becoming a recurrent dream. As usual, she was standing at the head of the front steps as Harry, dressed in full uniform, ran from the house. With a horrible finality, the great front doors clanged shut behind him. Clearly he hadn't seen her. 'You do love me, Harry?' she begged, catching his arm, detaining him with the one question always on her mind but only in her dream did she dare to ask.

He stopped, swinging towards her, impatience, exasperation and something else too, flitting across his face in rapid succession. 'Bron, I've always loved you!' he protested and then, to her delight, throwing his arms around her and holding her so tightly, her feet lifted from the ground. For long, delicious moments, they swayed together, his lips covering her face, her lips and hair before, wretchedly, he thrust her from him. And then, shaking her hand impatiently away, unmindful of her protests, which were numerous and heated, he turned away and ran quickly down the steps which, meanwhile, had become elongated, disappearing at the bottom into a curling yellow and choking mist, threatening to swallow him. Bronwyn's feet were rooted to the spot and though she called and called, he never looked back. It was heartbreaking. Why wouldn't he ever look back! Always the same sickening sensation, Harry fleeing into the distance, leaving Bronwyn afraid and alone and with only the growing awareness something terrible was waiting and of which they were unaware . . .

## September 1915

Bronwyn's eyes opened wide, her hands moving instinctively to encompass the mound once laughingly described as her stomach. The baby kicked so strongly she winced. The little blighter was announcing his presence! The bedroom swam into focus. It was unbelievable to think she was already five months into her pregnancy.

If only Harry were here, he might convince Katherine his wife wasn't a piece of porcelain, liable to crack at the slightest tap. Amused at the thought, she sat up, her glance, as always, falling to the portrait of Nell which, safe from prying eyes, hung on the wall by the side of her bed

'Only be thankful you never had my mother-in-law to deal with, Nell,' she muttered, and then smiling at her foolishness, even if the one-sided conversations she so frequently held with Nell made her feel better about so many things — the baby, Harry, the millstone of Loxley, so constantly around their necks. She told Nell everything and Nell, with her happy, smiling face, only seemed to encourage her.

She'd managed a good hour's sleep, enough to keep even Katherine from fretting she wasn't taking enough rest, Bronwyn mused. At the sound of a motor drawing up to the front façade, she jumped up, running a brush through her hair and smoothing down her dress before making her way downstairs in time to see Soames ushering her parents into the hall. She was delighted to see them. Katherine was an intimidating enough hostess to put anyone off and their visits were far too infrequent.

'Darling you're looking wonderful! Wait until I tell Tilly, who sends her love by the way . . . Now! We can't wait to hear all your news!' Nervousness was making her garrulous. Dorothea Colfax enveloped her daughter in a warm embrace.

'You do look well!' George Colfax agreed, happily and in his own quiet way, every bit as excited by the coming event as Katherine.

Bronwyn hadn't realised just how much she'd missed them. If only she could go home until Harry's return, how much easier this pregnancy would be . . .

'You should try telling Katherine,' she responded, rolling her eyes.

'That bad?' George Colfax whispered, chuckling. Bronwyn stood impatiently by, waiting for Soames to divest them of their coats before leading the way into the sitting room, only to discover Katherine was already entertaining a visitor this afternoon: Lawrence Payne, the vicar of nearby Harrington and the cleric temporarily in charge of Loxley whilst the Reverend Thomas, its usual incumbent, had answered the call and joined up. A thin, elderly man with a kindly face who sprang to his feet, his relief at their arrival only too evident.

'Wonderful to see you, your Grace. And I take it these good people are your parents?' he asked.

'Dr and Mrs Colfax . . . do sit down and make yourselves at home,' Katherine interrupted, taking charge before adding, bossily, 'Bronwyn, sit here, by the fire. You might take the chance of a rest; there'll be little enough time once our baby arrives . . . '

'My daughter's pregnant, not ill, your Grace,' George Colfax argued, testily.

'Certainly pregnancy's no illness,' Katherine agreed and not one whit put out. 'However, I'm afraid she'll make herself ill if she carries on as she is!'

'What's this?' George Colfax demanded, swinging back towards Bronwyn who grimaced. She wasn't ill. She was blooming in fact and even her father could see it. She knew exactly to what Katherine alluded. 'I'm merely concerned we're getting behind with the work round the estate . . . ' she prevaricated and referring to the list of things yet to do, so endless and time-consuming and which, an unnecessary distraction, had been playing on her mind.

'But surely it's not all up to you, darling?' Dorothea Colfax interjected.

She was under siege from all sides and matters could have deteriorated but fortuitously and with immaculate timing, Soames brought in the tea-things.

'I hope you're settling in?' Lawrence Payne

murmured, sensing Bronwyn's discomfort and thankfully coming to her rescue. He took his tea cup and sat in the chair by her side, angling his lean frame towards her and cutting her off thereby from the rest of the company.

'Life here is a little different to what I'm used to,' she acknowledged ruefully and at once liking this gently spoken man. 'I suspect, things as they are, we both have much to cope with, Reverend Payne.'

'Lawrence, please . . . '

'Lawrence then . . . '

Shortly, surprisingly, Bronwyn found the talk turning to the old man's hobbies and his interest in local history. It was too good a chance to miss.

'Do you know much about Nell Loxley?' she enquired and darting a nervous glance towards Katherine. Lord help the pair of them if Katherine heard her asking questions about Nell! The old man's face shone with interest.

'Our notorious Duchess? She was a most single-minded woman!' he enthused. 'Most folk roundabout flocked to the King's cause. Nell, of course, along with her husband, was a staunch Parliamentarian.' He leaned back, rubbing his chin with long, nervous fingers. 'Charles had a Catholic wife, and too many

163

loose ways for Rufus Hyssop's liking. He subscribed a large sum of money for the raising of Parliamentary troops, Nell's money it has to be said. He'd had an eye on her fortune from the start. A boon to an ambitious man determined to get on . . . '

'The marriage wasn't a happy one?' Bronwyn frowned, hating the thought Nell might have been unhappy. She'd looked so content in her portrait but that might have been painted before she fell so madly for Rufus Hyssop and the country had been plunged into a bloody and merciless civil war.

The rector nodded. 'Hyssop was a man of strong convictions and treated any Royalist unfortunate enough to fall into his hands with unflinching severity. They were troubled times, your Grace, tearing families asunder.'

'She was still on the wrong side.'

Lawrence Payne smiled. 'In her defence, she was a courageous woman, I do believe once taking up a musket to defend Loxley against attack.' The cleric sat back, regarding Bronwyn with a keen interest. 'I have a book, an in-depth analysis of the civil war, which happens to hold an eye-witness account of the attack against Loxley. I'll bring it, if you wish, the next time I'm round . . . '

★  ★  ★

Bronwyn did wish but she'd hardly expected it to be so soon. It was the following day and Katherine was at one of her interminable committee meetings. Fortuitously, she was alone and drinking her coffee in the morning room when, to her surprise, Soames ushered the elderly cleric, smiling broadly, into the room. He hurried towards her.

'You seemed so interested!' he said, handing her a cloth-bound book by way of greeting, his voice infused with a boyish enthusiasm to which she couldn't help but respond. 'I've marked the relevant page, containing extracts from a gentlewoman of breeding, by name of Eliza Pritchard, discovered in family papers after her death. She held the position of sewing mistress and provides a perfectly splendid account of a Parliamentary attack . . . ' Bronwyn sprang up, bidding Soames to fetch another cup and making her visitor comfortable before sinking back into her chair, eagerly opening the book.

'But don't you mean Royalist attack?' she asked.

Lawrence Payne's eyes twinkled. 'So family lore has it and a natural enough mistake given the household were such staunch Parliamentarians. But please . . . Read on. It soon becomes clear . . . '

Bronwyn read aloud from the relevant

page, her voice rising with excitement. But it was so interesting! And she did so want to know as much as she could of Nell . . . 'I watched from my chamber window . . . a sea of angry faces, gathering outside the gates, demanding entrance and, my dear, brave lady, musket in hand, calling for the gates to be opened before issuing boldly forth. How proud she looked, striding amongst them, their equal in courage so, as many as they were, they fell back, aye and looked ashamed of themselves too, as well they might. 'We harbour no Royalists here, good men!' she cried out. 'Away with you, else my husband hears of it and you live to rue the day . . . ''

Bronwyn's voice dwindled. There was something in this she still didn't understand. 'But how could they think she harboured a King's man?' she demanded, frowning and looking up from the page to her companion. Given Rufus Hyssop's support for the Parliamentarians, it hardly made sense. Lawrence Payne's thin shoulders lifted.

'Alas, as to that, we shall never know. The account doesn't specify. England was a hotbed of suspicion. The Royalists had been defeated at Naseby and were on the run. Rufus was probably away on Parliamentary business and was no doubt keen to hush it up on his return. There was no reason Nell would ever have gone against him. Houses were often ransacked for no other reason than a crowd of men banded together and seized their chance.' But they hadn't accounted on Nell. 'Oh, but I wish I could have seen her!' Bronwyn enthused, imagining the scene. Flame-haired, passionate, no care for her safety, a defenceless woman amongst so many men. The vicar's next words filled her with a rising excitement. 'I have a family portrait of Nell at the vicarage. An amateur daub I picked up at a local auction; I'd love you to see it, some time. Hyssop's manor isn't so far, either, if you've a mind to make a day of it one day soon . . . '

★　★　★

There was a huge whoosh of noise as the road in front erupted in a fireball of vivid yellow flame, bringing clods of earth and stone thundering down onto the bonnet of the ambulance. Instinctively, Ursula ducked, at the same time, slamming on the brakes to bring the vehicle to a screeching halt. The night's barrage had extended well into the morning, following on from a night impossibly spent picking their way over pot-holed roads to the Casualty Clearing Station south of Ypres. They'd been commissioned to pick up a wounded officer, a mission not without its dangers, Matron warned before they set off and fixing Ursula with a fierce gaze. 'Mind you follow orders, young lady!'

Such a mission meant someone high up had been pulling strings, Ursula hazarded, aware of the more usual route to the military hospital via the rail network. At least there'd been room in the ambulance to take another soldier of altogether lower rank, one of too many Tommies crowding the makeshift stations, the first port of call for any of the wounded. Standing in the tent-like structure, so lacking in equipment and basic facilities, Ursula had become only too aware of the appalling human cost of war. Inadequate, shame-faced, her impotence her undoing, she hurried away as soon as she decently could. But outside, how she cursed herself for her cowardice!

'Alright back there?' she called shakily.

First picking herself up from the floor, Dodi checked on their two patients, fortunately proving none the worse for their experience. 'Just about,' she grinned.

'Nearly got us there before the ambulance,' the young Tommy piped up, so typical of his lot. Black humour was sometimes the only way to keep going.

Carefully circumnavigating the crater left in

the road, they set off once more, arriving at the hospital in Saint-Omer a good hour late but without further incident. 'Am I ready for a hot bath!' Dodi grumbled, once they'd resigned their patients into the tender care of the hospital. She stretched her arms, throwing Ursula a curious look. 'Are you alright? You've hardly said a word all morning.'

'Not exactly,' Ursula admitted, following her friend outside into a bright wall of sunlight, the last lingering remains of summer seeming to mock the war, man-made and so puny and inconsequential in comparison. Dodi's brows rose.

'You're not still fretting about Freddie?'

'Of course not!' she answered, too quickly and fooling Dodi no more than herself. Thoughts of Freddie were incredibly painful. She hadn't heard from him for weeks, not even a postcard. He couldn't have made his feelings clearer if he'd told her to her face he never wanted to see her again.

'I thought you two wanted some time apart?' Dodi was clearly puzzled and so, she had to admit, was Ursula.

'I suppose,' she agreed half-heartedly and remembering now how relieved Freddie had seemed when finally, he'd realised she was setting him free. He must have a girl in every village he passed through, and wouldn't be

169

the slightest bit bothered whether he saw her again or not. And all the times he'd sworn he loved her!

A man was headed towards them. With a start of surprise, Ursula recognised Sam Tennant and an altogether different Sam from the last time she'd seen him; his uniform for once pressed and clean but better still, his easy-going manner returned, giving him a jaunty air so once again he appeared the forward young man she'd first met on top of a London omnibus. She'd heard so little from him of late; she'd almost forgotten his existence.

'What are you doing here?' she demanded.

He pulled off his cap, bowing theatrically towards the bottom of the long, sloping lawn and the gates by which he'd parked his bus, more dilapidated in appearance than ever. 'Your carriage awaits, mademoiselle!' he grandly informed her.

What ever plans he had, Ursula had no intentions of falling in with them.

'I'm on my way back to the digs.'

His face fell. 'But I've packed a picnic!'

'It'll do you good, you should go, Ursy . . .' Dodi murmured, teasingly. Nodding to Sam, who for some reason she liked, she trotted quickly away, leaving Ursula frowning after her.

'I'm sorry,' she muttered, turning back and

trying to let the young man down gently. 'I really am tired. We've had rather a time of it, of late . . . '

'And you think I haven't? Please Ursula. I only have a couple of hours. If you knew the trouble I've been to . . . '

He was impossible to resist. Shortly and incongruously, Ursula found herself perched on the front seat of a London Piccadilly Bus, hurtling through sweetly scented hedgerows, deep within the French countryside whilst, paying worryingly scant attention to his driving, Sam entertained her with snippets of his life since last they'd met. The battles he'd witnessed, the constant shelling, the weary troops. He was remarkably cheerful about it, it was impossible to be in his company and not feel cheered, even now, dead-beat and out on her feet. Passing through several villages of picture-book cottages and chateaus obscured by their cloaks of wine groves, finally they turned off down a winding country lane and onto a beaten track, the end of which tailed off into a meadow through which ran a gurgling brook. 'Water's always so romantic, dontcha know!' He grinned.

Before she could answer, he slammed on the brakes and jumped out, walking smartly round to the boot which, to her astonishment, he opened up to lift out a trestle table and two chairs. Next he took out a wicker basket containing a white cloth, glasses and a bottle of wine and even a tapered vase bearing a red rose, scattering petals, like confetti. There was food too, freshly baked bread, cheese, olives and tomatoes.

'Sam, stop!' she cried, unsure whether to laugh or cry. He was a crazy man and she was even crazier allowing herself to be dragged all the way out here. When he pulled out a chair, she sat down and gave herself up to a deep belly laugh. But he was incorrigible!

There was more. He climbed back on to the bus and, shortly, she heard the strains of a string quartet from a gramophone he'd purloined from heaven knows where. As if in competition, from a bush nearby, a nightingale burst forth. In all her short life, Ursula had never had such a strange and yet touchingly wonderful experience. One which, wonderfully, lifted her out of all the horror she'd experienced of late. Wishing life could always be this way, she kicked off her shoes and sat back and sipped her wine. Miraculously, all her tiredness had drifted away.

'I can't believe you've done all this for me,' she murmured with a rush of gratitude. 'It's good to see you smile.' Unlikely as it was, an odd introspection lurking under the bravado and forced wit, Sam was serious for once. He sat down, taking a fortifying swallow of wine.

'Life's for living, Ursula,' he urged softly, words she'd heard from his lips more than once. 'You do know I like you? I mean really like you . . . '

He was going to spoil things. Why couldn't he just let it be? 'Sam, don't . . . '

'You're so different from any other girl I've ever met.' He ploughed on regardless, ignoring her protests. 'And I know there's been far too many of those but I'd never met you before . . . ' He was the kind of man who would always flirt with a pretty face but he still had his head screwed on and was right about so many things, Ursula mused. Life was there to be experienced or why else would she have crossed the channel and immersed herself in this terrible war? When he kissed her, she didn't pull away as her instincts told her she should. Instead, she relaxed into it, enjoying the taste of wine and olives on his lips and, above all, the sense of letting herself go for once. It had been too long and life was too short with a habit of ending too abruptly. Music drifted over their heads, mingling with the sound of water splashing merrily over the stones and the nightingale nearby was still singing its heart out . . .

'For goodness sake, Bronwyn!' Katherine snapped.

'Be careful, your Grace!'

Taking an unprecedented liberty, Tom Compton grabbed Bronwyn by the shoulders, pulling her quickly away from the vicinity of the huge horse which, only moments earlier, had been standing by so benignly. They were in the stable yard. Alarmingly large hooves clattered against the cobbles and a large rump swung round towards them. Reuben, standing nearby and talking to Lizzie, jumped back, apparently startled. Bronwyn hadn't realised he was so uncomfortable around horses.

'I'll have him, your Grace,' Lizzie proffered, taking the reins and, talking to her charge gently, led him, docile as a baby, out of the yard and into the stables where a berth had already been made ready. Lizzie was looking well. Pregnancy suited her, Bronwyn considered.

'I'll get on then,' Reuben muttered, flushing and momentarily lifting his gaze to hers before walking swiftly away. No-one else appeared to have noticed his discomfort or, if so, had taken any account of it.

'But what a beautiful horse!' Bronwyn enthused.

Katherine had been haggling for days with

the gypsy women, presently camped on the edges of the estate, and had finally been successful. 'I knocked them down eventually,' she agreed, smiling complacently. 'We had need of a horse . . . so . . . there we are, my dear. There's no need to worry your pretty head any longer!'

The horse had been brought to stop Bronwyn fretting over the winter ploughing; that much was clear. 'We could certainly use one about the place,' she answered, not wanting to appear churlish yet still unsure she was comfortable with the idea of such largesse when surely, such a sturdy beast would be better employed at the front? 'It won't get us into any trouble?' She frowned, feeling duty-bound to ask.

Katherine's snort of disapproval was audible.

'I'd be upset to see such a beautiful animal making an end in France, if you don't mind me saying, your Grace,' Tom Compton replied, jumping in quickly and referring to the army's habit of commandeering every horse they could lay their hands on.

'There it is, then,' Katherine retorted, putting an end to the matter. As far as she was concerned, the estate was desperate for horse power and thus, they had a perfect right to make use of this one. Mayhap she was right, Bronwyn conceded. The little group dispersed. Momentarily at a loose end, she wandered over to the stables to see the newcomer bedded down and stood, arms draped over the stable door, enjoying the best of the afternoon's sunshine as Lizzie rubbed the huge beast down and found him oats and straw. How odd it was, Bronwyn conjectured, given their pregnancies running so concurrently, how differing were their respective experiences. Lizzie, carrying on as normal, running the car, keeping the stables going, even giving Tom Compton a hand when she'd time, whereas she, Bronwyn, Duchess of Loxley and owner of all she surveyed . . .

'I do believe Katherine will drive me mad,' she muttered, desperate to talk to someone and trusting this happy young woman implicitly. Lizzie stood up, rubbing her back, nodding her head in acknowledgement.

'She means well, miss. It's because she's so wound up about the baby. It means too much.' That about summed it up and perhaps she'd just needed Lizzie to point it out. Katherine cared too much and, given all the baby was likely to inherit, was it any wonder! Bronwyn smiled. It was impossible not to be happy around Lizzie and her obvious joy in her pregnancy.

'You're looking well, Lizzie.'

'And so are you, too, if you don't mind me

saying so, miss!' the young woman assured her, taking a liberty and suddenly not caring two hoots. Pregnancy was making her reckless but she did so like her young mistress, who'd grown more a friend than an employer and more, the sort of young woman she'd be proud to have as a friend. Bill was right; things were changing and the old order breaking down. Perhaps the time would come when she and such as this young woman here, could meet as equals, odd as that seemed right now. 'We'll be alright, miss, once our men folk are home!' she exclaimed.

'More children?' Bronwyn teased.

'Oh your Grace; I've always wanted a houseful!' Lizzie returned and taking Bronwyn's words at their face value. 'Just me and Bill and a whole houseful of children — what more could any girl want!'

The picture she painted was an appealing one. Of course Bronwyn wanted children, especially this one, but for itself she'd decided and not just for Loxley and its relentless succession, important as she knew that was. Just her and Harry and a house full of children. A smile tugged her lips upwards. Perhaps a little more than that! Something else to put her brain to use . . .

The afternoon was a warm one and she didn't feel like returning inside. Motivated by the thought, she made her way down the meadow, surprised to find herself on the path through the trees leading down to Reuben's cottage. He was outside, chopping sticks, chickens and pheasants running round his feet and in and out of the kitchen, making for a pleasant pastoral scene. Glancing up as she emerged into the clearing, he threw down the axe and tumbled the result of his labours into a basket at his feet. 'You're a stranger here!' he retorted gruffly, his earlier discomfort over the horse apparently forgotten. He looked pleased to see her. 'Are you alright?' he demanded, giving her a second and closer glance.

'I'm fine,' she replied, wondering why he asked. Now she was here, she hardly knew what to say. 'We hardly had chance to talk earlier, Reuben,' she tried cautiously and thinking to lead into the conversation. 'Father was wondering . . . He'd love to see your work sometime.'

Reuben heaved the basket up from the floor. 'No doubt,' he retorted dryly, heading inside, and then, seemingly aware he might have sounded rude, calling over his shoulder, 'Would you like some tea?'

Bronwyn nodded. After her spat with Katherine, it was comforting to follow him inside and sit down in the neat little kitchen with its smoky fire, casting the room in a flood of warm colours whilst Reuben busied himself with the tea things, perfectly at home in his domain. 'Is something worrying you?' he demanded at last, pushing a mug across the table towards her. He sat across, drinking his tea, apparently with all the patience in the world. Patience wasn't an attribute with which she normally associated Reuben and there was no way other than to come right out with her thoughts.

'I didn't realise you were afraid of horses, Reuben,' she blurted out, cursing her impetuosity the moment the words were out of her mouth. Instantly, their growing companionship ended.

'And what if I am!' he growled, getting up so quickly he knocked against the table and spilt the tea.

'Why . . . nothing; I only asked! Reuben, please . . . I meant nothing by it!' She sat, itching to help, yet afraid to offend him further as, tight-lipped, he mopped up. 'Reuben, we all have difficulties,' she pointed out, once she'd considered she'd given him time enough to compose himself. He flushed but at least sat down again, accepting the fresh tea she poured and watching her with dark, brooding eyes. The atmosphere prickled with a tension she didn't understand.

'You were injured by a horse in some way?'

she intuited, alarmed at the way he flinched at her words. Somehow she'd stumbled onto the enigma of this man. 'Please talk to me . . . ' she prompted, gently.

His eyes flickered with pain, like some dumb beast in distress. If only he'd tell her! 'I was a lad in the wrong place at the wrong time,' he muttered reluctantly. 'The horse involved always was a cussed beast. It trampled me underfoot. I was lucky things were no worse.' An accident with a horse — but there was no need for it to have remained such a secret!

'There was someone else involved . . . ' she muttered, thinking aloud, ignoring his start of surprise. Pregnancy, it seemed, had heightened her senses. She blurted out the first name to enter her head. 'Was it Harry?' Her eyes widened in amazement as she read the truth in his face. 'Reuben, it was Harry! You can't not tell me now!'

'We were only lads,' he muttered cagily.

'And?' she prompted, resisting the desire to shake the rest out of him.

'And Harry might have been quiet but like most his age, he still had a streak of devil in him,' he complained testily.

It was hard to reconcile the boy with the man she knew. 'Go on, please . . . ' she urged.

Surprisingly, he told her without further

demure. 'The horse was a thoroughbred the old Duke had won in a bet, and from the King himself would you please!' he began in a low voice, but one filled with emotion. 'A wild beast, but beautiful and Harry fell in love with it despite his father forbidding him to go anywhere near. Their relationship was an odd one, the Duke thinking his son a milksop, the boy naturally enough wanting to do anything to prove his father wrong. It seemed I knew him better than anyone!

'True enough, I caught him, the very next morning, at the crack of dawn, saddling the beast and leading it out into the yard! White as a sheet, he was. I reasoned, argued, begged him to go back and do as he was told, for once. 'Make me,' he said and him only half my size and, all the while, the beast clattering and snorting behind him, the look of the devil in its eyes. We must have been making a fair old noise. Old Ned's father, Joseph, who lived in the rooms over the stables, saw us and rushed out. Something must have startled the horse, perhaps it was just Joseph . . . ' His voice trailed away.

'Reuben, please tell me . . . ' Bronwyn demanded. 'You simply have to tell me everything now!'

'It reared up, suddenly,' he murmured, first taking a steadying swallow of tea. 'God knows how it missed Harry's head for he was rooted to the spot. All I could think was to get him out of it and . . . '

'You pushed him out of the way?' Bronwyn breathed, seeing all now.

'Aye.' Reuben grinned, weakly. 'That's about the size of it, only I wasn't as agile as I'd imagined . . . '

He didn't have to tell her more. Shock, pity, horror, welled up inside, his words explaining so much, so previously unexplainable. The horse had trampled Reuben instead of Harry, smashing his leg so badly it had left him with a limp for life. Why hadn't Harry ever told her? No wonder Reuben hated feeling so beholden to the Loxleys, whilst they, apparently, let him get away with so much. An independent man constrained to depend on others. How difficult that must be.

'Katherine must feel she owes you so much,' she murmured.

'Aye, so she says . . . ' he responded bitterly.

'Is that all there is?' she demanded and still unsure if it explained everything.

'Why, isn't that enough? What more should there be?'

The gamekeeper's voice had grown mocking again, an odd light dancing in his dark eyes, giving them a devilish light of which she couldn't make sense. She'd never get to the bottom of this man! There was more, she knew and, worse and so frustratingly, he had no intention of telling her what it was.

* * *

The men were worn out. They'd been too long at the Front with more expected of them than was humanly possible. Only too aware of it, Harry sat at the rough deal table, toying with the letter he'd been writing to Bronwyn and wondering if he'd managed in any way to convey what he so much wanted to say. He couldn't wait for this baby! But she surely knew that already! He couldn't wait for the war to be over so they could begin to repair their marriage, if only it weren't for Loxley.

Bronwyn would never understand about Loxley, that was the problem.

He leaned back, rubbing eyes, red-rimmed through lack of sleep before glancing round at his men, taking their ease in a farmhouse kitchen still bearing traces of the Boche who'd previously occupied it. The argument had been short and fierce, resulting in losses either side when it hadn't really mattered so much who occupied the blessed place! A gain here, a loss there, months of stalemate and more to come by the looks of it.

'At least we dined well,' Harry murmured,

to no-one in particular, giving up on the letter and crossing the room to Freddie and Bill who were sharing a companiable silence by the fire. The kitchen bore the tantalising aroma of the four hen birds Alf Walker had brought in earlier from one of his brief forages into the local countryside.

'Fell off the back of a wagon,' he chuckled, his grin so wide, it nearly split his face in two. No one asked where he'd got them, the men only being relieved at a change from their interminable diet of hard biscuits and bully beef. They'd had a feast, enhanced by the several bottles of wine inexplicably left by the Boche and which little Stanley Pickering had so happily discovered in the cellar. Good naturedly, Freddie and Bill budged up. Harry sat down, took out his pipe, taking comfort in their calm acceptance of his company. Back home, or within earshot of the big brass, normality was quickly resumed. Here was a different world.

'How's Lizzie?' he enquired and aware Bill had received a letter only that morning, via the soldiers bringing rations up the line.

'Bonny as anything, your Grace!' Bill returned and clearly delighted to be on his favourite subject. 'Not long now before the young un'll be here. Well . . . I've no need to say that to you, of all people!'

A smile passed between the two. Old married men with bairns on the way, both good-naturedly putting up with the banter amongst the men which baby was likely to put in first appearance. Feeling out of it, thinking of Ursula and how impossibly painful it was denying himself even the solace of a letter, Freddie rolled a cigarette and lit up. If only she wasn't so blessed pig-headed! She should know exactly how much he loved her without him having to tell her the whole while . . .

'Dunna take on, you'll sort it out. Ursula Compton was born stubborn,' Bill soothed, sensing his friend's frustration and patting his arm in a gesture, if awkward, infinitely well meant.

'Women are a different breed, Bill,' Harry concurred heavily.

'They're that, right enough, for all I love my Lizzie!' Bill grinned, standing up and stretching before crossing the room to draw the curtains. It was a fine evening, the moon already up and reminding him, in some way, of home. He stood momentarily, captivated by the scene. Great harvest moons shining over Loxley, man and beast alike! His roaming gaze fell to the little copse of trees at the back of the garden which was shrouded in the mist rising up from the ground and shimmering on the lake beyond. Why, how pretty it looked . . .

All at once, he breathed in sharply, rubbing at his chest as if something had hurt him before glancing down in puzzled surprise at the odd red stain spreading over his shirt front. There was a chair by the window. Aware his legs were about to give way, not understanding why this should be, he sat down heavily. His mouth had gone dry; his tongue clove to the roof of his mouth. By, but what wouldn't he give for a sup of summat! Dazed, he looked across to Freddie, his head suddenly full of Lizzie and the awful and inevitable truth; he wasn't going to see their baby after all. What a damn thing it was . . . whatever would she do without him? All the life . . . him and Lizzie . . . Oh, dear God help him but it wasn't fair . . .

He was still fretting over it when he stopped thinking altogether and nothing mattered then, not even Lizzie.

'Bill! Oh no . . . Bill.'

Freddie mouthed the words, stuck in his throat, choking him.

Outside, an owl hooted. Remembering only the pleasant face at the window, the single shot in his rifle dispensed, the German sniper who'd fired it in retaliation for the earlier loss of the farmhouse, ghosted silently away through the trees.

# 7

Lizzie was plunged into a nightmare from which she knew instinctively, she'd never wake up. Bill was dead and the wonder was the news hadn't done for her, too. She stood, staring foolishly at the postman, the letter he'd just delivered, and which she'd so eagerly ripped open, left trembling in her hand.

'My darling daughter, there's no easy way to tell you this . . . '

The postman's face was filled with a terrible compassion. Still in her nightdress and shawl, she pushed past him and with the tears pouring unchecked down her face, began to run, helplessly, helter-skelter down the road towards the hall, round to the great front door, beating her fists against it, shouting at the top of her lungs for someone, anyone, to wake her up and tell her this wasn't happening, it wasn't true. She couldn't believe Bill was dead — oh, she couldn't believe it was true!

The door swung open, gentle hands

ushering her inside, fetching a blanket with which to wrap her whilst someone held a cup of tea to her chattering lips. 'Oh my poor child . . . my poor child!' Katherine's face loomed large — or was it Bronwyn's? One merged with the other so poor Lizzie had no clear idea what happened next. And all the while, the terrible grinding certainty overwhelming her like a blanket of poisonous fog, invading every fibre of her being, she'd never see Bill again.

Dark days followed, turning to long and bitter weeks in which, kind and understanding as everyone was, no-one knew quite what to do with her. How could they when she'd no idea what to do with herself? Vaguely, she was aware of Bill's child growing inside her. She felt it kick. Sometimes, in her more lucid days, she even talked to it and told it what a good man its poor father had been.

She had to go on for the baby's sake, her only remaining connection to Bill, so it became like a religion to her, dragging her back to work to throw herself into all the tasks piling up in her absence. A driving force, which saw her rise, sleepless from her bed at first light, not returning there until darkness and exhaustion claimed her. Anything to keep her thoughts at bay! How could she bear it! She'd no idea how to go on and, if it wasn't for the baby, she would have wished herself out of it, too.

## Nov 1915

'I'm worried about Lizzie, Reuben,' Bronwyn murmured.

'Aye, poor lass.' The gamekeeper was whittling a piece of wood, one foot rested on the low stone wall by which they stood and across from which he'd parked the Rolls. Below them, in the valley, nestled Hyssop Manor, a long, low, half-timbered house, where Rufus Hyssop had grown up, happily too, by all accounts until the seeds of ambition had sprung to life and he'd cast ambitious eyes Nell Loxley's way. Lawrence Payne had told Bronwyn all about it when she'd called round at the vicarage earlier that afternoon. According to Lawrence, the Hyssop family line had long since died out, though their place of residence was still worth a visit, thus leading to their presence here. The American family owning the house had long since returned across the water and, given England's state of uncertainty, no-one could blame them. Somehow though, Bronwyn did and not just because she would have loved to see inside.

'She's too calm, as if she can't . . . won't accept it yet,' she mused and wondering again what she could do to help when the irreversible fact was that Bill was dead and there was nothing anyone could do. Their very worst nightmare, every single one of them, and that it should have happened to Lizzie — leaving her pregnant and alone was dreadful.

Harry had written. Lizzie had shown Bronwyn the letter, full of praise for Bill who'd turned out a splendid soldier Harry said, one admired and respected by all the men. Lizzie should be proud he'd been so brave and made the ultimate sacrifice . . . Words only words but what else could he have said, Bronwyn pondered, wondering sadly too, what it had cost him to write it and how many more similar letters he'd have to pen before this dreadful war was done. 'I do wish she'd come with us this afternoon, all the same,' she repeated, helplessly and turning her troubled gaze to Reuben. 'It might have helped to take her mind off Bill awhile. There's nothing else we can do for her.'

The form of a tiny bird was miraculously taking shape beneath Reuben's hands. As he whittled, his dark brows gathered, yet she knew he was paying attention to all she said. 'Don't take on. She's stronger than you

190

think,' he replied, after some consideration. It would never have crossed his mind he was being too familiar but he was right, in any case. Oddly for such a bitterly cold afternoon, Bronwyn was aware of the scent of lavender drifting from across the valley, a sensation that had followed her around all day. Pregnancy was giving her strange fancies. Feeling some of her cares drift away, she lifted her face towards it.

'Do you imagine Nell was happy, Reuben?' she mused whilst inwardly conceding happy was the last thing Harry's ancestor had looked in the first of the two portraits she'd viewed that afternoon and which took pride of place on Lawrence Payne's sitting room wall. Even given the sweet little boy, George Purcell, the future sixth Duke, spit of his mother and whose chubby arms clung around her neck, Nell's gaze had held a haunted look. Rufus Hyssop stood behind her, one hand clamped possessively on his wife's shoulder, his dark, saturnine face staring boldly from the canvas. The portrait next to it was of Rufus and his brother Alexander, as boys, painted in the Hall at Hyssop Manor. Even then, dressed in a plain, dark tunic and standing in front of the great stone fireplace, Rufus had looked brooding and intense. His younger brother was seated beside him, fairer and altogether more delicate, gazing up at his sibling as if seeking approval. There'd been no need to wonder which was the most dominant of the pair.

'I never imagine,' Reuben retorted sharply, shutting the blade of his knife and dropping it into his pocket. He held the little carving out towards her.

'Is this for me?' She took it, feeling touched.

'Aye, if you want . . . ' he muttered awkwardly.

She sensed his gaze fastening on her face, trying to gauge her response. 'It's beautiful, Reuben,' she said.

'So it is,' he answered and with not a shred of modesty.

'I told Katherine I'd heard about your accident.' She'd not had chance to tell him yet and seized on the opportunity now. They'd hardly had a moment together of late.

'Did you now!'

'It annoyed her.'

'Aye, I bet.'

Bronwyn frowned, unsettled by the memory of Katherine's expression when she'd confessed she'd wormed from him, the secret of Reuben's accident. 'It's none of your business!' her mother-in-law had retorted sharply, then pointedly changing the conversation to other things — the baby, Harry, the blessed war. Anything other than the subject under discussion and rattling on so quickly; frustratingly, the chance to find out more was gone. She was burning to know what Katherine thought about Harry's actions, boyhood prank as it was, leaving Reuben lamed for life! There was more to this business than she thought, and so much more to Reuben too, Bronwyn mused, if only she could coax him to open up.

He scowled towards the car, taking no pains to hide the fact he was eager to return to the work from which she'd dragged him. There was little to be learned of Nell here, and yet . . . In the early throes of her relationship with Rufus Hyssop, before she'd married him and discovered his true nature, Nell could conceivably have run down this very slope to the house, a young woman happy in love. If the painting was anything to go by, how sad to think, her hopes for her marriage had somehow all gone wrong.

'Why are you so interested in Nell and the Hyssops?' he asked.

'No reason.' She shrugged, wary of being mocked and not yet understanding it herself. She was drawn to Nell and that was all there was to it, her interest now expanding to encompass other people who'd inhabited the young woman's world.

There was nothing else but to let Reuben

drive her home. He returned to work whilst still thinking about Lizzie, Bronwyn hurried up to the stables.

The young woman was sweeping out the stalls, their single occupant having been released for the day for Tom Compton's use and the start of the winter ploughing. They were late this year with so many things.

'I do wish you'd have come with us, Lizzie. The fresh air would have done you good,' Bronwyn began, immediately alarmed at how pale the young woman looked.

'I'm alright, miss,' Lizzie replied, turning a strained face her way.

She was holding herself together and that was all that could be said for her. If only she could let go of her grief and Bronwyn could find some way to help her. Disconsolate, Bronwyn returned to the Hall and to an evening spent with Katherine, who, alarmed at what she saw as the afternoon's unnecessary outing, spent it reproving her for overtaxing her strength. She did her best to shut it out, relieved finally to escape to bed, where she slept deeply, awaking the following morning to the sound of raised voices downstairs when normally the servants would be going about their business quietly so as not to wake the rest of the house. Katherine's strident tones drifted upwards, infiltrating

Bronwyn's sleep-lagged state, followed by Tom Compton's more measured tone. A door slammed. Opening her eyes to the pale light filtering through a gap in her bedroom curtains, she registered something was wrong, rising quickly to throw on her dressing gown and hurry downstairs. Soames was on the telephone in the hall.

'Your Grace, what a commotion!' he said, hand over the mouthpiece. 'Her Ladyship and Compton have just gone up to the stables ... the blessed horse is gone ... stolen! I'm on to the Constabulary now though I'm afraid it'll be far too late ...'

It was the most he'd ever spoken to her. Cursing the news, Bronwyn returned upstairs to dress before hurrying over to the stables, where she found Katherine, white-faced with anger, standing by the open stable doors, letting her feelings be known to Tom who stood twisting his cap between his large, capable hands. Determined to make the best of the weather and crack on with the ploughing, he'd risen early, only to discover the place empty and the horse they'd named Merry, for his happy disposition and willingness to work, vanished from his stall.

'Gypsies!' Katherine bridled, with the kind of look that made Bronwyn fear for their safety should she ever lay hands on them.

'We have no proof,' Tom interjected and ever the voice of reason.

'Fiddlesticks man!' she erupted, staring grimly towards the empty stall. 'It must have rankled I'd knocked them down to such a low price. They mean to sell him on again, there's no doubt about it!'

'But your Grace . . . '

'Think about it, man!' she snapped angrily. 'Why else would they have let me have him? They've stolen him back; a well known ruse and I can't believe I fell for it.'

At that moment, through the doorway to her flat upstairs and roused by their voices, Lizzie's dressing gowned figure appeared. She came to a halt, her shocked gaze shifting uneasily from one face to another, finally settling on the empty stall.

'What's happened? Please tell me,' she asked. Her voice was trembling.

'Now lass, you're not to take on,' Tom Compton began, kindly. 'It's Merry. I'm afraid he's gone missing but we'll have him back before you know it. You see if we don't!'

'Please . . . calm yourself,' Bronwyn cried, in some distress herself.

It was too late. Lizzie's face crumpled, her whole body seeming to sag with the weight of the news. Her hand flew to her mouth, her body turning this way and that as if she didn't know what to do with herself. 'Oh, Merry! Oh, my poor horse!' she cried. 'Bill would have been so upset. My Bill loved his horses! Oh, if only he were here! Oh . . . Oh . . . What shall I do? What ever shall I do without him?' Burying her face in her hands, her breath emerging in great juddering gasps, she began to sob.

Something good had come from such wrong. Breathing a sigh of relief, moving swiftly towards her, Bronwyn took her into her arms.

★ ★ ★

Freddie's undeniable euphoria at seeing Ursula evaporated all too quickly.

'What do you mean, Sam Tennant kissed you?' he snapped.

'It just happened. I didn't mean it to.'

Inside, Ursula cringed. It had been a mistake, something she'd realised as soon as it had happened. She'd enjoyed kissing Sam, she couldn't deny it; it had been a pleasant experience, satisfying a momentary impulse, but it hadn't been the same as when Freddie kissed her. She stared at him in dismay, wishing now she hadn't told him.

The strains of 'Mademoiselle from Armentieres,' to which the clientele of the Café des Allies had joined in lustily, died away as the old man who'd been playing the squeeze-box reached for his glass of the rough, local wine and took a swallow, wiping his hand appreciatively across the back of his mouth. A hush fell over the room. Wondering wretchedly how many had just become a party to the most intimate of thoughts, Ursula blushed. Poperinghe, or Pops as the place was affectionately known to the troops, was the nearest thing to a social life the blacked-out salient offered and the first place the troops headed for should they be lucky enough to obtain a pass.

Artillery fire rattled, so close too; the tables jumped, sending a shower of dust from the ceiling. More normally, shells fell around the train station, aimed randomly, in the hope of hitting a passing train and only very occasionally, miscued, falling on the town itself. The Tommies on the next table, hardened men all, took no notice. Everyone else, villagers and Red Cross workers alike, dusted themselves down, glancing about them nervously.

Freddie took a gulp of wine. 'How could you!' he retorted angrily.

'I was trying to explain if only you'd listen,' Ursula answered, hanging onto her temper with difficulty. There was no use both of them letting rip.

'I wished you hadn't come here!' he muttered furiously, a downright lie they both knew, when he'd sent for her. Aware she'd seen through him, he looked away.

'You wouldn't believe the trouble I had getting here,' she returned evenly and in a valiant effort to channel his thoughts to safer ground. She gulped her wine. For the first time in all the while she'd known him, she was unsure of him. It simply wasn't fair . . .

★   ★   ★

The floor in Matron's office had a curious opaque pattern. Ursula stared at it fixedly.

'Young girls today! The world falling down around your ears and your only concern is a love affair?' Matron retorted sharply and in outrage at what Ursula had just told her. Ursula's head shot up, anger at such injustice loosening her tongue and lending her an unusual eloquence.

'But that's not it at all, Matron! Freddie . . . Mr. Hamilton . . . is a childhood friend. He sent a message . . . by the supply wagon . . . his company have a few hours off. There's so much we have to say to each other and we may never get another chance . . . '

Something of her desperation must have penetrated even Matron's hardened heart.

'I have to agree, it is a while since you've had leave . . . ' she mused and then, miraculously to the ears of the young woman hovering in such agitation in front of her desk, 'you can take the day — no more, mind!' she warned.

Even given the dreadful state of the pot-holed roads, the random shells and constant troop movement, it still left time to get to Freddie and back to the hospital again, leaving, hopefully, a couple of blissful hours to spend together. Resisting the impulse to fling her arms around her and before she'd chance to change her mind, Ursula fled. That the old curmudgeon wouldn't have been so agreeable if she'd realised her driver's only form of transport was her ambulance, Ursula was only too aware. She had no intention of hanging around to find out.

'You'll cop it,' Dodi warned.

'Tough,' she'd retorted, no longer caring, consumed only with a desire to see Freddie to tell him that Sam had been a terrible mistake. What's more, it was Freddie she loved, and always had loved, she now realised. She only hoped, given the way he'd been behaving over these last few months, she wasn't too late.

★  ★  ★

'Why did you want to see me?' she asked curiously.

200

Freddie's gaze slid away. This was the difficult bit, he acknowledged, if only to himself. 'I wanted to tell you . . . You were right after all. I must admit . . . at first I only went along with us not seeing each other because I thought you'd get fed up with it. But I see now it was for the best. There's really no other way.'

'What poppycock!'

'It isn't poppycock! Does this . . . this Sam bloke love you?'

The conversation wasn't turning out a bit as Ursula had planned. The change of conversation left her floundering and at a disadvantage. Worse it left her with the suspicion that that was what Freddie had intended all along. 'Sam? Of course he doesn't love me!' She scowled. And then, the cursed honesty, so integral to her nature and so often her undoing, leapt to the fore, causing her to divulge information better kept to herself. 'Or at least . . . He only thinks he does. I don't have feelings for him, Freddie, and I mean to tell him so the very next time I see him.'

'You mean you haven't told him already?' he demanded, scandalized.

'I hardly got a chance . . . ' she stumbled, finding it unaccountably hard to meet his gaze. But it wasn't as if she hadn't tried. Sam, it appeared, sensing what might be coming, had deflected the subject with admirable precision every time she'd tried to open up and tell him how she really felt. She had no idea where he was now. She'd heard nothing, other than the hastily scrawled note she'd received two weeks ago, typically Sam-like professing his undying love.

Freddie glared. For the first time now, she took note of the dark shadows under his eyes and his haunted look. 'What's wrong?' she asked, more gently now and then chiding herself for being so obtuse. Given what he'd been through, what all his company had been through, things couldn't be anything other than wrong.

Trying not to notice the way his hand trembled, Freddie drained his glass. They all had the shakes to some extent but how could he tell her the horrors that had caused it? What would she think of him for being such a coward! He'd do anything rather than Ursula should think that of him. Wearily, he forced down the feelings he didn't dare to let out. The fear he'd lived with for too long, the strangest of feelings he wanted to grab her hand and run away with her, as far as he could. As if they could ever outrun this blasted war!

Sensing some of his state, pity overwhelmed her. 'It's Bill, isn't it?' she stated bluntly, relieved to get his name out into the open. 'I'm so sorry, Freddie. Mother wrote. You two had known each other so long . . . '

Bill's face loomed before him. He swallowed, biting down hard on his lip, forcing the image away. 'It isn't just he was an old friend, Ursy. There's a kind of comradeship out here,' he muttered. 'It's like losing a close family member. You're devastated, wondering if you'll be next. You can't understand unless you've spent weeks, months on the Front line . . . '

She reached for his hand, relieved when he took it and some of the strain left his face.

Time was moving on and she had to go. They didn't seem to have sorted anything out. But then, their eyes locked and abruptly everything else faded so they might have been back at Loxley again, roaming the fields and with nothing more in their heads than how long it was until tea-time. How happy they'd been and how much they'd taken for granted!

When, if, they ever got home, she'd never take anything for granted again.

Freddie walked with her back to the ambulance, no longer the brash Freddie Hamilton who would have shouted his love out loud, she realised and pained by it. 'Ursula, I do love you,' he muttered hopelessly, under his breath. Despite the crump of artillery fire, there was nothing wrong with Ursula's hearing.

'I love you too,' she answered, simply and trying not to see the hope leap instantly into his eyes. She loved him and he loved her so why did it feel so hopeless? They embraced, clinging onto each other, not wanting to let go.

In sombre mood, she drove the torturous route back to the hospital. It didn't do to think, thinking only made things worse. Freddie, the war, what was happening back home. Work was her salvation, an endless succession of back-breaking days, sliding too easily into weeks, bringing the winter with it, flecking the fields around with morning frosts and scatterings of bright, brilliant-white light, illusively pretty, a hard, barren landscape, reflecting the mood amongst the girls.

'I'd forgotten it's nearly Christmas,' Dodi complained.

They were waiting on the station platform for one of the endless succession of troop trains due. Ursula shook her head. The Christmas festivities were the furthest thing from her mind. They'd been so busy of late; she was beginning to wonder if there was anyone left to fight.

'I expect we'll have some time off,' she proffered.

It wasn't a given fact. She grinned weakly as a grey ribbon of smoke in the distance told them the train for which they were waiting was on its way. All around broke into a frenzy of activity. Red Cross workers, nurses and orderlies from the hospital and bustling French housewives, here to serve the troops with tea and cigarettes, gladly doing the little they could to help. Shortly the platform was littered with stretchers and walking wounded whilst in the midst of such chaos, the girls tried to prioritise the more seriously wounded.

They'd loaded two stretchers, returning for a third when one of the ambulance drivers, a pretty girl by the name of Diana, and a young woman more suited to the debutante's life she'd left behind than her current occupation of ambulance driver, came rushing across. 'One of the men over there swears he knows you, Ursula. I said I'd fetch you . . . '

Her words grew faint. Instantly, dreadfully, Ursula's world crashed in. It was Freddie. It had to be Freddie! Her worst nightmare, the one moment she'd feared since first she'd arrived here in Saint-Omer, a young, thoughtless girl with whom, it seemed to her now, she no longer had any connection. Staring resolutely at the girl's back, delaying the moment when she'd be forced to face her fears, she followed her, tremblingly, back across the platform.

A man lay on a stretcher, covered by a grey army-issue blanket, smiling weakly up at her.

She could hardly acknowledge his greeting for the huge whooshing tide of relief engulfing her, telling her, if nothing else, exactly whom she loved and always had. How could it be wrong to feel such relief it wasn't Freddie? How could she not feel a great swelling pity for this man, so full of life the last time she'd seen him? She knelt down, taking his arm, alarmed to discover the hand attached to it was swathed in bloody bandages.

'I was beginning to think you'd deserted me . . . ' Sam Tennant muttered peevishly.

'Whatever's happened?' she demanded, panic edging her voice.

Somewhere the young man found a small, tight smile. 'Blasted artillery fire's done for my bus. I'm blessed if it hasn't done for me too . . . '

## Boxing Day 1915

'Mind, dad!' Mary grumbled, nudging his feet with her brush. My, but she was glad Christmas Day was over and the house was finally back to normal. It hadn't seemed right celebrating Christmas and their Ursula not there to share it, too. Good-naturedly, Ned swung his feet up whilst she swept the floor beneath. That done, she propped her brush against the table. 'I'll make us a cup of tea. We'll sit and put the world to rights . . . '

'Hah! Chance would be a fine thing!' the old man retorted, his mind still on the snippets she'd read him from the paper over breakfast. The government in disarray, the Allies so stretched; it seemed the blessed war would go on forever. And as for that poor nurse Edith Cavell . . . 'I wish we'd pull out of Gallipolli.' He sighed. 'If we left Serbia to take care of itself, happen we'd get to grips with the Western Front.'

'Now dad,' Mary returned wearily and to whom it was all so much hogwash. Too many men fighting over things they'd be better leaving alone, to her mind. They should have more sense, the lot of them.

At that moment, Tom rushed in, his face bristling with excitement.

'You'll never believe it . . . ' he began, scarcely pausing to draw breath.

'We won't, lad, if you dunna tell us . . . ' Ned chuckled.

'The police have rung . . . up at the house . . . they've found Merry!'

Ned thrust his hands on his knees, leaning forwards happily.

'Where, lad? Tell me!'

'Eastwood way,' Tom returned airily, if inwardly conceding he wasn't exactly sure where. Indeed he'd been too fired up at the news to stop and listen to all the ins and outs of the business. 'The gypsies tried to pull the same stunt on a local landowner but he was too canny for 'em! Blessed if her Ladyship wasn't right all along, wouldn't you know it! This time they've been caught red-handed.'

'And serve them right!' Mary interjected, smiling grimly.

'Soames has taken her Ladyship in the car.'

With Lizzie being so near to the end of her pregnancy, the elderly butler had taken to ferrying Katherine wherever she needed to go. 'What!' Mary retorted and scandalised at this news more than any other. 'And her poor Grace left alone when she's on the verge of giving birth herself?'

'Aye, well, now there's that posh nurse installed. I expect Katherine wouldn't have gone otherwise.' Tom began to chuckle. 'Even the future heir of Loxley won't dare make an appearance now her Ladyship's decreed he's to wait until she gets back.'

'Nature waits for no-one, not even her Ladyship,' Mary said, busying herself with the tea-things and nodding her head wisely. Shortly Tom's arms slid around her waist, his head inclining to kiss the nape of her neck.

'Alright, my love?' he crooned.

'Give over!' she muttered crossly, still

turning her ample frame back towards him and snuggling into his chest. All discord over their Ursula's defection to France had long since been smoothed over. They both knew, to their cost, their precious child had a mind of her own. They tried not to worry, that was all they could do.

'She'll be home soon,' he murmured, lifting her thoughts.

At that moment, the door nearly flew off its hinges and Reuben burst into the room.

'Mary . . . you must come . . . quickly!'

Mary's kindly face dropped.

'Whatever's the matter, man? It's never her Grace?'

'It's Lizzie, you crazy woman! The baby's on its way . . . '

Taking no count of his rudeness, Mary grabbed her coat from the hook on the back of the door. 'Go and fetch Doctor Coates from the village,' she ordered, quickly. 'Hurry, Reuben, as quick as you can!'

'Anything I can do?' Tom demanded.

'Whist man, away with you. Keep from under my feet if you can!' Stopping only to throw her arms around him, she rushed out of the door.

★ ★ ★

209

Bronwyn had nearly shouted for joy when Katherine informed her she meant to fetch Merry back herself and wouldn't return until nightfall. So long as Bronwyn was well, her baby not due for two whole weeks and Mrs. Ridley here to keep watchful eye on her, she couldn't see any reason not to go. It was wonderful news, even if it filled Bronwyn with guilt for thinking that way.

Katherine's nagging interference over the pregnancy, although well meant, was wearying. And Bronwyn was utterly weary, disturbed over their muted Christmas celebrations by an ache at the base of her spine she hadn't dared to mention to Katherine. Gently, she laid her hands around the swell of her stomach. This child meant so much, most of all the chance to make things right between herself and Harry when he returned home, which surely couldn't be much longer, despite all and sundry declaring this dreadful war would go on forever.

'Thank you, Rose!' Stifling the thought she'd rather have made her own coffee, she smiled towards the maid who'd just entered the room to deposit her morning tray on the little inlaid table by her writing bureau. She took her cup over to the window, staring down reflectively onto the garden below whilst she drank it. Lacking outdoor staff, how untidy everywhere had grown, she mused. But still the morning sunshine winked merrily on the frost adorning the boxed hedges and lacing the footprints Tom Compton had made earlier, on his way up to the house to receive his day's orders. Loxley land stretched into the distance, as far as she could see, encompassing the crumbling turrets of the old hall, the lazily rolling river and the snow-flecked hills behind which looked so pretty.

She'd had a cramp this morning. She put down her cup and rubbed her stomach, aware at the same time of an odd and unexpected feeling of ownership, a growing pride in all she saw. A strange passion which took her breath and brought with it an inkling of exactly what this place must mean to Harry, born and bred here. What it would mean to their child too, born to so much, knowing nothing else and needing nothing else, according to Katherine, who would have it no other way.

It would be down to Bronwyn to make sure their child's world expanded to include other, equally important things.

Fighting for calm, she took one deep and shuddering breath.

Rose reappeared to remove the coffee tray, peering across at her uncertainly.

'Your Grace ... Are you quite well? Is

there anything I can do?'

It would have to happen now and Harry so far away. If only her mother was here and not looking after their Robert, recovering from the shrapnel wound he'd received at Loos. The decibel of pain Bronwyn had been struggling against all morning rose sharply, causing her to cry out.

Remembering who she was, maintaining her dignity at all times, she sucked in her breath and straightened up, steeling herself for the ordeal to come.

★   ★   ★

At that moment, Mary was laying Lizzie's son into her arms. The poor lass was exhausted and no wonder, everything happening so quickly so even Mary had only just got here in time. The doctor had been delayed with another call. Mary beamed. There'd been no need of any fiddle-faddle doctors here!

Gently, she laid the back of one hand against the baby's cheek; soft as thistledown, bless him. Something had at last gone right for this poor girl when the Lord alone knew, she'd been through enough of late.

Tears streamed down Lizzie's face. Too choked up to speak, her gaze fastening hungrily on her little son's face, the one thought rising, no matter how she tried, she couldn't keep at bay. If only Bill was here. If only he could see the miracle they'd created between them. But he ought to be here for the birth of his first-born! He'd have been that made up.

The inner strength that had sustained her since Bill's death suffused her, sustaining her anew, as if he'd been with her all along, telling her she must bear up and live her life for the both of them now. Bill wasn't here and she accepted he never would be. At least now, in his son, she had every reason to go on.

As if on cue, the tiny form stirred and, opening eyes she couldn't help but think were remarkably like his father's, frowned up at her thoughtfully. A wise child, his mother sensed, one who would think carefully before acting but, once making up his mind, would be ever steadfast and unwavering. 'He's Bill all over,' she murmured and her heart filled with such a rush of love it took her breath.

★ ★ ★

'Is this the woman who sold you the horse, lately stolen, your Ladyship?' Police Sergeant May, of Nottinghamshire Constabulary, nodded towards the ragged gypsy. She had been brought up from the cells, struggling, arms pinioned, between two young police constables. The

213

jagged scar Katherine remembered so well ran the length of the woman's cheek, marring an otherwise surprisingly pretty face. Wisps of curly, black hair sprang from under a bright red scarf. She was younger than Katherine remembered, her eyes flashing a defiance she'd taken care to hide the last time they'd met. Prompted to an unexpected sympathy, Katherine nodded, reluctantly. The woman had swindled her, wantonly selling her a horse she'd even then had every intention of stealing back and at a time when the country should be pulling together. Still, the horse had been well cared for and was waiting, even now, in the stables of the landowner he'd been so wickedly sold on to. One, fortunately, prepared to allow the matter to be settled amicably between them and for Katherine to make arrangements for it to be taken home. With the outcome so satisfactorily arranged it had seemed churlish not to carry out her civic duty and have Soames drive the extra five miles over here to the police station.

The gypsy's struggles increased.

'Aye! Such a fine lady!' she spat. 'You'll rue this day's work, mark my words! Curse you!'

'That's enough!' The sergeant spoke sharply, indicating to his men to return the woman to the cells and waiting until the door clanged shut behind them before speaking again. 'Six months' hard labour will give her the chance to ponder the error of her ways . . . '

So long? Ill at ease with the thought, Katherine returned outside to Soames, her mind made up to something with which she'd been toying since she'd arrived here. Fifteen miles wasn't so very far. There was perfectly no need to go to the inconvenience of putting one of the servants out when it would surely make more sense to ride Merry back herself. 'Do we still have the tack in the back of the car, Soames?' she demanded abruptly.

The old man glanced at her curiously.

'We have, your Grace.'

Katherine's heart leapt. Shortly and despite all arguments to the contrary, Soames was consigned to drive, unaccompanied, back to the sanity of Derbyshire whilst his mistress, riding side-saddle, made her contented way through fields and country lanes towards her beloved Loxley. There was no need for maps or guides. Unerring instinct drove her on. But how wonderful to have a horse beneath her! Biting cold flushed her cheeks but she exulted in it, bringing with it memories of other, more congenial Boxing Days when the Loxley hunt, splendid in pink, spent all day in the field. A tradition she'd once thought cast in stone!

Given this wretched war, even Katherine

accepted things couldn't possibly return to those halcyon days. Loxley endured, surviving even worse, even Harry falling so ridiculously in love with that chit of a child so eminently unsuitable to her role as bearer of the heir of Loxley. Suddenly, Katherine chuckled, a deep belly laugh startling a bird from the hedgerows with a clatter of alarm. Thoughts of the coming child brought with it such a fierce stab of joy; she cared nothing for the arduousness of her self-imposed task.

The sun sank low over the horizon, Loxley's horizon, drawing her ever onwards and staining the frosted ground a dusky pink. It was late by the time she reached home, guiding her weary charge over the bridge to the winking lights which called out to her. She was so pleased to see them and pleased too, to see her faithful old Soames, on the lookout for his mistress this long while, hurrying down the steps towards her, the woman he'd made the centre of his world, as had all these loyal people here. She was here. She'd make things right. She always made things right.

Accepting she'd done too much and would suffer for it in the morning, she climbed stiffly down.

'Thank goodness you're here, ma'am! Such a to do . . . '

'Why, whatever's the matter, man?'

'Her Grace, your Ladyship . . . the baby . . . the doctor's with her now . . . '

Visibly startled, pausing only to throw him the reins, she hurried swiftly up the steps and into the hall. Inside, heavenly joy, the thin mewl of a newborn child drifted down the stairs towards her . . .

★ ★ ★

'A beautiful child, your Grace . . . ' A smiling Nurse Ridley placed the baby, gently, into Bronwyn's arms. Looking down into the small, crumpled, red face, Bronwyn had no expectancy of the overpowering rush of a love she experienced, so overwhelming, it consumed her. A troubled gaze stared solemnly into hers, seeming to understand, even now, the weight of expectancy awaiting the Duke of Loxley's firstborn. Tenderly, Bronwyn kissed the little face. She was emotional, exhausted. The birth had not been an easy one.

'You must rest, your Grace. Isn't that right, Doctor Peters?'

Doctor Peters, a middle-aged man with a shock of iron-grey hair, fastened his Gladstone bag.

A shadow flickered uneasily across his face. 'Rest is essential, I should say,' he answered, briskly.

217

'What nonsense, Peters! What's more natural than giving birth? The girl's stronger than she looks!' Catching the tail end of the conversation, Katherine swept into the room. Bronwyn sank back against the pillows, watching anxiously as her redoubtable mother-in-law came towards her to draw back the shawl hiding the baby's face. Loxley's heir at long and wonderful last. The girl had managed something right and instantly, Katherine's expression softened. 'He's the look of his father, don't you agree, Peters?' she retorted, happily.

Seeing Bronwyn disinclined to speak, a fact for which he couldn't blame her, Roland Peters braced himself. 'Your Ladyship . . . That's a beautiful, healthy granddaughter you have there.'

'Fiddlesticks man, of course it's a boy!'

The silence following her outburst told her more than words ever could. Her fierce eyes flashed towards Bronwyn, who squirmed under their force. Once, it would have undone her completely but suddenly, a wave of fiercely maternal love came to her rescue, telling her, whatever the circumstances, she'd fight tooth and nail for this child.

'Aye, she's the look of Harry,' she retorted, stung. 'He'll be so proud of her!'

'Will he indeed!' The sharpness of the

words was offset by the crushing disappointment besetting Katherine's face. Loxley, always Loxley. It meant too much to her. Foolish woman, building her hopes so high!

'We're both young. We'll have a boy next time,' Bronwyn whispered softly and, weak as she still was from her labours, still unaccountably sorry for the wretched woman. Peters coughed discreetly, aware this time, there must be no misconceptions.

'Your Grace, I'm afraid I have to tell you, under no circumstances must there be more children. We must thank the Lord you have such a healthy little girl . . . '

Katherine's sharp intake of breath ripped through them. Grim-faced, taking no account of Bronwyn, left to digest this unhappy news, she brushed past Peters and silently, her back stiff and full of reproach, she swept from the room.

# 8

<u>July 1916</u>

'For Heaven's sake, Tom! How am I expected to lay the table?' Mary dumped a handful of cutlery onto the table where Tom sat, poring over a board on which he'd drawn a map of the Western Front. Coloured pins highlighted the troop movements.

'There's trouble brewing here, see, round the Somme,' he muttered, taking no notice. 'It'll take pressure off the French and that blessed business at Verdun . . . '

'Tom! I won't tell you again!'

'There have been enough casualties already . . . '

Mary's face dropped. 'Aye, there are casualties right enough! The papers are full of 'em. All those fine lads . . . That's all they are! A list of bloomin' casualties. Must you go on, pushing pins in as if it's nothing! I hate it . . . ' she cried and, pulling her apron up over her face, at last gave into the tears that had been threatening all morning.

Tom's face fell. Cursing himself for his thoughtlessness, he jumped up and took her into his arms. 'Whatever's the matter, love?'

How good it felt to lean in against him, Mary thought, drawing strength from his warm solidness and relieving the burden she'd carried for too long. 'Give over, I'm alright,' she murmured at last, gently disentangling herself. She took a deep and steadying breath.

'Now what's to do?' Ned muttered, coming downstairs from his wash and instinctively aware something was up.

'Our Mary's got herself in a bit of a state,' Tom explained, unnecessarily. Of course he knew the real problem. They all knew and the house was like a morgue because of it. 'We'll hear from Ursula soon, you'll see, my love,' he soothed, patting her shoulder awkwardly. 'She'll be busy, rushed off her feet and not had time to give us a thought . . . '

'Aye, she always was a thoughtless one,' Ned grumbled peevishly and more worried about their Ursula's lack of communication than he'd ever let on. 'Just a line to let us know she's alright. It wouldn't take much!'

'So it wouldn't, grandpa and I am very sorry . . . ' came a familiar and so wonderfully unexpected voice. Simultaneously the three heads swung towards it.

'But where . . . what . . . Oh, my darling child!' Mary's leap from the chair into which she'd just sunk, sent Tom's board flying. With a wild cry, she rushed across the room to fling her arms around the young woman who, unobserved, had just walked in. Pandemonium ensued, Ned getting under everyone's feet, Tom, in his joy, attempting to throw his arms around them all, so no-one noticed the young man, dressed in hospital blue, hovering awkwardly at the door. He stood frowning, watching the scene distantly, as a stranger, uncomfortably aware he didn't belong here. He would have retreated too, even at this late stage if only Ursula, sensing his reticence, hadn't disentangled herself and, by way of introduction, held her hand out towards him.

'Sam, meet my parents and grandfather, Ned . . . '

Made aware of the stranger in their midst and managing to hang on to their curiosity with admirable restraint, the Comptons did their best to make him welcome. 'Here lad. Come in and make yersen comfy . . . ' Tom took the young man's case and sat him down, taking note of the deformed hand and the pink skin around it, showing it to be a recent wound.

'Can you put Sam up, dad?' Ursula asked. 'I couldn't think of a better place to bring him than home.'

'Why, of course, lass! But why didn't you say, tell us you were coming, like . . . ?'

She flashed him a warning glance.

There was more to this than was immediately obvious, Tom thought, ever sensitive to his daughter's moods.

'I think the stew should stretch,' Mary murmured anxiously, her mind already on the practicalities of two extra mouths to feed.

Over the hastily contrived meal, spun out with the vegetables Ned was despatched to the garden to dig up, and carefully prompted by Mary, determined to get to the bottom of what their Ursula was doing with a young man she'd never thought to mention before, Sam's story emerged — his meeting with Ursula in London and his bus used as a makeshift troop transporter until the Boche had blown it up, blown him up too, blast them. He didn't know what he'd have done if this wonderful young woman here hadn't fetched him from the hospital in Bristol, where he'd been ever since he got back to blighty. The smile he threw Ursula at this conclusion was plain for anyone to see.

'Of course it's to be expected when the hospitals are so full,' Tom mused. 'It's the price we have to pay for war, I'm afraid . . .'

Ursula was horrified. 'Young men in hospital or worse?' she interjected, unable to believe her ears. Her father's shoulders lifted complacently. Her mother bustled off to fetch the pudding. She had to escape outside, leaving the company to the rest of their meal, disbelieving how angry the casually spoken words had made her. She stood, leaning against the wooden fencing surrounding the veranda, watching the rapidly darkening sky turning pink-mauve at the edges and thinking how odd it was that, for once in her life, there was something she knew more about than her father. It threw her, made her want to rush back immediately to the sanity of her friends in France — simple girls who knew the truth about the war if only because they spent their days dealing with its consequences. This militancy at home, everywhere she turned, was so very hard to take, unforgivably so to her mind.

'Take no notice, our Ursula. He means nothing by it,' Ned murmured, hurrying out after her and upset because he knew, intuitively, she was upset.

She turned towards him heatedly. 'He doesn't know the half, gramps!'

'Aye, well, maybe he doesn't want to know,' he pointed out.

They spoke quietly, not wanting those inside to hear, Sam included, who, despite Tom's ignorance, was getting on famously with her parents.

'What is it, my love?' the old man coaxed.

Ursula frowned, not sure herself. 'It's really

bad over there, gramps,' she began and fumbling for words to describe it that didn't sound too shocking. 'The hospitals are crammed. 'We're rushed off our feet. And I haven't seen the worst of it. You should hear the stretcher bearers on the front line.'

Whatever had happened to their Ursula in the time she'd been away, she'd grown up. Ned's old heart swelled with pity and pride too that she had coped with so much and at such a young age. 'And the hospital pastor wrote to you about Sam, like?' he probed, curious about the young man and where he fitted into the scheme of things.

'No-one knew what to do with him,' she agreed. 'He lost his parents before the war and he has no other family; there was nowhere else to send him. All his friends are at the Front. His hand's so messed up, grandpa, he'll never be able to drive again.' Matron, surprisingly sympathetic once Ursula had explained Sam's predicament, had given her leave to return to England to take him home. And a right time Ursula had had of it too. Wounds healed on the surface took no account of a man's mind, she mused, remembering her shock when she'd seen him, lying so quietly, so un-Sam-like, in his hospital bed in the Bristol Royal Infirmary. Gone was the carefree young man she remembered.

'I knew mother was the one to get him back on his feet. She won't mind . . . will she? I mean, me going and leaving Sam here?'

'Mary? No, lass, of course she won't.' Ned's head nodded rapidly. 'She'll be glad of the company. We all will. Help take our mind off things. Are you sweet on him, our Ursula?' he finished abruptly and asking the one question he'd been left wondering.

'I love Freddie. I . . . I think I always have, only I was too stubborn to see it,' she replied, her voice threaded with the earnestness that underpinned her character and leaving the old man smiling to himself. A good part of her would never change and he wouldn't want her to. 'Sam's a friend I happen to think a lot about,' she went on, sounding troubled. 'We should look after our friends, shouldn't we, gramps?'

'We certainly should,' he answered solemnly.

'He needs every friend he can get. It's just . . .'

'He's sweet on you?' the old man finished. His sight might be gone but he hadn't lost his faculties or misheard the young man's tone whenever it was directed towards their Ursula. She cast an anxious glance behind her, relieved to hear Sam's laugh drift through the open doorway, a sound she'd not heard in a very long while.

'I've told him about Freddie and that

226

there's no way I'd ever feel that way about him. It's friendship I'm offering, that's all. I'm just not certain he's listening.'

'Perhaps he doesn't want to, lass.'

'What am I going to do?' she agonised.

'Tell him again and make sure he's not holding out hope you'll change your mind,' he answered simply.

She turned towards him gratefully.

'Gramps . . . ' she began hesitantly.

'What, my love?'

She was struggling for words, trying and failing to let out what was in her heart. But the war had made her think about so many things she'd never considered before. 'I never . . . I never . . . ' She stopped, suddenly too choked up to speak. She'd never acknowledged his blindness was what she'd meant to say and couldn't. And now the moment was gone though she drew comfort from the thought that, somehow, he knew how she felt.

★   ★   ★

'What are you trying to tell me, Nell?'

Unaware she'd spoken aloud, Bronwyn spun round full circle. The long corridor, leading to the great baronial hall below, lined with portraits of Loxlians both past and present, appeared reassuringly the same. She must be going out of her mind. How else to explain a scent of lavender, so overpowering, it had brought her crashing to a halt?

There were no vases of flowers to account for it, nor her strange fancy it meant Nell was trying to communicate with her in some way. Directly in front of her line of vision was a portrait of Nell's cousin. She knew because shortly after they were married, Harry had walked with her along this very corridor, explaining the history of every portrait they'd passed. There'd been so many, she'd scarcely had the chance to take it all in but she'd taken a particular liking to this one, she remembered, of a personable young man with laughing blue eyes and the flowing locks so favoured by the cavaliers. Harry had told her he'd been killed, fighting for the King's cause at Naseby. Was Nell trying to tell her something particular about him, or merely pointing to the fact he was a Royalist and therefore had fought on the opposite side? Why remember now Lawrence Payne's account of Nell defending Loxley against Parliamentary forces? Rufus Hyssop had been firm for the Parliamentary cause, after all . . .

'Nell, whatever is it?' she murmured.

A glance at her watch reminded her, both the morning's post was yet to arrive and that she'd been on the way to the nursery to take

Hettie for her morning's walk. She hurried downstairs, arriving in time to find Reuben, bursting through the front doors and waving the letter for which he'd waylaid the postman, his lack of breath denoting his haste to get it to her. The sight of Harry's handwriting on the front of the envelope caused the young woman's heart to leap.

'There you are!' He beamed. 'A letter from Hal. I knew you'd be pleased!' He hovered by her eagerly, satisfied to be the bearer of good news. Everyone on the estate knew how Bronwyn longed for a letter from Harry, as did Katherine, Bronwyn acknowledged, determining still to have a moment to read her precious letter alone.

'Reuben, thank you, that's wonderful!' she retorted, her face shining with happiness.

'Good to know he's alive!' he replied, pragmatically, putting into words something most would have had tact enough to keep to themselves. He hurried away. The door slammed shut behind him.

All they could be sure was, Harry was alive when the letter was written, Bronwyn reminded herself, continuing on her way to the nursery where the sunshine, streaming through the window, illuminated both the poker face of Loxley's elderly nanny and, by way of contrast, the chubby limbs of the adorable baby girl, Henrietta Arabella Loxley, her most precious charge, cooing happily in her cot.

'I'll take Hettie for her walk, Mrs. Norris. It's such a beautiful morning.'

'If you say so, your Grace,' the woman replied stiffly and not troubling to keep her disapproval to herself. It was too early in the morning. Nursery routine would be put out and wouldn't she just like to tell Bronwyn so!

Battle lines had long since been drawn between Bronwyn and the elderly woman who'd seen both Harry and Georgina successfully through their first years and who had no intention of being told what to do in her own nursery! Katherine, a stickler for tradition, had insisted on her appointment and not realising what she was letting herself in for, Bronwyn had too easily agreed. As if she hadn't enough with Katherine to contend with, without the addition of this old termagant, she now realised.

It didn't mean Hettie should be tied to the wretched woman's obsessional routine. 'It will be a chance to put your feet up, Mrs. Norris,' she added firmly, before pointedly holding open the door and waiting, with what patience she could muster, whilst the woman stalked indignantly from the room.

Stifling the irrational desire to laugh out loud, a worrying impulse she'd experienced too often of late, she threw herself down on the window seat and ripped open Harry's letter, eagerly scanning the single sheet of paper it contained. Since Hettie's birth, her husband's missives had taken on a deeper, more mature tone as if the responsibility of parenthood had raised a new and unexpected tenderness in his psyche. It seemed for a moment, he stood beside her, his voice murmuring words for her ears alone.

'My darling wife, if only you knew how often I think of you and that precious daughter of ours. I treasure the photograph you sent me and keep it with my things, here in the dug-out. But if only I could see you both! How cruel is this war to keep us so far apart when I long, above all else, to see our daughter's face . . . '

Bronwyn blinked rapidly, her eyes so suddenly swimming with tears, she could no longer read the print. Seven months old and her father had yet to see her. Did Harry really mind she was to be their only child? Bronwyn's thoughts too readily drifted to her husband's response to news of his daughter's birth and the sad fact there were to be no more children. No doubt he hadn't meant to sound so reproachful, even given his natural euphoria about the birth. 'You mustn't worry,' he'd written, 'it can't be helped. We'll cope somehow.'

What can't be helped must be endured. Disappointment and disapproval, all she'd met with since she'd got here. Since then, it had never been mentioned but did he, as his redoubtable mother so obviously did, blame her? Harry was too even-minded for such unfairness but even he, deep down and no matter how determined not to, must feel Bronwyn had somehow failed.

Worse, she blamed herself. Hettie cooed, inspecting her toes with which she was currently fascinated. Watching her, Bronwyn was aware of conflict. Who could look at such a sweet little body and fail to feel joy? Her gaze returned to the letter and the hurried, cramped writing denoting how much it had been written in a rush.

' . . . as I write, I can hear our snipers and the ping, ping of the Boche reply — two old men squaring up to each other. At least being here, on the horseshoe of the salient, and the enemy lines so close, the Boche won't risk shelling. So you see, my darling, you mustn't worry. I'm here, doing my duty, as are all these valiant men from Loxley. We're as safe as we'll ever be in this laughable theatre called war . . . '

He made too light of it, a way of keeping the horror at bay, Bronwyn sensed. As he made light of her inability to give him the son he'd so longed for.

In a sombre mood she took her daughter downstairs and laid her in the perambulator which, much to Soames's disapproval, was parked permanently in the hall. At that moment, Katherine and Mrs. Norris appeared from the direction of the drawing room. That they'd been talking about her was obvious. The nanny's features were smug and Katherine's set with more than the ordinary disapproval to which Bronwyn was so used; she was fast becoming immune.

'I'm taking Hettie out for her walk. I need to see Tom about mixing rye with the wheat when we plant the meadows up, next year,' she retorted firmly and determined to get in first. It was time they expanded and made better use of the land. Hettie's birth had given her a renewed sense of purpose to keep this estate thriving until Harry's return.

'I'd have imagined you'd enough on, without taking on extra,' Katherine countered swiftly and, not even troubling to look inside the pram, turned away.

'Oh, but why don't you come with us?' Bronwyn's offer was impulsive but Katherine's attitude towards Hettie was beginning to unnerve her. If only she could unbend and show some natural affection towards the child! To her dismay, her mother-in-law's face stiffened. She'd been let down. She had no intention of softening.

'I have a committee meeting. The hospital board,' she answered coldly.

'Of course, I remember now,' Bronwyn returned, suppressing her natural indignation. So be it. She'd tried. She could do no more. Cheeks flaming, aware of disapproving glances boring into her back, she manoeuvred the carriage out of the house and, on impulse, headed it towards the stables, where she found Lizzie busy washing the car and little Bill, happy and content, playing with a peg bag on a checked rug by her side.

'There you are, your Grace!' Lizzie smiled and, as it so often did, her gaze stole proudly towards her little son.

'Goodness, Lizzie! He grows every time I see him,' Bronwyn enthused.

'Hettie too, miss. What a bonny pair!' Lizzie looked pleased as Bronwyn lifted Hettie from her perambulator and plonked her down next to Bill. The two women stood companiably as, chuckling happily, the little boy passed pegs to Hettie, who took each one, inspecting it carefully before letting it drop, unceremoniously, into her lap.

Bless them, what a joy they were and how

sad Katherine was to so wilfully be missing out! Something of Bronwyn's face must have reflected her frustration. Lizzie dropped the cloth into the pail by her feet. 'Is everything alright, miss?' she asked tentatively.

Bronwyn frowned. It would be good to talk, especially to Lizzie of whom she was so fond. 'Oh . . . it's nothing . . . '

'Just her Ladyship . . . ?' the young woman coaxed, sure it must be either Katherine or Harry causing Bronwyn's mood and plumping for Katherine as the likelier. Bronwyn breathed in deeply.

'Wouldn't you think she'd be thrilled she has such a beautiful little granddaughter instead of complaining she's the wrong sex!' she burst out heatedly.

So that was the problem. Given the fact it had taken the old curmudgeon so long to get used to having Lizzie as driver, instead of Lizzie's father Alf, it had struck the young woman as odd Katherine had so easily accepted little Bill should accompany them on their journeys.

'He's a fine sturdy boy,' the Dowager had murmured, more than once and with such a yearning in her voice, Lizzie had gazed at her sharply through the driver's mirror. If only she wasn't so fearful for her job, she would have given her a piece of her mind.

Self-preservation had made her swallow her words as she sensed this much put-upon young woman often did, too. Lizzie only hoped it had helped her to talk. She longed to reassure her and yet wasn't sure how to go about it.

'Don't take on so, miss, please!' she pleaded. 'Her Ladyship's such a stickler. You know she doesn't mean anything by it.' But she did, that was the point. Lizzie frowned, sensing she wasn't being much help. 'Besides . . . if that's really all she's upset over . . . It's hurtful and wrong but you'll have a little boy next time round, miss, you see if you don't!'

Bronwyn blanched visibly. 'But that's just it, Lizzie, I can't have any more children,' she admitted, her voice calm but, inside, something twisting as it always did whenever the subject of her infertility came up.

Lizzie's face crumpled.

'Oh miss, I'm sorry! I never realised . . . But it only makes this little one all the more precious!' she uttered fiercely, her gaze lingering on Hettie, before moving past her and settling on little Bill. She shook her head sadly. 'I shall never have another, either.'

'Lizzie, you might!' Bronwyn protested, immediately putting her own problems aside. 'You're young. You'll meet someone else, given time. Bill would never want you to be alone for ever.'

Lizzie's denial was prompt. 'Little Bill's my life now. There's nothing . . . no-one else I want. It seems to me, miss, if you don't mind me saying . . . We've only to give all our love to the bairns we have!'

Bronwyn turned towards her gratefully.

'Lizzie you do me so much good! That's just it! Why should it matter what anyone else thinks when I think Hettie the most precious little girl in the world?'

'That's the ticket, miss!' Delighted she'd been able to help after all, Lizzie beamed happily.

★  ★  ★

Katherine was late for her meeting, a thing she despised and yet, despite it, she lingered at the window of her dressing room, watching as Lizzie drove the car the short distance from the stables to the front of the steps and Bronwyn, pointing the perambulator in determined fashion towards Tom Compton's cottage, took off in the opposite direction. Bent on this ridiculous scheme she'd taken into her head over next year's planting when the ground more naturally needed to lay fallow. Interfering when Compton had the work already organised! Everything in its place, a place for everything, as it had been since time immemorial. And a male heir to Loxley for nigh on two hundred and fifty years until Harry had seen fit to defy his mother and marry a girl so far below his station in life.

The wretched girl couldn't even get that right, Katherine fretted, remembering, with a bitter stab of discontent, her crushing disappointment on the day of Hettie's birth. Mutinously, she rammed the final hat pin into position, even yet, in some small corner of her being, aware she was being unfair. She lingered, struggling to control her emotions. Duty, pity, a great well of sorrow overwhelmed her — events couldn't be as she ordered. She watched as the young woman stopped, leaned over the perambulator and with a tender gesture, tucked the blanket more firmly around the sleeping child. A tiny hand appeared. Seeing it, an unexpected feeling surfaced in her grandmother's breast, an emotion she scarcely recognised for what it was. Something soft, tender and so fierce, it momentarily took her breath. Vexatious child! But Loxley needed a firm hand, a man's hand as tradition allowed. A thing cast in stone never to be broken and Bronwyn seemingly with no idea how badly she'd let the side down.

She was late. It wasn't like her to be so indecisive. Worry over Harry and this blessed war would be her undoing. In some irritation, grumbling quietly to herself, Katherine hurried away downstairs.

★　★　★

Early the following morning, far away in the heart of the industrial north, two large wrought-iron gates belonging to the prison there, swung wide: a sprawling and dingy Victorian edifice that should have been pulled down long since. Two burly wardresses appeared, dragging between them with some relish, the bedraggled, emaciated figure of a gypsy woman. Unceremoniously, they dumped her in the road.

'Don't bother coming back, neither,' one laughed, taking a well-aimed kick in her direction. The gypsy woman yelped. They returned inside. The gates clanged shut, leaving her figure sprawled, motionless in the road some long moments before, gathering her senses, she scrambled slowly to her feet. Eyes burning fiercely in their sockets, she stood swaying and rubbing under her breast where the boot had painfully connected. She turned, shaking a clenched fist at the prison before lifting her face southeast towards Derbyshire and Loxley.

'Aye, you'll pay for this too, Katherine Loxley,' she spat. 'Wait and see if you don't!' A look of peculiar malevolence cast a shadow over her features, despite the scar cutting a

239

swathe so cruelly along one cheek, some had once called pretty. Hissing softly and scaring a blackbird taking roost in a tree nearby, she limped away down the road.

★   ★   ★

'That's it then, mother!' Carefully, Ursula folded the last of the clothes she'd brought back from France and which Mary had insisted on washing, into the case open on the kitchen table. Ned, sitting in his usual place by the fire, sighed heavily. Tom, similarly dreading his daughter's departure but affecting indifference, took refuge behind the morning's papers he'd just fetched down from the house.

'Oh, love, I do wish you didn't have to go,' Mary murmured. She was at the stove frying bacon. Hastily, she stifled the sob which caught in her throat.

'Me too!' Ursula laughed shakily, recognising the churning in her stomach exactly for the nerves it was. She was torn, desperate to get back to France and yet, dreading it too. This time at home had been wonderful, reminding her exactly of what she was missing. If only her family knew what they were sending her back to! But there, it was better they didn't. Leave them to their innocence. With an air of finality, she shut the lid of the case and fastened the catches. She hated this next bit, everyone keeping their emotions so tightly under control, it somehow only made things worse. 'Where's Sam?' she asked and surprised he wasn't there to see her off.

'He's out in the orchard, love. Tell him breakfast's waiting!' Mary called to her daughter's retreating back.

She found him leaning against a tree trunk, staring moodily into space. At her approach, he straightened up, letting go the leaf he'd been twisting round the two good fingers remaining on his left hand. The scent of blossom was overpowering.

'Pretty, ain't it,' he grimaced, holding up his hand.

'I thought we'd decided to keep positive,' Ursula countered briskly, not seeing the wound, so angry and puckered at its edges, instead seeing only a justifiably angry young man and wondering how she was going to find the right words to tell him what she'd come out here to say. He'd allowed her no opportunity to catch him alone, so determined had he been, she realised now, on putting members of her family between himself and the unpalatable truth he refused to face.

'Don't say it, Ursula!' he muttered fiercely. 'Leave me with some hope, do . . .'

'Sam,' she moaned, exasperated, perplexed, pity swelling in her heart and then discovering, with a huge surge of relief, the words were there all along. 'It would never work,' she began, quietly. 'I like you so much; you're a lovely man and some day you're going to make some girl really happy but . . . not me. I don't love you, Sam. I'm sorry but I have to tell you. It wouldn't be fair, either to you or to me . . . '

His face creased with pain. 'Or to this blessed Freddie, either!' he snapped.

The truth was hurtful but it was the truth.

'I love him. I think I always have, Sam, only I was too pig-headed to see it. I am sorry.' She repeated it, hopelessly, wishing there was some other way than to hurt him like this. Impulsively, she threw her arms around him and hugged him close. 'You'll be alright,' she soothed. 'Mother will get you back on your feet. Sam, I do care about you! Promise me you'll look after yourself?'

He was struggling with emotion but with a valiant effort, he managed a smile and hugged her back. 'I promise,' he muttered.

It was wretched to leave him at such a time but there was no other way. He was on her mind during all the painful, drawn-out goodbyes, every bit as bad as she'd imagined. On the train down to Southampton and across the channel to Le Havre where she caught the overnighter to Saint-Omer, arriving at the hospital crumpled and weary, yet still, miraculously, in time for the morning's shift. Eight hours on, eight hours off, unless there was a rush of wounded, in which case, they carried on regardless.

'I could do with a bath,' she groaned, dropping her case onto the bed to pull out her uniform and change quickly into it. Doors banged, girls' voices could be heard in the corridor outside, chatting earnestly about the coming day.

'We'll be late,' Dodi urged and for some reason appearing on edge. She stood by the door, tapping her fingers against the jamb.

Ursula, lingering by the mirror, straightened her cap. 'Do you feel we do enough here, Dodi? Don't you ever wish we could do more?' She frowned, giving voice to a worry increasingly on her mind.

'More than driving the ambulances, you mean?'

Ursula nodded. It was precisely what she did mean. Something more than fetching and carrying and administering the basic first aid which was all they knew. Being away had given her a chance to think and put life into some kind of perspective. Inadequate as it was, all you could do was your best. Giving her cap a final tweak, she turned to go. 'Come on. We'll catch it if we don't hurry.'

Dodi took a deep breath. 'Wait . . . I've something to tell you. We had a visitor whilst you were away. Freddie . . . '

All thoughts of their shift fled. 'Freddie? Here? But why didn't you say?' Ursula retorted sharply and already unable to bear the thought she'd missed him.

'I did mean to tell you.' Dodi frowned, relieved she'd decided to cough up now and not leave it any later. 'It was only a fleeting visit. You know how it is, Ursy.'

Ursula did know. 'Is he alright?' she demanded.

'He seemed to be. Desperately sorry to have missed you, of course . . . '

He'd been lurking by the stairwell of the girls' quarters as Dodi had come from her shift, his groan at the news she'd just imparted about Ursula's absence, loud enough to make the girls who'd gone on ahead, turn round and stare.

'Please tell me that's not true!' he'd implored.

'She's back tomorrow . . . '

'But I only have a couple of hours!' Freddie's gaze had fastened miserably on hers, reading some of what she'd been so desperately trying to hide. Whatever he was, he was no-one's fool . . .

'Is everything alright?' he demanded abruptly.

'Why . . . yes . . . of course . . . ' Sorry for him as she was, the conversation was becoming uncomfortable and she would have rushed on after her friends, who would bag all the hot water if she didn't get a move on. His hand fastened on her arm, delaying her.

'You have to tell me, Dodi. I've come all this way!' His eyes sparked with ill humour. 'It's that blasted Sam, isn't it? She's gone off with Sam!'

Dodi's spirits sank. What a mess she'd made of things! 'No! Yes. I mean not exactly . . . She's taken him home, back to Derbyshire. There was nowhere else to go, apparently.' She pulled her arm free. 'It's not like it sounds, Freddie. Don't read something into it that isn't there . . . ' It was too late. Not giving her a chance to explain the truth, he spun away furiously and headed out of the door.

* * *

'Spit it out,' Ursula prompted, sensing, whatever it was, she wasn't going to like it.

Dodi looked longingly towards the corridor and escape. 'The thing is, Ursula. I told him you'd taken Sam home. He kind of guessed and wheedled the rest out of me.'

'Oh Lord!' The exclamation was long and drawn-out, bringing with it the wretched realisation, in all the worry over Sam, the rush to get him back to England and make things right with her mother, that she'd omitted telling Freddie her plans. He knew Sam had been injured because she'd written and told him so. He said he wouldn't have wished that on anyone, even Sam. As if he'd thought she'd assume he would! 'And what interpretation did he put on it, exactly?' she demanded, and yet knowing already. She knew him too well. Dodi looked away.

'He stormed off before I could explain the situation. I did run after him but it was too late. He'd gone, vamoosed.'

'I see.' She did and too clearly.

'I am sorry.'

'It's not your fault.'

'Why don't you write? Explain it all yourself?'

Ursula's first instinct was to fly to him but how could she? What else could she do but write? Blast this war! Wretchedly, there wasn't time to do anything now. Her day was to be spent ferrying injured soldiers, sufficiently recovered from their wounds to survive the journey, to one of the many hospital ships anchored off the coast. For once and perhaps unforgivably, her mind too full of Freddie, Ursula carried out her duties mechanically, removed even from Matron's tirade at their tardy time-keeping. Freddie professed he loved her and yet he always thought the worst. If only he was here now, she'd give him a piece of her mind!

She couldn't wait for the day to end but end, it did. Paper, pen, how inadequate it seemed when all she wanted was to see him and explain properly. She sat, hunched on her bed, wondering hopelessly how best to start and, worse, what tone to adopt. She chewed the top of her pen. Admonitory that, so Freddie-like, he'd jumped so readily to the wrong conclusion? Or ought she to be more understanding and accepting of her share of the blame? She only understood they couldn't get this right, no matter how they tried.

Willingly, her head bent over the paper. 'My dearest, darling Freddie . . . '

## March 1917

At long and bitter last, the artillery fire had ceased. Twenty-four hours of relentless pounding with shrapnel and high explosives, softening the enemy lines and lifting the barbed wire to ease the infantry's access. As if everyone didn't know already, to their cost, it never worked.

'Fifteen minutes boys. Ready to go . . . '

Harry's face, laced with tiredness, loomed out of the mist.

No-one had slept. Dawn, and tension all around. At least the rain had stopped. Freddie pulled Ursula's last letter out of his top pocket. Was it the fourth or fifth? Crazily he'd lost count as he'd lost count of so many things. She must have given up hope of hearing from him because he hadn't received another for a while. All that silly business over Sam as if she imagined he didn't know the truth already! She'd become increasingly desperate as to why he didn't reply, something he was no longer sure about himself. Pride? Wanting to punish her for what she'd put him through? Too late now to wish he'd written back! Nothing seemed to matter any more. Weeks sliding into months, autumn turning to the wettest winter on record so Christmas had come and gone, unnoticed, consumed in this empty sea of mud when all he longed for was home and the farm with the larks sweeping high over the meadows and his heart full of Ursula — if there'd ever been such a time and he hadn't dreamed his life before the war!

Desperation did odd things to the memory. Tenderly, he tucked the letter back into his top pocket. A keepsake, a lucky charm. Alf Walker shook his hand and wished him all the best. More faces loomed. Arthur Davis, his pale face and trembling lips at odds with his attempt at a smile. Little Stanley Pickering, filled out like even his mother wouldn't have believed, hopping about with excitement, silly lad. And crazily, the sense of his old friend Bill by his side, urging him on. Divine retribution. A life for a life. So many wasted lives!

His thoughts were wild, shooting off at random, anywhere other than here and now and the horror that lay before them. If only Ursula could see him now! If only Ursula was in his arms and not this hateful weapon of war. No soldier he. Oh, dear God, what was he doing here!

The silence grew, worse than the guns, blossoming cruelly, a terrible sound so his instinct was to clamp his hands over his ears and blot it out. Sing, laugh, scream out loud, anything to blot it out.

The shrill blast of the whistle, when it came, was almost a relief. Freddie inhaled deeply and steadied himself. He was a soldier, here to do his duty for King and Country. Loxley too, he remembered, grimly. 'Over you go, boys,' Harry cried, urging them on and jumping up and over before them all. In that moment, the men would have followed him anywhere.

What worse hell could there be than this? Thoughtlessly, oddly joyous, a sudden, creeping artillery fire edging that strange no-man's place, the men scrambled up and forwards, bowed backs weighed down by battle gear, a line of grey merging into a sea of mud.

# 9

The attack had descended into an explosion of shells and raking machine-gun fire so Harry had no idea how many of his company had heard the retreat. As they waited for nightfall and the chance of escape, he was left with Freddie, shivering and freezing cold and edging away from the pool of icy mud in the bottom of the shell hole into which they'd thrown themselves. At least they were alive.

The screaming in no-man's-land had stopped. Whoever it was, friend or foe, there'd been no way of getting to him, poor devil. The flashes of shells in the slate-grey sky grew more brilliant, one following hotly on from another. Freddie winced. The shoulder wound Harry had earlier packed with bandages was giving him some gyp. Only a flesh wound, Harry said, aware that was the last news Freddie would want to hear. A blighty wound was something for which all the men longed, even Harry.

'Any water left?' Freddie muttered, easing himself round.

Harry shook the flask and threw it across. Freddie drank and wiped the back of his hand across his mouth. 'How much longer?' he demanded tetchily. The guns were beginning to spook him.

'Not long,' Harry soothed, aware of his own rising panic. They were in a pretty pickle and that was the truth. 'You and Ursula back together again, yet?' he demanded, in an effort to take their minds off things.

'Not exactly,' Freddie muttered, feeling uncomfortable to be talking about something so personal with anyone, never mind his commanding officer. He retrieved his last biscuit from his kit, wiping the mud off onto his tunic before taking a bite, wondering then what his mates would think to hear him talking to Harry Loxley like this. It didn't matter. They were just two soldiers stuck in a shell hole, that was all they were. Why shouldn't they talk man to man? He munched doggedly. 'I wish I had a wife and child to go home to, Harry. You don't know how lucky you are,' he ventured, between bites.

Harry grimaced. Lucky was hardly how he'd describe it. So desperately wanting things to be right with Bronwyn yet knowing they weren't, no matter how hard he tried, or Bronwyn either, for that matter. He leaned back, wondering how much of this apparent idyll it was right to expose, even to Freddie Hamilton, a man he'd learned he could trust with his life. He stared down at his boots. 'We can't have any more children,' he blurted out all at once. 'Rather puts the lid on the succession, don't you see?'

Freddie pursed his lips into a silent whistle. How would that make him feel? he wondered. Children were important but after all they'd been through of late, he realised there were other things in life. 'You have a child,' he reminded him, gently.

'Aye, a beautiful little girl!' Harry agreed fiercely. 'And I'm longing to see her. I . . . I do love my wife.' He glanced up quickly, wondering if Freddie understood. Loxley needed an heir and now it wouldn't have one. How it complicated things!

There was so much more to this than trouble with Bronwyn Loxley, Freddie sensed.

'I love Ursula,' he muttered, feeling foolish saying it, but feeling oddly better for it too. He couldn't easily find the words to explain the mess of his relationship with Ursula. 'We can't get on, no matter how we try and yet . . . I hate it when we're not together. I can't stop thinking about her, Harry!' That just about summed it up. With a sudden aching yearning, he looked up into the darkening sky, the stars appearing one by one, tiny pinpricks of light, finding comfort in the thought, somewhere out there, Ursula might be gazing up at them too. Oh, if only they were safe in Loxley and the whole of the blasted Western Front was only a bad dream!

Wretchedly, he was aware of a rising hysteria. How crazy it was, stuck out here in no-man's-land, in danger of being blown into so many pieces and discovering Harry Loxley was just another bloke with women problems too!

The two men lapsed into silence, waiting as patiently as they could as darkness fell around them and the artillery fire from their own lines gathered into a crescendo. At last they edged upwards towards the rim of the crater, peering over it cautiously before scrambling up and creeping forwards into the slippery sea of mud and the direction they prayed held Allied lines.

Earlier that day

'Look darling! See the pretty lady . . . '

Scooping her little daughter from the bed, where she'd been playing happily with the contents of her mother's jewellery box, Bronwyn carried her over to the portrait of Nell Loxley hanging on the wall across. In such close proximity, there was no doubting where her little girl had inherited her striking red hair and the good Lord help them if Katherine, who had banned mention of Nell from the house, ever discovered it!

'Lady,' Hettie lisped happily, holding out a chubby hand. The child was adorable and, grandmother apart, charmed everyone with whom she came into contact. The thought reminded Bronwyn how annoyed Katherine was that she'd chosen to go to Ned Compton's seventy-fifth birthday party that afternoon, instead of the tea-dance for wounded Officers Georgina, Harry's sister, had arranged at Belfield Castle, her home. Her parties were legendary and Katherine, who always attended, liked nothing better than the chance to order everyone about.

But someone from the family should attend Ned's birthday party! Thoughtfully, Bronwyn kissed Hettie's little face. 'We'll be able to see grumpy Reuben, darling!' Her smile held a hint of exasperation. Reuben who, for reasons best known to himself, had been decidedly stand-offish with her of late, whenever she'd happened to bump into him, complaining of too much to do to stand around gossiping. How exasperating when she'd begun to see him as a friend! Harry away, she needed as many friends about the place as she could get, she mused. Back downstairs in the hall, she was surprised to discover Katherine with her coat already buttoned; checking her face in the mirror, the small valise on the floor by her feet, suggesting her departure was imminent.

'Are you off, already?' the young woman asked, taken by surprise.

Katherine nodded coolly, the set of her face outlining her irritation at what she saw as Bronwyn's intransigence. 'It's never too late to change your mind,' she coaxed.

'Katherine I am sorry but . . . '

'But you have no intention of putting yourself out?'

'Not that exactly.' Bronwyn frowned, aware this constant bickering was getting them nowhere. Hettie was weighing heavily in her arms. Unhappily, she put the little girl down, where she stood, taking a tight grip on her mother's skirt to peer shyly round at her grandmother. Lagging behind little Bill in walking, she'd yet to take her first steps, instead demanding imperiously to be carried wherever she wanted to go.

'You might still come to Ned's party?' her mother challenged and amazed she'd had the temerity as soon as the words were out of her mouth. The very idea of Katherine lowering herself to attend Ned's party! The older woman's snort of amusement showed how ridiculous the thought was. Colour flooded Bronwyn's face. It was obvious her redoubtable mother-in-law was prepared to go to any lengths rather than be faced with an afternoon in the company of the little grandchild in whom, if only she was a boy, she would take such a pride. What a thorn it was becoming between them, destroying any chance they might have had of mutual companionship and providing a support for each other whilst Harry was away.

The thought was quickly followed by another — that poor Lizzie would be the one left to chauffeur this jaunt to Georgina's. 'Lizzie and little Bill are invited to Ned's party, too,' she ventured, frowning over Katherine's sigh of irritation and aware Katherine hated the fact Hettie and Bill shared the nursery together; a red rag to a bull as far as Katherine was concerned. With Lizzie working, it seemed only common sense to Bronwyn, who sensed too, that what Katherine most disliked about the arrangement was the obvious bond developing between the two children. They adored each other, a fact both mothers thought wonderful. 'If we set off now, she'll be back in plenty of time.' Katherine smiled, making it clear that as far as she was concerned, the matter was resolved.

It was true enough but did that make it any better? 'But then she'd have to fetch you back tomorrow,' Bronwyn continued doggedly and determined to have this out.

'And?' Her mother-in-law's tone was icy.

'And she'll be using double the petrol ration!' Surely she didn't have to point this out? Given Lloyd George's frequent exhortations, they all knew every drop of petrol saved was precious and needed for the front.

Katherine snorted. 'Georgina's chauffeur shall bring me home,' she informed, grandly. And that should be an end to it! Katherine had decreed and so it should be done, regardless of however much petrol it should take. Bronwyn hung onto her temper, only too aware to lose it would give this incorrigible woman further proof that the girl her precious son had married wasn't quite . . . top drawer. But she wasn't top drawer and if Katherine were example of the way the top drawer behaved, then she very much doubted she wanted to be either! Giving her hat one last check, Katherine turned away, her gaze suddenly fastening onto the child clinging so tenaciously to her mother's skirt. The Lord alone knew who she favoured with that ridiculous hair but even so . . . The thought springing immediately to mind took her by surprise. Blessed if the chit hadn't

Harry's eyes — a sea green, suggestive of hidden depths. How odd she'd never noticed before . . .

For once, the stern features, so normally prohibitive to Hettie, softened. 'Gwanny!' the little girl happily announced and, all at once, letting go her mother's skirt and holding up her arms, set off on tottering legs towards her.

'Hettie! Oh, clever, clever girl!' her mother cried, clapping her hands and watching her in delight.

'Gracious,' Katherine muttered and left with no other option than to take hold of the child's arm and wait, with a thinly veiled impatience, whilst her mother should reclaim her. Looking down into the little face, staring so determinedly up at her, an inexplicable pang in her breast gathered force. She was bound to acknowledge that whatever sex, this small being was still a Loxley, and with a Loxley's spirit and heart in her too, by the looks of it.

'But isn't she wonderful!' Bronwyn laughed, sweeping the little girl up aloft until she squealed to be put down.

'I fail to see why you're making such a fuss,' Katherine grumbled, a curious look flickering across her handsome face, but so quickly that Bronwyn wondered if she'd imagined it. It seemed she had. In full control of herself once more and, without another glance, Katherine picked up her valise and departed the house.

★  ★  ★

Matron's head, encased in its crisp white cap, thrust itself through the ambulance window, her gaze sweeping imperiously over the vehicle's two occupants.

'You're clear as to your orders?' she demanded.

'We're to pick up Major John Somerville at the Clearing Station, south of Ypres,' Ursula intoned happily. A hastily converted church in a village situated close to the main railway line. Dodi had the map and the list of directions which, given the two girls had made the journey numerous times already, was scarcely needed.

It was mid-day. It would be dark by the time they got back.

'And mind you treat him with the respect due his rank!' Matron snapped, as a parting shot before retreating briskly back to the hospital.

'Not if I can help it,' Ursula muttered mutinously.

'He's Brass. You can hardly expect him to travel back via the nearest troop train,' Dodi pointed out complacently.

Ursula frowned. She hated the way privilege was abused so the officers were always so much better treated than the men. Even if, as now, it gave the two girls a chance to remove themselves from the claustrophobic confines of Saint-Omer for a much-needed break from routine. If only the Loxleys and Harringtons weren't stationed at Ypres. As soon as Matron had mooted the trip, she'd been dreaming of the chance of bumping into Freddie, a forlorn hope, she knew but one she couldn't help harbouring. It was so long since she'd seen him; she simply ached to throw her arms around him, thereby proving to herself, he was still alive and in one piece. 'It isn't as if he'd want anything to do with me,' she muttered, thinking aloud.

'Freddie?' Dodi shifted in her seat. 'When are you two going to sort things out?'

'Given how many times I've written and never had a bean back, it's pretty sorted, don't you think?' she replied glumly. The fact Freddie hadn't answered any of her numerous letters led her to think all kinds of unpalatable thoughts, the least of which was he wanted no more to do with her. No matter the difficulties she had in imagining herself as a farmer's wife — the last thing she wanted to be — it still hurt.

She sighed, aware as they set off and the journey wore on, that their discomfort was increased by once-passable roads changed to pitted, shell-blown tracks, churned to mud by the constant rainfall. They ploughed on, lurching past supply wagons, armoured personnel carriers and troops and horses, all passing wearily to and from the Front. The sound of artillery fire was tremendous, signifying something big on, so all the while, they were on the constant look out for stray shells. Shortly, Ursula's hands were clamped tightly to the steering wheel whilst her eyes felt gritty with tiredness.

'Will this blasted war never end, Dodi?' She frowned. It seemed it had gone on forever, longer than she'd a memory to remember.

'Dunno, girl,' Dodi responded cheerfully. 'Buck up, do. We mustn't give in.'

They both knew Ursula was no quitter. They finished the journey in a companiable silence which only seemed to intensify the burst of shells, whiz bangs and artillery fire, lighting the gloom and pushing at the edges of the pall of smoke hanging so ominously over Ypres. 'We're here for Major Somerville,' Ursula informed a harassed orderly, once they were inside what she guessed had once been a pretty little church. Now the windows were boarded up and the roof smashed in and it was hard to think of men receiving any decent medical care here. Both girls tried hard not to stare at the stretchers and their groaning occupants which lined the corridor leading to the makeshift wards. And still they came, a constant stream of stretchers carried in by field ambulances from the Regimental Aid Posts. 'Is it always this bad?' she demanded of the orderly and wondering, forlornly, why she hadn't got used to it by now.

'There's a push on.' The man grimaced, leaving them shifting uncomfortably in the corridor whilst he went to make enquiries, returning moments later shaking his head. 'I'm sorry. You've had a wasted journey. According to the Medical Officer, Major Somerville left this morning. Private transport was arranged. They've taken him straight to the hospital ship.'

'And no-one thought to tell us?' Ursula fumed, back outside and reduced to watching, with a growing frustration, as yet another ambulance drew up. Two privates from the medical corps, uniforms splattered with mud, jumped out, hurrying round to the back to unload their patient. 'Anything we can do?' she called out, wishing desperately there was. How horrible it was to stand there so impotently when, all around, there was so

263

much which needed to be done. One of the men paused, pushing his helmet to the back of his head.

'I wish there was, darling. We've more casualties than men to get them here.'

'And what a waste does that make of us?' Ursula muttered, through clenched teeth, standing helplessly by as the men pulled the stretcher out to manoeuvre it, with a surprising gentleness, into the shattered building. A certain look, one Dodi knew only too well, crossed Ursula's face.

'Ursy, don't even think about it,' Dodi warned, her spirits already sinking.

It was too late and she knew it. Fuelled by a sudden wild energy, Ursula was already running back towards their ambulance.

They latched onto the tail end of a field ambulance which was crawling, at a snail's pace, behind a munitions wagon and a long, straggling line of exhausted men marching back to the Front. The night was falling already, the sky cracked with vivid explosions of light, illuminating their way along shattered roads lined with blighted trees and past villages where scarcely a house stood upright, testament to how dangerous their path was. Nothing mattered, only that they'd travelled all this way for nothing and must make some use of themselves. Finally, the road narrowed into little more than a muddied track where, to one side of it, a line of field ambulances waited. The vehicle in front pulled up and its owners jumped out, hurrying quickly away.

'I expect it's shanks pony from here on in,' Ursula commented cheerfully, manoeuvring them onto the side of the verge, next to the rest of the ambulances, and leaping out after them, leaving Dodi with no other option than to follow suit.

The direction the men had taken led to duckboards, laid across a narrow, twisted ditch, lined with sandbags, the first of a line of communication trenches leading directly to the Front, Ursula assumed, at the same time aware of an odd sweet smell that turned her stomach. The noise was deafening, a constant barrage of whistles and bangs, so there was no point in even trying to talk. In the dark, no-one took the slightest notice, only a sentry, momentarily barring their way and staring at them in startled surprise.

'We're ambulance personnel!' Ursula snapped, failing to add the obvious when he could see it well enough for himself. He was too shocked to stop them. Pausing only to grab hold of Dodi's sleeve, she brushed past him and hurried on after the two men in front until, all at once, they vanished from sight. The two girls hastened to the point. Closer inspection revealed it to be little more than a huge hole dug into one side of the ditch, supported by precarious-looking wooden props. In trepidation, they ventured in, horrified to see in the dim light cast by a storm lantern hanging from a hook in the ceiling, that stretchers were crammed into every conceivable space and, worse, yet more were being brought in as they stood, though it seemed impossible there'd be room enough. A huge explosion nearby, so sudden and fierce it made them jump, rattled the walls, bringing dust and debris raining down on its occupants. No-one took much notice, quietly carrying on with their task of tending to the wounded. Feeling themselves in the way, suddenly unsure of themselves, the girls hovered helplessly.

'What the hell are you waiting for!' snapped a strained voice belonging to a middle-aged man, a medical officer by his uniform, who knelt by a stretcher, applying a tourniquet to the remains of an arm belonging to a boy who didn't look old enough to be out of school. His tired, rather kindly eyes widened in surprise.

'But you're . . . '

'Women?' Ursula bridled, suddenly angry. What did it matter so long as they did something to help? They had to do something now!

Taking his silence as assent, they sprang

into action. It was no different to what they were used, after all, just rawer, more immediate and in the thick of things. Seizing on the nearest stretcher awaiting transit, they manoeuvred it carefully, between them, outside into the trench where, slipping and sliding in the gathering darkness and oblivious to the frightening explosion of shells bursting overhead, they headed determinedly back towards the direction of the ambulances. It was heavy, back-breaking work they gladly undertook, standing back in satisfaction once they'd loaded their precious cargo into the nearest vehicle.

'What are you waiting for, a medal?' a voice snapped, belonging to an officer from the medical corps, too stressed to care who they were or where they'd come from.

He was tired and angry and who could blame him, Ursula conceded miserably. There was so much to be angry at here. His hastily spoken words at least jolted them back into action. As the night lengthened, they stumbled back and forth, their way illuminated here and there by the moon scudding between clouds or, sometimes, a particularly huge explosion which lingered like a starburst, flooding their immediate surround with light and for which, momentarily, they were grateful. Once filled, each ambulance miraculously acquired a driver and co-driver and headed off into the night, only to be replaced by another, its hungry, gaping mouth yawning ever wider. An endless, thankless task. At last and unbelievably, the line of injured had reduced to a steady trickle and a pale dawn was raising its head above the sandbags lining the trenches.

Ursula lifted a weary face towards it. 'The birds are singing . . . ' she murmured, more shocked by it than anything she'd witnessed so far. It was as if even the birds should hang their heads in shame at such carnage done this night. They stood outside the dug-out, grateful for the tin mugs of hot, sweet tea someone thrust into their hands; too deadbeat to acknowledge the astonished glances from passing Tommies beginning their day. Their friend the Medical Officer emerged, leaning against the sandbags and lighting his pipe, his face drawn and shadowed with fatigue.

'You have no right to be here, you know,' he murmured quietly, still a grudging respect in his voice. 'Your superior . . . '

'Won't know if you don't tell her!' Ursula interjected quickly. Thoughts of Matron aware of this little escapade sent shivers racing along the length of her spine. With a rush of relief she saw amusement spring into his eyes.

'You'd better disappear then, double quick,' he advised before returning inside.

They were in the clear. Relieved, they

finished up quickly, noticing then, from the opposite direction, four soldiers advancing over the duckboards, carrying a stretcher carefully between them. A fifth soldier led the way. Mud-splattered, weary, scarcely strength enough to put one foot in front of another, something about the man caused Ursula to take a second look followed quickly by another and sharper glance. At once, her heart began to pound and there was a thunderous rushing in her ears. She'd have known that figure anywhere! Moving as if she were sleepwalking, her stumbling steps gathering pace, she flew towards him and threw her arms around him, taking no care of his howl of pain.

'Freddie! Thank God but you're alive! I've been so worried!'

'Ursula? But what the blazes . . . '

'Oh, but you're injured!'

'It's nothing. Don't fuss.'

'Dear God and when I thought . . . '
Precisely what she thought was buried into his tunic, as his good arm folded around her, crushing her to him and, all too briefly, holding her close. She could hear his heartbeat, so steady and reassuring; if only they could have stayed that way forever. Horribly, he was already putting her from him, his gaze raking her face before turning fretfully to the stretcher and its motionless cargo.

'It's his Grace,' he muttered, his voice hoarse with tiredness. 'He's taken a shrapnel wound to the head. He's badly injured, I'm afraid . . . '

## Ned's birthday party

Harry had been on Bronwyn's mind ever since she'd woken, a constant niggling worry, so much so that she was glad to leave the Hall and escape outside.

'There you are, your Grace!' Mary beamed, opening the door to the cottage.

The young woman had walked, pushing Hettie in her perambulator, so they could both enjoy the sight of the newly opened crocuses lining the road all the way over there, hinting at the spring. Smiling, Bronwyn lifted the baby out before turning to her host, looking past her and into the cottage and relieved to see Lizzie already there and that she wasn't the first to arrive. There was Reuben too, sitting at the table talking to Tom and Sam, the nice young man the Comptons had so willingly taken under their wing.

'You'll never believe this, Mary,' she murmured happily as she stepped over the threshold, 'but Hettie's taken her first steps this morning — across the hall to her grandmamma. I don't know who was the more surprised . . . '

'But miss, what a clever girl!' Happy for yet another cause for celebration, Mary patted Hettie's little cheek.

Inside, the cottage shone with the kind of gleam only a week's scrubbing with household soda could give it. The table was laid. Ned, protesting he was too old for such fuss, was prised reluctantly into his Sunday suit and sitting in his usual place by the fire, which this afternoon and especially for the occasion, was roaring halfway up the chimney back. Making their guest of honour welcome, happy to see her make straight for Lizzie and little Bill, happily playing on the hearth-rug, Mary smiled in quiet satisfaction. So what if she'd had to barter eggs for enough sugar to make the cake when that nuisance Lord Davenport said every housewife in Britain must feed their family as sparingly as possible. Keep calm and carry on! It was Ned's birthday and the old man deserved some happiness at this time of his life.

'Good news about our friends across the water,' Tom announced to the general company, puffing on his pipe and referring to Woodrow Wilson, the American president who had just broken off American relations with Germany, so enraged was he at their brazenly declared intention to blast all shipping out of the channel, irrespective of nationality.

'Serve 'em right. They were asking for it. Blasted U-boats . . . ' Sam chipped in.

'They'll happen broker for peace now,' Reuben murmured, unlikely peacemaker himself and rewarded by a smile from his host for his pains.

'What's that?' Ned retorted, sharply. 'I'll give 'em falling out and thinking that's an end to it. Why don't they get stuck in, same as the rest of us?'

'Lord, don't start,' Mary grumbled, momentarily forgetting whose day it was and that she'd promised to keep her temper. She mashed tea and filled the cups, all the while worrying there'd be enough to go round. But shortly and to her satisfaction, everyone was seated around the table, heartily reducing all her hard work to a pile of crumbs, even her Grace, bless her, dangling Hettie on one knee and feeding the child fingers of bread and butter, as if to take tea with those so far beneath her was the most natural thing in the world.

'I wish our Ursula was here!' Mary blurted out, surprising everyone, even herself. She put down the large green family teapot with a thump, her eyes inexplicably filling with tears she wiped away, in some embarrassment, with the corner of her apron.

'You must be desperate to get her home again!' Bronwyn burst out in sympathy.

'Now lass, don't take on,' Tom said, though whether to his wife or Bronwyn wasn't altogether clear.

It appeared only Lizzie had noticed Sam Tennant's start of dismay at the sound of Ursula's name, remembering then that Mary had told her that the young man was sweet on Ursula; only Ursula, being Ursula and still carrying a torch for Freddie, Raith Hamilton's lad who was away at the Front, didn't feel the same about him.

Nowadays, Lizzie couldn't bear pain, neither her own, nor anyone else's. When he got up, she thrust little Bill onto Reuben's knee and, ignoring the gamekeeper's start of surprise, followed him through into the scullery where she found him staring moodily through the window into the garden beyond.

'It's Sam, isn't it?' she asked, receiving only a brief nod for her pains. Undaunted, she reached for one of Mary's aprons dangling over the chair, and put it on, then fetched the kettle and filled the sink with hot water. 'Care to lend a hand?' she demanded briskly.

'This one?' he retorted bitterly, holding up his bad hand.

'Looks alright to me,' she replied, not one whit put out.

He sighed heavily, nevertheless reaching for the cloth. 'Sorry, that was cheap.'

'It was rather,' she agreed pleasantly, handing him a plate. 'I am sorry about your hand though.'

Sam was suddenly ashamed. So what if he couldn't stop thinking about Ursula and the fact she didn't love him. It wasn't this young woman's fault and when, from all Mary had told him, she'd trouble enough of her own. 'I'm sorry about your husband,' he muttered awkwardly. 'Ypres, wasn't it?'

Nodding, Lizzie plunged her hands into the water. 'At least you are still here,' she reminded him. Unlike Bill who wasn't and never would be. Momentarily, memory of Bill's big cheesy grin blotted out everything and it was only with a huge effort she pushed it away. She was only thankful thoughts like that were receding.

'I understand you're helping Tom out?' she asked quietly.

Sam nodded. The Comptons were good people and he owed them, he knew. 'It's surprising what I can do now I'm getting used to being one-handed. Its good therapy and I . . . I like to feel I can repay Tom and Mary in some way. They've been wonderful. They didn't have to take me in.'

'And you're enjoying the work?'

He stopped, regarding her in surprise. What a lot of questions she asked.

'I am,' he said, sounding surprised about that, too.

Lizzie handed a teacup over and smiled. 'The way you feel about Ursula . . . It will get better, I promise.'

If anyone knew about that, Sam guessed this girl would. She was so kind, so much concerned to put her own problems to one side and help him. 'If only I could be sure,' he admitted.

As usual, the pragmatic side of Lizzie's nature took over. 'There's nothing else for it, Sam. We have to go on,' she urged, spilling the one thought which had sustained her over Bill's loss more than any other.

She was right, he knew. Much as he loved her, Ursula only had eyes for Freddie Hamilton and there was an end to it. Somehow, he had to put her behind him and get on with the rest of his life.

★　★　★

Left to his own devices, Reuben sat awkwardly dangling little Bill on his knee, feeling only relief when Bronwyn, seizing the moment, suggested they let the children play together. 'You'll make a good father someday, Reuben,' she teased, once they'd settled themselves down either side of the hearth-rug where the children sat with a bag of Mary's pegs. He looked away quickly, leaving her wondering why he'd taken the remark so amiss.

'What's wrong?' she asked quietly.

'Nothing.' He scowled.

'You have been avoiding me of late,' she went on lightly.

'I never have!' His denial was vehement and too loud, causing Mary, who was stacking pots at the table, to throw him a worried frown.

'Alright?' she called.

Reuben's eyes blazed.

Casting another and more fretful glance in his direction, Mary acknowledged quietly to herself that Reuben had been in an especially odd mood of late. How awkwardly he sat, his troubled gaze resting on Bronwyn . . . Something about the sight gave her a jolt. Why! If she hadn't known any better . . . Mary's lips pursed firmly together. But what a patently ridiculous idea! Why of course Reuben wouldn't be so foolish as to develop feelings where he never ought . . .

'What is it, Reuben?' Bronwyn persisted.

The gamekeeper's ruddy colour deepened. The sight irritated her and she would have pushed him further if only Hettie hadn't chosen the moment to repeat her party trick, suddenly rearing to her feet and setting off determinedly towards Mary, who made so great a fuss, there was nothing else for it but that the little girl must do it all over again.

Watching the scene, Reuben shrank in on himself, only annoyed now that he'd allowed Mary to force him into coming here in the first place. How heartily glad he was when the enforced festivity was over and the party-goers were free to disperse. Outside, he hung back, waiting until he saw Bronwyn catch up with Lizzie and make room in the perambulator for the two little ones to share the journey home.

'And what would her Ladyship say about that, I wonder?' Mary muttered, coming to stand beside him to wave them away and glad now Katherine hadn't put in an appearance. She'd only have put a damper on proceedings, Mary thought and aware of Reuben watching the two women with such a haunted expression, all her worries came tumbling back.

'Are you alright, lad?' she gently probed.

'Leave it, I'm fine,' he growled but so patently not true, even Mary could see. But that was Reuben: man and boy, he always had been as tight as a clam. Before she could say more, he'd nodded good night and limped away, his cap thrust to the back of his head and his hands in his pockets so anyone who saw him would think all was well, only Mary who knew him better than most and more, to be a good man if one sometimes got confused.

A breeze had sprung up, keeping off the threatened rain and sending clouds scudding across the darkening sky to reveal a full high moon. In the woods, a dog fox barked, as usual at this time of evening, a time more normally Reuben loved, if only it weren't for the taste of bitter gall in his mouth. His boots struck against the road, sending sparks flying, his sense of unease deepening and bringing with it the oddest of feelings he was being watched. He stopped, looking about him sharply before spinning round on his heel and catching, out of the corner of his eye, the shadow of a human form shrinking back into the trees. Glittering eyes, so dark and malevolent, so bent on revenge. It was pure nonsense of course for who should ever bother over Reuben Fairfax? He'd taken a glass too much of Mary's elderflower.

'Who's there?' he demanded, peering uneasily into the gloom.

There was nothing and no-one, only the wind, whipping his words away high over the swaying tree-tops as, wings outspread and hooting mournfully, an owl glided by.

He was glad to get home where he built up

the fire and mashed tea, whiling away the time until bed whittling at a piece of wood, then horrified to discover when he looked down that his subconscious had taken over and it was the slim figure of a girl taking shape beneath his hands. Throwing it from him with a cry of despair, he stumped upstairs to bed to lie long, sleepless hours, staring sightlessly into the darkness until at last, exhaustion claimed him and he dropped into a troubled sleep.

It was still dark when he awoke. He lay quietly, aware of an odd scent in the room and thinking strangely, meanwhile, of when he was a lad and he'd used to take off with Harry for the day, over the moors to a meadow threaded with lavender and their favourite spot to eat the food they'd sneaked from the kitchen.

It was the scent of lavender around him now — how odd that was! He'd never forget it, or the happy days of which it reminded him. Levering himself up on his elbows, he stared at the thin streaks of dawn already filtering through the window, wondering at its rosiness. At once, he leapt from his bed, rushing over to stare in dismay at the fiery dawn throbbing over Loxley. Dear God! That was no dawn! With clumsy, trembling fingers, he threw on his clothes and rushed downstairs, stumbling from the cottage and cursing his bad leg which would slow him down, so driven by madness and fear, the smell of burning so strong in him now, he thought he would die of it. Through the trees and over the bridge he ran, gasping as he rounded the corner and saw for real, the bright red flames flickering through the windows of the south facing front of the Hall.

Of its inhabitants there was no sign. Why weren't they awake? Were they murdered in their beds? Almost out of his wits, he ran wildly up the steps to the front doors, cursing to find them locked and banging on them with his fists and feet. He'd gone mad, become enmeshed in some nightmare from which he couldn't awake. All to no avail! Thwarted, he leapt back, glaring upwards into the clouded night sky and, in his madness, shaking his fist at it. 'Rain! Rain blast you!' he cried.

Looking around him, his desperate gaze fell on the two pillars next to the stone lions at the bottom of the steps, each topped by a ball of stone. With no thought now but to get inside and waken the hall's inhabitants, he heaved one up into his arms, staggering with it to the top of the steps to fling it, with every morsel of strength he could muster, against the nearest downstairs window.

The glass shattered, letting out a puther of smoke. Balling his hands into fists, he beat out the rest, throwing himself heedlessly through the aperture to land, in a tangle of arms and legs, on the stone floor beneath. Momentarily, he lay winded but in a trice, he was up again, taking no note of the tapestries aflame over the stairs, or the flicking tongues of red and orange flames snaking across the beams of the great oak ceiling. He opened his lungs and yelled, something, anything, rushing back to the front doors where the fingers of fire so lovingly caressed that which it would consume. Heedlessly, he knocked back the bolts, flinging them wide and letting in a rush of air, only adding thereby to the crackle of flame and conflagration.

At least his efforts had effect. Coughing and spluttering through the smoke, figures loomed. Mrs. Norris, in her nightgown and sleeping cap tied under her chin, clutching a squalling, frightened Hettie to her breast. From the servants' quarters below, cook and Rose, the kitchen maid, emerged, followed by Soames in his dressing gown, his hair on end. Fiercely, Reuben seized hold of him.

'Her Grace . . . Bronwyn . . . where is she!'

'Why . . . why still in her bed,' the old man moaned, staring at him stupidly.

Reuben knew the place like the back of his

hand and always had. Angrily, he thrust him away and tore away upstairs into a choking smoke, much denser here and fused with a heat so fierce it forced him to his knees. There was no time to think. Instinct drove him on, eyes streaming, choking and coughing, crawling, head bent, to the door of Bronwyn's sitting room, springing up then and dashing it open before running heedlessly into her bedroom beyond.

She was still in her bed, lying half in and half out, overcome by the smoke which clung like a shroud over the furniture, obscuring his vision. Alive, he prayed, having no time to stop and find out before heaving her up into his arms. He staggered, righting himself before gathering her more fiercely to him, his precious burden, exulting when he felt her stir. 'Oh my love,' he moaned, before head bent against the heat, he blundered back towards the door. In the hallway outside, an insidious choking smoke clawed the back of his throat, filling his lungs so he swayed, turning this way and that as the smoke folded around them and he knew then that they were lost . . .

# 10

March 1917

Safe inside the sanctuary of Mary Compton's little cottage, Bronwyn sat with her head in her hands, trying to recall the slightest detail of how she had survived the raging fire that had so very nearly destroyed Harry's beloved Loxley. Momentarily she roused to stare vacantly at Ned who sat across the hearth, aware that all she had were the barest of impressions — heat then cold, burning light then darkness, and then Reuben's arms around her, holding her safe. Lizzie, rushing down from the stables with little Bill clasped in her arms, had found her wandering, dazed, from the direction of the meadows, and with only wits enough to implore the one question hammering in her brain — wherever was Hettie? That her little girl was safe with Mrs. Norris had taken long, agonizing minutes to discern.

'At least the poor wee things are settled,' Mary murmured, returning downstairs after sitting with them until they'd fallen asleep, two little angels in each other's arms. It hadn't taken long either, poor mites, so rudely awakened. A rude awakening for them all, Bronwyn more than any, Mary hazarded, feeling again her amazement that her young mistress was here and alive and not, as first feared, trapped inside the blazing Hall.

Of Reuben there was no sign. Dear God, they all prayed Reuben was safe!

No-one knew how any had managed to get out alive and, judging by her reaction since Tom had ushered the little party in here, Bronwyn least of all. Mary threw a fretful gaze towards the young woman sitting so dazed by the fire, still dressed in the rough skirt and blouse she'd borrowed from Lizzie. Mercifully, the stables and the flat over it, where Lizzie lived, were untouched.

Wearily, Mary lifted the kettle onto the range, her head still raging with the night's events which, along with most other folk roused by the unnatural glow shining through their bedroom windows, had seen her jump from her bed, stopping only to throw a coat over her night-dress before rushing out to help. Folk dashing to and fro, cries and screams, the crackling, dancing flames and all suffused with the terrible, acrid smell of burning which would remain with her for the rest of her life. Mary shuddered.

An organised effort to pump water from

the lake in the gardens had been attempted but it had soon become obvious that the flames had taken too great a hold. Then just when all had seemed lost, as if in answer to their heartfelt prayers, of which there'd been many, the skies had opened and the longed for rain arrived. A heaven sent downpour, quenching that which had seemed insatiable only moments before. Mary believed it a miracle but there'd been no time to dwell on it since. Practicalities had taken over, most importantly that of the villagers opening up their homes and offering willing sanctuary to the Hall's evacuees so none were left without a roof over their heads, at least until other and more permanent arrangements could be made.

'Try and not fret, lass. I'll make us a drop more tea,' she murmured, wishing there was something else she could offer. The ability to put the clock back — if only she could!

'We've supped nowt but tea,' Ned grumbled.

'You've no need to drink it, dad,' she pointed out.

The old man sighed. 'I ought to be helping out.'

'And what could you do?' she snapped, unforgivably.

'There must be summat!' he retorted, offended. He shifted in his chair. He was frustrated.

Folk were doing so much and he could do so little. But he should do something! 'How long will her Ladyship be?' he demanded, needing some outlet for his temper. Lizzie had been despatched to Georgina's to bring Katherine home. No-one envied the poor girl, trying to explain to her mistress that in her absence, her home had all but burnt down.

'How should I know, dad,' Mary fretted, already dreading Katherine's arrival. There was nothing she could say. What anyone could say. Things, on the whole, Mary reckoned, couldn't have been worse.

The door opened and Tom and Sam trooped in, delayed by the police who'd needed to talk to them. Both men looked out on their feet but their appearance at least roused Bronwyn from her reverie. Her head jerked up. 'Any news of Reuben?' she demanded.

'Not yet, lass,' Tom muttered.

'He's safe! I'm sure he's safe!' Wildly, half out of her mind, she sprang to her feet.

Suddenly, she was anything but sure and sank back helplessly into the chair again, where she folded her arms around herself and began to rock. She hardly knew what she thought.

'Blessed if I know where he is,' Tom remarked unhappily.

The two men threw off their coats and sat

down at the table. Mary ran the tap to refill the kettle. The sound made Bronwyn start, concentrating her mind on an odd memory, just surfaced — the sound of water dripping with a steady, methodical pulse. And a whooshing, slushing noise! Rain? More than rain, and Reuben's voice, as if from a distance. 'Go now, you're safe,' he'd murmured and with such a lilting softness, she'd imagined it was Harry . . . Harry who was soothing her, holding her safe . . .

Tom's gaze sought Mary's and, as always, found a world of comfort there. He frowned, wiping a hand around the back of his neck, wondering how to put it and deciding he could only be blunt.

'He's not in the house. At least there's that.'

'There's no body, you mean?' Mary demanded and equally bluntly. She breathed in heavily, gripping the back of the chair. 'Oh dear lad, the flames were awful fierce.'

'Not that fierce there'd be nothing left,' Tom muttered. 'Wherever he is, he got out of the fire. I'm sure of it.'

Bronwyn moaned softly.

'I'll make that tea,' Mary murmured, pulling herself together; someone must. Her hand brushed Bronwyn's arm, a gesture of sympathy, all she had to offer. Poor girl, what a night she'd endured. What a night they'd all endured!

'Any idea yet how the fire started?' Ned enquired, voicing the one question in everyone's minds.

'I wondered if it was a spark from the fire . . . I dunno, it's a mystery, dad.' Tom was relieved to turn his mind to practicalities, even if he'd yet to make sense of it. Raking out the ashes was generally Soames' last task before he took himself off to bed but the old butler swore blind he hadn't been so careless as to forget. A lamp knocked over? And no-one noticed, which was a point stretching credibility, Tom knew. His face lifted; remembering now, at least, he did have some good news to impart. 'Things aren't as bad as we feared,' he told the company eagerly. 'There's superficial damage, of course. The south front roof's gone and the first floor's caved in but as far as I can see, the rest has held up remarkably well.'

'But the paintings, Tom, and the furniture and the tapestries — all that history!' Bronwyn cried, thinking of Harry and Katherine and unsure which would take it worse. Only now, the full calamity of what had happened was sinking in.

'Ah, history . . . that's a different matter!' Tom frowned.

Thoughts of Katherine's imminent arrival worried them all to varying degrees and it was a sombre group who sat together around the kitchen table drinking the tea Mary so constantly supplied. It took the sound of childish babble, drifting downstairs, to rouse them from their respective reveries. Hettie and little Bill had woken; hearteningly, neither apparently the worse for their adventures.

Normality was in her child. Upstairs, Bronwyn lifted her daughter and hugged her close, drawing strength from her solid little body, her tiny hands reaching out to pat her mother's face as if, young as she was, she sensed something dreadfully bad had happened.

'Don't cry, mummy,' she lisped frowningly.

Mary gathered up little Bill. Together, the two women returned downstairs. At that moment, the kitchen door burst open and Katherine rushed in, Lizzie not far behind. Swaying slightly, she stood, in obvious agitation, her wild gaze roaming over the sea of faces until, finally, it came to settle on Bronwyn. And then, oddly, the last thing anyone in that little kitchen had expected, emitting a soft cry, she hurried towards Bronwyn and put her arms around her and the child she held so tightly in her arms. Some long moments followed but at last she recovered herself enough to speak.

'Oh my dear girl! Thank the Lord you're safe. I couldn't bear to think . . . ' Her voice, normally so forceful, trailed away, as if what she'd been thinking was a thing too terrible to contemplate.

'Katherine, the Hall!' Bronwyn said wretchedly, after recovering from the shock of finding herself so embraced. 'Such a dreadful, terrible fire . . . '

Katherine's face showed the strain of great emotion. 'You're safe and that's the most important thing,' she answered, gently stroking the young woman's cheek before tremblingly moving to Hettie's bright curls. Hettie held out her arms. Shocked as everyone already was, it was to more general astonishment when, gently, Katherine lifted the granddaughter she'd scarcely acknowledged up until this point, unresisting into her arms. 'There now, darling,' she soothed, clutching her tightly to her. 'Grandmamma's here and will make things right.' Feeling the weight of the child in her arms — her grandchild, she reminded herself — Katherine Loxley made a concerted effort to pull herself together. There was no doubting things were bad but, she was only just beginning to realise, they could have been unbearably worse. She breathed in deeply, bringing emotions so wildly, so uncommonly unrestrained, firmly back under control.

'Now, Tom,' she commenced briskly. 'Are you going to tell me what's happened?' A disaster no matter how he tried to make the best of it. Tom nodded unhappily. Whilst Mary settled everyone down, he filled his mistress in on events as far as he knew and his unshakeable belief Reuben had managed to get out and was somewhere safe. No-one knew where, as yet. Sent out of his wits, he expected, after all that had happened, and who could blame him for it was enough to turn any man's mind.

'But haven't you seen the Hall yet?' Bronwyn demanded, shocked when, bad as it sounded, she'd have expected Katherine to have been more concerned with that than anything, even Hettie. It appeared she was wrong.

'Only fleetingly,' Katherine conceded, not elucidating on the panic which had caused her to avert her eyes as they drove past. She couldn't bear to look and see the ruin of all her dreams, that was the truth of it. She sat, Hettie on her knee, unable to explain her feelings at this point. Shock, horror, disbelief and yet something else too which, during all the wretched drive over here, had made her deaf to Lizzie's protestations that Bronwyn and Hettie were both safe, until she could get here and see for herself. Loxley was her life but it had taken thoughts of losing the grandchild of whom she'd so stupidly thought so little, to bring her to her senses. Her gaze lifted to Bronwyn. Neither could she bear thoughts of losing this young woman either, she realised, with a start. 'Thank the Lord you're safe,' she repeated, helplessly, as if she couldn't say it enough. Her arms tightened around her granddaughter's chubby little frame, finding, unexpectedly, her eyes full of tears.

'Katherine, please don't distress yourself,' Bronwyn muttered awkwardly. 'We must take a walk up to the Hall so you can see the damage for yourself?' Unpalatable as it was it did have to be faced.

The panic Katherine was struggling so hard to suppress resurfaced and this time she couldn't hide it. 'You'll come with me?' she asked querulously.

Katherine had never before asked for her help and Bronwyn was determined not to fail her now. There was no time like the present. 'Of course!' she returned, jumping up. Shortly, dressed in an old coat of Mary's, she was headed Hallwards with Katherine and Tom. Katherine's agitation was palpable. She didn't want to go because she couldn't bear what she'd find when she got there, and who could blame her, Bronwyn surmised. She took her arm, surprised when the older woman made no protest.

Despite the rain still falling, a thick pall of smoke hung over the damaged south front and, as they drew nearer, they saw that the windows were burnt out and the walls beneath discoloured with ugly scorch marks. The roof had all but gone. Two police constables stood guard by the front steps where a small knot of villagers stood, unable to believe what had happened and turning anxious glances Katherine's way when they realised who she was. 'Oh dear God . . . ' Katherine moaned, aware of their need but, for once in her life, with nothing left to give them. Reassuringly, Bronwyn's grip on her arm tightened. 'It'll be alright,' she soothed. 'Isn't that so, Tom?' She looked across eagerly. 'Aye, your Grace!' he agreed, wanting more than anything to take that look from Katherine's face. 'Please believe me. It's not as bad as it looks!'

They had to take his word for it. A middle-aged man with whiskers, in a threadbare coat and a bowler hat, was walking towards them. With obvious reluctance, he touched his hat with one grubby finger.

'Your Graces . . . I'm Inspector Digby. A bad business this!'

'Any news?' Tom Compton demanded.

The Inspector's gaze shifted towards him. 'Aye, you could say,' he replied evenly. 'We're nearer to piecing events together at last. There's been a break-in, I'm afraid, a window smashed downstairs, round the back.'

'But I don't understand!' Katherine's voice was sharp.

'I mean you've had an intruder,' the inspector responded.

'We've been burgled as well?' None of this was making sense to her.

'Someone broke in and started the fire by the looks of it . . . ' the little Inspector agreed.

'But what madman would do such a thing?' she demanded imperiously.

'Someone with a grudge?' he hazarded. 'Maybe one of the servants perceived themselves wrongly treated. One's gone missing, I understand?'

He'd been asking round already and getting the wrong impression too, by the looks of it.

'Take no account of Reuben. He's a law unto himself,' Tom broke in, hastily.

'Whoever else could there be?'

Katherine frowned, for some unknown reason thinking back to Hettie's birth and the crazed gypsy woman, mouthing curses. She'd never given her another thought, until now.

'Tell me!' Digby ordered, sensing something and determined to winkle it out.

Amazed to find herself doing exactly that, Katherine communicated all she knew about the gypsy who'd been jailed over the theft of

Merry and the part she'd played in her downfall. It was little enough. 'You know what gypsies are like.'

The inspector apparently did, though he made no comment on the story or Katherine's involvement in it. There was nothing else to go on. Katherine's gaze settled on the damaged Hall. The one moment she'd dreaded above all.

'We've yet to give it the all clear,' Digby muttered, following her gaze.

He didn't know Katherine, however, or he'd have saved his breath.

'I'll come with you,' Bronwyn said, who did.

'I'd rather be alone,' she replied, her voice thick with emotion. First taking a deep breath, she headed with quiet dignity towards her burnt-out home. Digby departed, leaving Bronwyn and Tom kicking their heels until her reappearance, minutes later. She was visibly shaken.

'Is it so very bad?' Bronwyn demanded, then cursed herself for her tactlessness. Of course it was bad. It was catastrophic. Fire consumed, destroyed, made pointless, centuries of endeavour.

'Bad enough,' Katherine muttered, her gaze, whether by chance or direction, turning back towards the shattered building and the family crest hanging over the front doors. A stag and lion rampant, signifying the courage and strength of heart for which the Loxleys had always been renowned. Miraculously untouched by flames, still keeping a watchful eye on whomsoever entered or departed the Hall.

If she was no Loxley by birth, she was one by nature and design. Courage coursed through Katherine Loxley's veins, giving her strength, just when she needed it most. 'It could have been worse,' she admitted quietly. 'There's nothing that can't be repaired, given time. Now . . . ' Her face stiffened, taking on the identity of the Katherine of old, the one Bronwyn knew only too well and was oddly gratified to see back. 'We'll need somewhere to stay,' she retorted briskly. 'Georgina's, I think, at least until the place is made safe. Once that's done, we can put up somewhere closer and oversee the repairs. It's certain, things as they are, we shall have a battle finding the manpower but we shall manage, never fear.'

Bronwyn had no doubts of it but first there was something else. 'Hettie and I won't be going to Georgina's,' she returned quickly, the firmness of her voice nowhere near betraying her agitation in arguing with Katherine. Within the course of time, she could well see the sense of being nearby but not for the immediate future. 'We're going home,' she went on, her heart leaping at the thought and wondering now why she hadn't insisted on it already. 'My mother will be only too delighted to see us and . . . Oh Katherine! I'm sorry, I just need to go home!'

'I see.' Katherine stood, digesting the news; finally and shockingly, to Bronwyn, nodding her head in agreement.

'Your mother's it is. Lizzie shall take us! There's nothing we can do here, for now.'

'You mean you're coming, too?' Bronwyn blurted out, shocked at the idea.

'Of course I'm coming with you!' Katherine smiled grimly. Good should come from bad. From the ashes of the old, something wonderful should rise, better than all that had gone before. Her head nodded rapidly. 'After what we've been through, I've no intention of letting Hettie from my sight again . . . '

★   ★   ★

'You need a hand,' Katherine asserted briskly, coming through into the kitchen of Doctor Colfax's neat little villa and seeing Tilly, his servant, sitting at the table, peeling vegetables for the evening meal. Rolling up the sleeves of her dress, she pulled out a chair and sat down.

Tilly's mouth dropped open.

'I helped out enough in the kitchens when I was a girl,' Katherine bridled, sensing opposition and bent on finding occupation for her hands, whether this curmudgeonly old serving woman desired it or not.

At the far end of the table, where she stood kneading the dough for the day's bread, Dorothea Colfax bent her head to hide a smile, her first since the little party of refugees had arrived two days since. Lizzie had brought them, returning afterwards to Mary Compton's who'd been left in charge of little Bill. Everyone was doing their best. All it needed now was for the all clear to be given and a start could be made on the rebuilding of the Hall. Easy enough said, not so easily accomplished, Katherine conceded, suppressing a sigh.

Bronwyn came in from settling Hettie to her nap upstairs.

'Tilly, help me lay the table. We'll eat in the dining room to-night,' Dorothea murmured, wiping her hands on her apron and sensing the two women would appreciate some time alone.

'That's it, wear the old 'uns out first,' Tilly muttered spitefully, under her breath, nevertheless rising to her feet to follow her mistress out.

'You look tired,' Katherine observed, her keen eyes fastened on her daughter-in-law's face. Bronwyn knew it perfectly well already; the aftermath of shock from which they were all suffering to varying degrees, even her mother, the house sent topsy-turvy with so many extra mouths to feed. Gratefully, the young woman sank into Tilly's vacated seat, finding solace from the restlessness which had been plaguing her since their arrival, in resuming their old servant's work. The incongruousness of sitting at the kitchen table, peeling vegetables with Katherine Loxley, of all people, passed her by. She was too tired to care.

'What are we to tell Harry?' she demanded fretfully, neatly slicing a carrot and dropping it into the bowl. And, more to the point, how were they to tell him and when: given the small matter of a world war, he wasn't so easily reached.

'It would be terrible news to receive by post,' Katherine conceded, who'd been wondering as much herself. Harry had enough on as it was, without such calamitous news from home.

'Do we have to tell him?' Momentarily, Bronwyn clung to the vain hope they might not.

'The news is bound to spread even out there . . . '

'But it's such a shame he needs to know before the repairs are underway! That's all I'm thinking,' she fretted. 'What a mess it is! Reuben . . . '

'Aye, Reuben!' Katherine sighed so heavily, Bronwyn shot her a second and sharper glance.

'Where could he be? I don't understand,' she fretted. There was still no clue as to their gamekeeper's whereabouts and it simply didn't make sense. Nothing made sense, she thought, brushing a weary hand across her forehead. She was tired, upset and consumed by an unexpected anger that Reuben, of all people, should be so thoughtless as to put them through this extra worry when they surely had had enough already. What if he'd injured himself in some way? There was no sign of him at the cottage and a thorough search had already been made of the surrounding woods, turning up no further clue as to his whereabouts.

Katherine put down her knife, giving air to the thought over which she'd been struggling.

'There's a perfectly obvious reason why he's disappeared, child!' she exclaimed. 'All this talk of gypsy curses when the solution is so very clear! Why else would he have disappeared if it wasn't because . . . he was the one who started the fire in the first place?'

Bronwyn stared at her as if she'd taken leave of her senses. 'Reuben started the fire?'

'You think the police haven't reached the same conclusion?' Katherine retorted, bitterly.

'But why? What possible reason . . . '

'I can think of plenty,' she snapped.

Any closeness Bronwyn had imagined between herself and Katherine vanished instantly.

'You're wrong!' she returned vehemently and offended for Reuben when he wasn't here to defend himself. She took a deep breath, proceeding more calmly. 'You're so wrong. Reuben was the one who raised the alarm and got everyone out. How could you think he'd do such a terrible thing?' She stared at Katherine, sensing, if not understanding, she was struggling with an emotion engendered by something more than the crazy idea that he'd set fire to the place. Something so terrible, it would make him want to burn the place down around their ears? It was an outlandish notion but as she opened her mouth to express it, the sound of raised voices emerged from the hall. At once, the interior door burst open and her mother hurried into the room, swiftly followed by Lizzie.

'Oh, my darling girl . . . '

'Oh miss, I had to come!' Lizzie jumped in. She looked distraught.

Deep within Bronwyn's breast, the flicker of a fear constantly with her, but which she more normally suppressed, flamed into a terrible and vibrant life.

'What is it?' she cried, rising quickly to her feet.

In answer, Lizzie held out the telegram with which she'd hurried straight over. 'It came this morning, miss,' she fretted. 'With no-one up at the Hall, the post man delivered it to Tom's. He didn't know where else to take it.'

'Oh dear God . . . ' Katherine's hand flew to her mouth.

Bronwyn realised she'd been waiting for this moment all along and, now it had arrived, it didn't even surprise her. All thoughts of Reuben forgotten, her world crumbled and dissolved. No cataclysmic earthquake but more terrible, a folding, a disintegrating from within. A single sheet of paper, folded over. So simple and yet so terrifying. Here and now and meant for her.

Trembling, she took it and, before her courage should fail her, slid her finger under the seal and opened it.

The words jumped up to meet her, hammering at her consciousness, so a little soft sigh escaped her lips. Fervently, she scanned the two lines of print. 'We regret to inform . . . your husband, Harry Loxley . . . injured on active service . . . currently in the military hospital at Saint-Omer, France. No further information available.'

'Is he dead? Please tell me.' Katherine's voice came from far away.

Unsure if it was relief she felt, Bronwyn

handed her the telegram. He wasn't dead. It must mean something? 'He's injured. I don't know how badly. I must go to him, Katherine.' Her voice trembled with emotion.

'How can you?' Katherine answered wretchedly.

Harry was injured and needed her. An unexpected courage rose up, sustaining her and giving her strength. She hadn't an idea in her head yet as to how she would get to him. She only knew she must.

★   ★   ★

Sunset at Cape Gris Nez, spinning golden threads over the darkening white capped waves and turning the sea pinks and thrift lining the cliff top to a deep and rosy red. Ursula wished the day would never end. Perhaps it never would.

She reached for Freddie's hand, tucking it comfortably under her arm, grateful to see more colour in his cheeks than when he'd first been discharged from Saint-Omer. That he'd opted to spend his week's recuperation in a pension overlooking the Strait of Dover, rather than taking the time to go home to his family, hoping against hope Ursula might, at some point manage to join him, told her so much.

She couldn't believe she was here and,

better still, she'd wangled a forty-eight-hour pass from Matron. Miraculously, Dodi had one too, but Matron would have a seizure if she'd guessed either girl was spending it with a man. They had found lodging in a farmhouse on the outskirts of Audingham, where the farmer's wife, whose husband was away at the front, had been only too pleased of a few extra francs to help her feed her children.

'Happy?' Freddie smiled.

She nodded. She was and not just because Dodi, ever tactful, had disappeared to do some sight-seeing in Calais, leaving her alone with Freddie to spend the day blissfully wandering along the impossibly white-sanded beach and enjoying both sight and sound of the waves crashing in. Later, they'd discovered a secluded sand-dune to sit and eat their bread and cheese and drink the rough red wine the farmer's wife had pressed upon them before they'd left. The climb up here to the cliff top, with its spectacular views and ruins of the fortress built by Henry VIII, they'd saved until the last.

'I wish we had more time, Freddie.' She sighed, her grip on his hand tightening.

'Tomorrow I'll be back at the hospital and you'll be stuck at Officer Training Camp in Boulogne . . . '

'Aren't you proud of me?' he teased.

'Of course I'm proud!' she responded quickly and aggrieved he might think she wasn't.

Freddie's actions after he'd got stuck in no-man's-land with Harry Loxley were such that he was now considered suitable officer material. Not that he'd talked about it much, only that in trying to get back to the lines, Harry had been hit by shrapnel. That he'd carried him on his back the best part of the way, she'd only just learned.

'I hope Harry's going to be alright,' he murmured, quietly.

'He's in the best place, Freddie.'

Her words sounded hollow even to Ursula's ears. Harry Loxley was in the hospital at St Omer, where the women who worked there were run off their feet, and where there was such a chronic lack of facilities that, much as everyone fretted over it, the staff could only offer the most basic of care.

They came to a halt, standing to look out over the sea shimmering in the sunset and bringing the white cliffs beyond so tantalisingly close, Ursula felt she could almost reach out and touch them. A sight so magnificent, it filled her with strength, just when she needed it most, and engendered in her an ache deep inside of which she was only now aware. Home, England and Loxley. And when she'd once so longed to leave it! It tore at her heart;

making her long for things she sensed would always be with her, no matter where.

Freddie's gaze roamed her face. 'It was so odd you were there at the Front, waiting for me, Ursy,' he muttered and talking, she sensed, to hide his emotion. 'Do you believe in fate? It was as if you knew you were needed and were determined on getting us out, no matter what.' She nodded, admitting then to something that had been troubling her ever since that terrible night. It did seem like fate but . . . 'That's just it though, Freddie!' she moaned. 'I abused a privilege bringing you out. I've always decried anyone doing that and yet, there was I, when it came to, prepared to do exactly the same. And I'd do it again, a thousand times if . . . '

He turned her gently towards him, stopping her words with his lips so she leaned into him, giving herself up to his embrace, amazed that this time, it felt so right.

'You don't have to go back to the farm to-night,' he whispered roughly.

His breath fanned her face. Her hand stole upwards, caressing his face, his dear face, the sight of which, when they were apart, she'd so longed for it was like a physical ache.

'Freddie, you know I have to go back. Dodi . . . '

'Dodi would understand . . . ' he urged.

'Why shouldn't we snatch a little happiness? We may never get another chance.' Tenderly, he kissed the top of her head. 'We'll make it right when we get home.'

She wouldn't listen. 'If we get home . . . '

'Of course we'll get home!' He frowned.

She only knew, before they had a chance of going anywhere, they had to sort this out, once and for all. 'I still don't know if I can be a farmer's wife!' she blurted out and sure in the bones of her she'd never take to the life. Look how she'd been before the war! Bored, itching to get away; sure there must be more to life. Caring for the farm and Freddie, bringing up a brood of children, would it ever be enough? But how could she tell until she'd tried? Back came the insidious voice, whispering treacherously in her ear. What if she failed, making herself miserable in the process, worse making Freddie miserable too?

She'd never forgive herself after all he'd been through.

'I haven't asked you yet,' he teased, trying vainly to lighten the atmosphere when all he really wanted was for them to be together, now, this moment and more than he'd ever wanted anything in his life.

'Freddie Hamilton, you jolly well have!' she raged, nearly in tears, wanting and yet not wanting him, so confused she felt nothing other than a slow and burning anger which, with nowhere else to go, she turned in on herself. 'I don't know what we'll do,' she moaned, wondering now if the war had driven her ever so slightly mad.

'We have to get through this first,' he pointed out, evenly.

Freddie Hamilton being practical! He'd changed, become less hot-headed, a new Freddie she guessed it would take her time to get to know. More time than they had now. The only man, Ursula admitted, no matter what their respective futures, she could ever truly love.

★   ★   ★

'His Grace will be alright, miss, you see . . . ' Lizzie coaxed though both she and Bronwyn knew he might not be. But her poor young mistress was eaten up with anxiety and she only wanted to help.

They'd driven down to Portsmouth overnight, begging petrol rations from Dr. Colfax who'd managed to pull in a few favours amongst his patients. In the sea-salt air, the seagulls wheeled increasingly frantic circles whilst the owner of the fishing tug, 'The Jaunty Belle', bobbing gently in the harbour, waited impatiently by. Dover to Calais would have been nearer, Portsmouth to Dieppe safer enough to compensate for the longer journey across the French countryside to Saint-Omer. Bronwyn had paid the man handsomely. Crossing the channel was a dangerous business with German U-boats a constant threat.

She'd discovered she didn't care about anything, only Harry and getting him home again. She was learning; money and position moved mountains. Why shouldn't she take advantage, using every power at her fingertips?

'Miss, I wish I was going too!' Lizzie implored.

Bronwyn caught her hands, giving them an impatient shake.

'We've discussed this already. You have little Bill . . . '

'And you have Hettie, miss.'

'Katherine will look after Hettie.' Katherine's growing devotion to Hettie was the only good to come out of the whole sorry business as far as Bronwyn was concerned. 'I'll be quite safe, Lizzie. Please believe me.'

Lizzie sighed heavily. 'I wanted to see where they've put my Bill, miss, only . . . '

'Only you'd rather wait until after the war?' Bronwyn murmured perceptively.

The young woman bit down hard on her lip. 'I want to go in peace. Does . . . does that make sense?'

It made perfect sense when so little did. Oh, blast this war, making such a mess of their lives.

They'd never be the same again, any one of them! Impulsively, Bronwyn threw her arms around Lizzie and hugged her close.

'We'd best be getting off, mum, if we want to catch the tide,' the fisherman interrupted, gruffly.

Some of the famous Loxley spirit must be rubbing off. She was going to Harry to bring him home and nothing, but nothing, would stop her. Smiling a reassurance she was far from feeling, Bronwyn picked up the small valise bearing her change of clothes and followed the man onto the boat.

★  ★  ★

The journey had all the qualities of a dream, her palpable anxieties at one with the grey, choppy sea which stretched so far into the distance. The endless skies, streaked with gold, merging into a horizon where it was so hard to tell where the sea ended and the sky began. Bronwyn stood at the prow, eyes supposedly peeled for German U-boats when all she could think about was Harry and how he'd be when she finally got to him. At least he was alive, or had been when she'd received the telegram. The thought sent shivers racing down her spine. At last the coastline and the elegant frontage of the tall houses hugging Dieppe's water-front rose into view. They disembarked onto the jetty, her companion leaving her alone awhile whilst he disappeared into one of the houses, returning a short while later with a swarthy, thick-set man he informed her had agreed to drive the distance to her journey's end. The price was extortionate but she didn't care.

'I'll pay it,' she agreed, too quickly, wondering only then if he'd realised she'd have paid anything he asked. She settled herself in the passenger seat of his battered automobile, clutching her valise and relieved when they set off, hugging the coastline through Le Treport and Montreuil before turning off for Saint-Omer at Boulogne. She sat, trying to remember the schoolgirl French her father had insisted on and which at least left her able to follow her driver's increasingly volatile discussion about the war. It would last forever. The people here were suffering severely. How lucky she was, she had the channel between her people and the worst of the threat! Another time, and if only Harry had been with her, she would have enthused over the richly decorated façades of the town houses of Saint-Omer and the majestic tower of the cathedral. Now she was only relieved to pass through it onto the narrow country roads, winding through the rough countryside beyond and bringing her, at long last, to her destination. Trembling, she got out of the car, scrabbling in her purse for her money, aware of evening setting in and to the west, the sound of a distant rumbling so at odds to the bird-song from the trees nearby. The scene was familiar, so much like home and yet not home, only to Harry. The thought brought a flood of emotion almost overwhelming. Bracing herself, she picked up her case and walked, with a steady tread, towards the monastery building upon which the falling sun was even now winking. As she drew near, a group of ambulance girls emerged from the entrance to make their way down the front steps, watching her curiously as they passed. One face, oddly familiar, stopped and came back.

'Your Grace?' she asked quietly.

Bronwyn's heart leapt. 'Ursula? Ursula Compton!' The last person she'd expected and yet, she might have thought Ursula would be here. It made things better somehow. 'How's Harry? His Grace . . . please tell me!'

'I'll do better than that. I'll take you to him, if you'd like.' Gently, Ursula prised the valise from the young woman's nerveless fingers and led her back up the steps and inside.

Nurses in uniform. The smell of antiseptic and soap. A harassed-looking woman in a white coat emerged from a room full of beds, all occupied, hurrying away without a glance. The sound of footsteps slapping the tiled floor, her own, she realised with a start.

'You must be so desperate to see him, your Grace!' Ursula babbled and uncertain what else to say to this pale-faced young woman, the last person she'd expected to travel all this way, and unaccompanied to boot.

Doors, more nurses, an endless succession of faces and a longish corridor which, even in her distraught state, Bronwyn acknowledged still bore an odd, lingering sense of voices at prayer. It gave her comfort when she needed it most. Silently, she added another of her own. Light spilled through stained glass, warming their faces. A flight of stairs brought them to another door, their destination. Ursula knocked and opened it, poking her head round before, smiling encouragement, yet still unable to disguise her concern, she stood back to let the visitor through.

She'd love him however he was. No matter how bad. After her reckless headlong flight here, sure of this if nothing else, Bronwyn took a deep and steadying breath and, smiling bravely, walked past Ursula and into the room.

# 11

Bronwyn would never forget the tide of relief which overwhelmed her when she walked into that little room and discovered her husband's face on the pillow, turned towards her, fully conscious and filled with a wild and disbelieving joy. Scarce matter the ugly scar running from his forehead and cutting a deep furrow across his cheek. Harry was all she saw. The old Harry, the boy she'd fallen in love with and lost along the way. His war was over and when she heard of the horror of the British advance to Passchendaele, how could she be any other than heartily glad of it.

How willingly she stayed to nurse him, buoying his spirits during his long and painful incarceration in the hospital, and even longer convalescence in the run-down villa with the peeling paint she had found to rent, under the shadow of the Cathedral — a haven, a place to rediscover each other and, wonderfully, fall in love all over again.

Once the doctors considered him strong enough to travel, arrangements were made to transport him home, via a French fishing boat and a troop train from Portsmouth to Derby, where Lizzie was to meet them and take them the rest of the way home. Despite the arduousness of their journey, when he came within sight of his beloved Loxley, he determined to come upon it on his own two feet, leaning forwards to order Lizzie to drop them both by the bridge.

Disembarked and the car receding into the distance, Bronwyn slipped an arm around his waist, coaxing him to lean his weight on her. 'Sure you can manage? You know what the doctors said . . . ' Her flow of words was ceased, halted by a passionate kiss which once might have surprised her.

'If you only knew how I've longed for this moment, Bron,' he murmured, looking past her to Loxley, looming out of an autumnal mist. His breath caught in his throat, raw emotion filling his face, plain for Bronwyn to see. He was back where he longed to be and, in his darkest hours, thought he would never see again.

'Have you forgotten about Hettie?' she teased. Katherine had returned some weeks earlier, writing frequent and surprisingly lengthy letters informing them not only about the progress of the restoration, but also their little daughter's every achievement, no matter how small. Harry's grip tightened. Bronwyn knew he longed to see her and yet there was pain in his expression too that, through no fault of his own, he'd missed so much of her life.

There was no way she could have prepared him for the havoc the fire had wreaked but at their halting approach, even Bronwyn was heartened to see how much had been achieved in their absence. She knew because Katherine had told her, and all apparently under the guidance of a bluff Yorkshireman, a master builder by name of Huggins who, at her mother-in-law's instigation, had been only too grateful to emerge from retirement and undertake such prestigious work. Even a quick glance round told her the roof had been repaired, the windows replaced and the stone work re-pointed. Their dear home had become a hive of activity of overall-clad women, so bent about their business they gave the new-comers barely a glance.

The great front doors burst open and a beaming Soames, who'd been watching out for their arrival, came hurrying down the steps. A Soames they'd never have believed, dressed in workman's trousers and a paint-splattered shirt, scarcely recognisable from their reserved and immaculate butler of old.

'Oh master Harry, how wonderful!' Seizing

Harry's hand, he shook it heartily, only stopping to pull a handkerchief from his pocket and noisily blow his nose. 'Her Ladyship sends word you're to come round to the servants' quarters, your Grace,' he said, once he'd recovered enough. 'We're lodging there temporarily . . . '

'My mother too?' Harry asked, sounding faintly astonished. Thoughts of Katherine living in the servants' quarters took some believing but it seemed it was true. Soames chuckled quietly.

'Even her Ladyship, your Grace!' Eyes twinkling to be reporting such a happy turn of events, he hurried ahead, leaving Harry and Bronwyn to follow through the archway into the yard to Loxley's kitchens, heartbeat of the house, where yet another surprise awaited. Hettie knelt on a chair at the table, frowning in concentration and laboriously buttering slices of bread she passed to Katherine, who waited to receive them, sleeves rolled and ready to lay the ham.

'You're early' she commented, glancing up, only the faintest of tremor in her voice giving away her great emotion.

'It's been a long time, mother.'

This family were masters of understatement. Harry's attention was fixed firmly on the little girl whom Katherine was already

317

helping down from the chair. 'Look who's here, darling. Say hello to mummy and daddy nicely, just like grandmamma told you . . . '

Seeing the little girl hang back shyly, she gave her one gentle prod forwards. Bronwyn ached to run and hold her but this was Harry's moment for which he'd waited a lifetime. Looking unsure — scared, Bronwyn guessed, he'd frighten her — he moved slowly towards her. Hettie, in her turn, stared hard at this man her grandmamma had told her so much about. She pouted. Harry paused. Long unbearable moments passed when none present were sure what the little girl's reaction would be. And then, wonderfully, she held out her arms.

With a glad cry of joy, Harry bounded forwards to sweep her up into his arms, the tears he could no longer restrain spilling down his cheeks, confirmation, if ever Bronwyn had needed it, that the matter of Loxley's succession was the furthest thought from his mind. Pandemonium ensued, the following moments one long blur of laughter, hugs and kisses she'd a mind, at some point even Katherine had joined in. She must have imagined it because at last order was restored and Katherine, as in days of old, sat presiding, straight-faced, over the table.

Over the meal, faltering now and then

whilst she feasted her eyes on the son she'd thought, in times of despair, she'd never see again, the older woman filled them in on the happenings at the Hall. Reuben's continued absence, her disapproval of it and the items disappearing from his cottage suggesting his occasional return. She told them about the renovations underway, the army of women workers raised by the simple procedure of advertising in the papers so the floors were now repaired, the roof all but finished and the worst of the fire damage rectified, though there was still much to do. It was amazing what women could achieve when they put their minds to it. Katherine's head nodded in satisfaction.

'Oh mother, it is good to be back!' Harry murmured. He was drained; the day had been too much, even the longed-for inspection of the improvements would have to be put off until tomorrow. A bed had been made up in one of the servants' old rooms, Katherine rightly assuming, even if her son was to take no part in the ongoing renovations until he'd regained sufficient health, that he and Bronwyn would both wish to be here, on the premises.

The problem was holding him back, as Bronwyn discovered to her cost over the next few days, causing a return to the friction she'd thought long since behind them. There was still much to do and Harry wanted desperately to be a part of it. Katherine set him to work in the ground floor rooms where the fire-damaged objects were stored, many of them priceless and irreplaceable. It was a heartbreaking task. Tables by François Hervé, George III chairs, petit-point seats, tapestries, paintings, books, china, Indian silk curtains, priceless ornaments and bed-spreads, a portrait of Mary Queen of Scots miraculously unscathed though some, if not all, of the portraits of the old dukes were destroyed.

'I'm not sure how much more I can bear,' he said, kneeling to sort through a crate of Berlin china plates and dishes, collected by his grandfather. Some were cracked and scorched, some, unbelievably, pristine as ever. How arbitrary was fate! He stood up, cradling the remains of a once-pretty milk jug, the scar on his face a deep and vivid red, as it was in times of emotion, Bronwyn had learned, on the lookout for it. 'I thought I was fighting to keep Loxley safe, Bron,' he said sorrowfully, 'but the danger was here all along!'

It was hard to swallow, she had to agree. 'You're not strong enough for this yet,' she scolded. Deftly, she removed her coat and rolled up her sleeves. She'd just got back with

Hettie from a visit to her mother's and had left the little girl downstairs with cook whilst Katherine held discussions with Huggins about installing electricity. Loxley was to be dragged into the twentieth century, it appeared! All around came the sounds of hammering and sawing, bangs and knocks and voices, women's in the main and singing lustily, 'It's a long way to Tipperary', a favourite of the troops. They had to take heart. Bronwyn stood, hands on hips, surveying the wreckage of centuries of history, it coming to mind then, exactly why Loxley was so important. No arid monument this, as she'd so wrongly assumed, but a living, breathing connection with the past which should be cherished and upheld.

Her gaze fell to Nell's portrait, propped up against a heavy gilt-edged vase which had suffered only minimal damage. If only the same could be said of Nell, alas!

'Look, Harry,' she murmured sadly, crossing the room to pick it up and inspect its blackened edges. Beyond repair, she guessed, and it was a crying shame! How much had happened since her innocent longing to discover Nell's past.

'Your famous Duchess,' Harry returned, taking it gently from her. 'Bron, I am sorry.'

From the hall came voices, Katherine's and another's, vaguely familiar.

'What now, I wonder?' She sighed, reaching up to drop a light kiss on his cheek before going to investigate and finding Katherine talking to a man she recognised instantly.

'Inspector Digby!' She frowned.

His manners had undergone no improvement. He lifted his hat, nodding a curt and ungracious greeting. 'Your Grace . . . As I was telling her Ladyship here, you'll be relieved to know we've discovered our arsonist.'

'The gypsy woman after all!' Katherine broke in sharply, still looking shocked by the news she'd just received.

'The gypsy jailed for stealing Merry?' Harry demanded, hurrying in after Bronwyn in time to hear. Bronwyn had long since filled him in on all the happenings during his absence. 'But why's it taken you so long to find out, man?'

'We had to wait for a tip-off,' Inspector Digby bridled. 'Another gypsy our suspect got on the wrong side of, and some business over a horse. Gypsies are a vindictive lot and they never learn. She's confessed. Even she had no real desire to burn the place down around your ears, you'll be surprised to learn. It was only to teach her Grace a lesson for the time she'd spent in jail.'

'Live by the sword, die by the sword . . . ' Harry frowned. It was some time after the

Inspector had departed and they sat round the kitchen table, drinking the tea Katherine had made without a second thought.

'Perhaps Reuben will come home now!' Bronwyn replied, relieved he was vindicated by the news the Chief Inspector had brought. She drained her cup, waiting whilst Katherine refilled it. 'I never understood why he disappeared but I think I know now why he kept away,' she mused. 'There's no doubting the police wanted to talk to him about the fire. He was their chief suspect once upon a time . . .'

'I shouldn't have believed such wrong of him,' Katherine admitted graciously, relieved as any it wasn't Reuben who'd started the fire and yet, as always, hating to be proven wrong.

'You shouldn't,' Bronwyn retorted. She tended to say exactly what she thought to Katherine nowadays and found they got on all the better for it.

Whether Reuben returned home again had no bearing on the work still needing completion. To their varying degrees, they applied themselves diligently, Katherine in particular occupied with the man Huggins introduced to carry out the electrical work, a compact, quick-witted Welshman by name of Broderick Faraday, and whom she found to her liking. The price he'd quoted was steep.

Insurance covered the cost of the fire damage but this was something else. 'We'll find it somehow.' She frowned. But it would have been criminal, so much other work underway, not to seize the opportunity to drag Loxley into the twentieth century.

Accordingly, Faraday and his small, highly trained workforce — men too old for active service — set to, increasing the sense of thriving industry within the ancient walls. Imagining the place lit up so delightfully on a dark winter's afternoon, Bronwyn watched with increasing interest.

'Can you spare a moment, your Grace. I've something to show you!' It was a few days later and Broderick Faraday's voice was filled with excitement. The little Welshman stood in his overalls, thumbs hooked in his braces, rocking back on his heels. Mrs. Norris had taken Hettie into the village; Bronwyn had fetched steps from the pantry and was busy measuring the windows of the drawing room for new curtains. There was no chance of replacing the yellow Indian silk with which they'd previously been draped but she had a trip to Derby in mind. Smiling good-naturedly, she climbed down and followed him through into the hall.

'I've discovered something I imagine you'll find of great interest,' he said, intriguingly going over to the fireplace and the point where the mustard-coloured deal wainscot ended.

'It's a shame it has to go but it is badly damaged . . . '

Bronwyn joined him, looking over his shoulder, as his blunt, capable fingers busily prised one of the panels away from the wall, revealing, she saw now, a leaf-shaped scroll of wood, still attached to the brickwork beneath. Carefully he replaced the panel around it. 'It fits into the pattern of the wood perfectly, see? You'd have to know it was there but look you what else . . . ' Faraday's lilting voice filled with a rising excitement. So saying, he lifted the base of the leaf upwards and there followed a grating noise like stone rubbing against stone, causing Bronwyn to jump back in surprise. To her amazement, and proof that she wasn't hallucinating, she realised that incredibly, the fireplace was moving, slowly inch by inch, away from the wall, the space between gradually widening until it was of large enough width for a slim person to squeeze through.

'I don't believe it . . . '

'Please do!' Seeing her shocked expression, the electrician laughed. 'It's a secret passage-way! This old place must be full of them.'

She ran to fetch Harry, certain he must

know of it, further amazed to discover he didn't. He stood shaking his head, genuinely shocked.

'Father always said there was a secret passageway somewhere.'

'But where does it lead?' Bronwyn frowned. And, more to the point, who had built it, so cunningly it had existed undiscovered, at least by the Hall's present inhabitants?

'There's only one way to find out,' Harry urged. First trimming and lighting the wick, he fetched the lamp from the table nearby.

'I'm coming with you,' she warned, when she realised his intentions, still in shock at the unexpected turn of events their afternoon had taken. Leaving a clearly disappointed Faraday behind to keep guard, Harry squeezed through the gap, turning to help Bronwyn through after him.

She discovered they were in a narrow, low ceilinged and claustrophobic corridor, lending a distinct feeling of the walls closing in. But she hated enclosed spaces! There was a smell of damp and rottenness and, horrors, she felt something scurrying over her feet. Rats? Mice?

'Are we safe?' she muttered, brushing a cobweb from her face. Her voice echoed. Suddenly she wasn't so sure. How many centuries since other feet had trodden this path?

Mingling with the smell of decay was something else too, something completely out of harmony with this place. She was awash with the scent of lavender, she realised, even more shocked by this than the discovery of the passageway. Always lavender, only this time, bringing with it the greatest sense of Nell's presence she'd experienced yet so far. The thought calmed her racing thoughts, leaving her with the growing, if unsubstantiated, conviction they were on the point of a discovery of great importance to the history of the hall. Nell had something to do with this, if only she could make Harry believe and he could understand and feel it too!

As if sensing her agitation, his grip on her hand tightened.

'Sure you want to go on?' he asked, his voice rising, disembodied, from the darkness.

'Of course!' she returned sharply and stung he thought her such a coward.

Picking their way amongst the stone and rubble of the floor, they ventured on into the darkness, their progress illuminated by the lamp which flickered crazy shadows onto the walls, bringing with it a strange and disturbing memory, one spinning deep from the depths of her consciousness. How odd to think now of Reuben, his arms holding her close and keeping her safe . . .

'Harry, I've been this way before!' she told him, her voice throbbing with urgency. Harry's eyes glittered strangely in the darkness, like cat's eyes. 'The night of the fire!' she went on excitedly. 'Reuben carried me here. It was how we escaped the fire even if, at the time, I never realised it.' Drifting in and out of consciousness, it had seemed a dream.

'Reuben knows of this?' He sounded amused and incredulous; as if it was so patently ridiculous he wouldn't even give credence to the thought.

'Reuben must know!' she told him, crossly. Nothing else made sense and it explained so much. Reuben knew of this tunnel, perhaps discovering it by accident and keeping the knowledge to himself. How could he have known it would one day save their lives?

The scent of lavender was so strong, Bronwyn was sure Harry must remark upon it. He didn't and she realised, sadly, he had no idea. What he'd say if she brought the subject up, she hated to think. His wife must have lost the little sense she had, no doubt! They were travelling due south and she guessed they were already leaving the Hall some way behind. They pressed on, shivering under a growing dampness and a bitter, biting cold and instinctively, they moved closer to each other for warmth. The walls were running water, whilst at their feet lay pools of stagnant water, growing more difficult to negotiate as they progressed. Unnervingly, over their heads came the sound of rushing water.

'We're under the river!' Harry muttered in surprise. He stopped, holding up the lamp, and reassuring himself the tunnel was of sound construction. It was a relief to press on until, all at once, they came up against a solid wall of stone, blocking any chance of future progress.

'This must be the end of it!' he muttered, passing Bronwyn the lamp. He laid his hands flat, feeling around its massive solidness. Moments later, he emitted a happy cry of triumph. That which his fingers sought, an indentation at roughly shoulder height, yielded to his touch. At once, a small door, concealed within, swung wide. There was a rush of fresh, cold air and daylight flooded their faces.

'The Old Hall, I believe!' he muttered, laughing and bounding outside, through the crumbling remains of the fireplace and into what had once been old Loxley's dining hall. That was the length and breadth of it, only there was something else, too. Bronwyn's heart pattered fast within its ribcage. The scent of lavender was heady, pressing in on her senses and almost overpowering to her now. Something was here Nell was desperate she should see. Instinctively, she spun round to face the opposite wall. The lamp flickered wildly, the better to reveal what lay hidden there; a narrow recess cut into the wall, large enough to hold what she realised, with a frisson of shock, was a catacomb. But why and in such a dreadful place? The sight of it sent an icy finger of fear travelling the length of her spine. The light flared, nearly went out, distorting the shapes of the words carved in the stone at the foot of it.

She called Harry, waiting with barely suppressed impatience until he rejoined her and all the while, the one thought hammering in her brain and obliterating all else. The wrong brother! It was the wrong brother and none of it made sense!

'What is it?' Harry sounded exasperated.

Her voice trembling with fear, excitement, disbelief, she read aloud. 'Here lies Alexander Hyssop, born 1619, died 1645, father to George, and fifth Duke of Loxley. In death, as in life, beloved of Nell, Duchess of Loxley . . . '

★　★　★

The proprietor of the café nestling under the shadows of Saint-Omer's Cathedral placed a fresh pot of coffee on the table. Ursula flashed him a grateful smile. A man of diminutive stature with kindly eyes. It was odd how nowadays, she noticed such things. Sitting across the table, Matron poured. The last person Ursula had expected to discover on her few precious hours off. Dodi was catching up on some badly needed sleep so, for once, Ursula had ventured into town alone, wandering into the cathedral so deep in thought, the hand on her shoulder had made her jump. Marshalled in here, coffee ordered whether she wanted it or not, leaving her with the distinct impression there was more to this encounter than met the eye.

'I don't bite.' Matron smiled and took a sip of coffee, regarding Ursula, meanwhile, like a hawk sighting prey, about to swoop.

'But I never thought you did!' Ursula returned. She blushed, only too aware that was exactly what she'd thought.

Matron snorted, though whether with amusement or ire, it was hard to tell. 'I hear your young man's won himself a medal?' she remarked.

Ursula nodded. She was so proud of Freddie, she thought she would burst. Not that he'd given a hint of it. Raith Hamilton had mentioned it to her mother, who'd written a couple of days since. The news had spread — an act of bravery and courage in rescuing his commanding officer from enemy territory. Typical Freddie.

'He's still at Ypres?' Matron prompted.

'He's been for officer training.' Ursula frowned.

'You're worried, of course?'

That went without saying. But Freddie was only the same as the rest of the young men asked to do too much and suffering the consequences of their inexperience. 'I see the results of it every day of my life!' she retorted sharply, forgetting, for a moment, to whom she talked and that the woman across from her knew it more than most. Her voice had risen. A couple of VADs on the next table turned to stare curiously. She'd been rude, unforgivably so. 'I'm sorry,' she muttered.

An odd light appeared in Matron's eyes.

'You young girls have had to grow up fast!'

The sympathy was unexpected. 'Will this blasted war never end?' Ursula burst out, desperate to know if her employer, today so inexplicably approachable, might know the answer to something the girls had often discussed amongst themselves.

'Everything has an end,' she replied thoughtfully, Ursula would have said dreamily, if only she could have apportioned to the old dragon any such startling an emotion.

'Now the US has joined in, it may be over sooner than we think,' she continued. 'You'll marry your young man and have yourself a brood of children, no doubt.'

'But that's just it!' Ursula complained heatedly; unlikely confidant as her companion was, now she'd begun, she was desperate to unburden herself completely. 'Oh Matron, I'm not sure I want family life. After witnessing all this suffering, it's left me feeling I ought to be doing something else, something more worthwhile . . . ' She drank her coffee which was piping hot and surprisingly good, helping to steady her racing thoughts. 'If I have to wait until after the war, then so be it,' she went on, more quietly. 'But I must try to make something of my life. I owe it to all the men who've suffered . . . ' Her voice ground to a halt. Did she sound too earnest — or worse, pompous? As if anything she could do would ever alter what had happened! Her gaze lifted, seeking reassurance. 'Does that make sense?' she asked, feeling suddenly foolish and wondering what this forbidding woman must make of it.

'It makes perfect sense,' she responded and surprising her again. 'You love this young man?'

Ursula nodded, sure of this at least. 'I love him so much,' she agreed quietly. 'But after all this carnage . . . Is even love enough?'

Miraculously, Matron appeared to know exactly what she meant. 'You have a choice to make,' she responded dryly. Reaching into the pocket of her coat, she took out a paper and pencil, scribbling on it hastily before pushing it across the table. 'Once we're finished up here, a group of us mean to set up a teaching hospital for women. Join us if you like?' So casually, she'd dropped a bombshell into the muddy waters of Ursula's consciousness. 'Let me have your answer after the war,' she countered, seeing her about to issue a swift rebuttal.

She rose to her feet, her lips lifting into the ghost of a smile, a return to the Matron Ursula knew so well.

Ursula stared after her retreating back in dismay, reflecting now how the conversation had revealed a side to the woman she'd never imagined. How odd life was and how there was so much more to folk than you ever knew! The door swung too behind her.

Around rose the voices of people taking a break from the horrors of war, enjoying a return to normality, no matter how short. Had she the slightest chance of making any sort of a career in medicine? Was it what she wanted and what would Freddie think of such a crazy idea?

Thoughts of Freddie jolted her thoughts into their more usual processes. Dear God keep him safe. Rising to her feet, none the wiser for the morning's events, she buttoned up her coat and followed Matron out into the cold.

★ ★ ★

What a mockery time made of a man. Doing his best to temper his understandable enthusiasm, Lawrence Payne reached gently into the newly opened grave to remove the small, silver casket they'd discovered lying at the feet of the pitiable bleached bones inside. Even worse, the circle of bright red hair tied about the wrist. Nell's hair, Bronwyn knew. A prayer had been said, a blessing asked. Shadows flickered over the faces of the party grouped around.

'Perhaps now we'll learn Nell's secret,' Harry whispered.

'It's certainly an intriguing find,' Lawrence Payne agreed pleasantly before carefully passing the casket across to Bronwyn who clasped it tightly to her.

'I still don't understand,' Katherine retorted and her voice made sharp with the evidence of her own two eyes. Bronwyn shot her a wary glance. Even with Harry's backing, she'd felt herself disbelieved when first, and in great excitement, they'd told her about the existence of the secret passageway and what they'd so startlingly discovered there.

It was late in the afternoon of the following day, the wintry sunshine already fading as they trooped back through the passageway and re-emerged into the Hall. By common consent, they'd made their way down to the kitchens where a bright fire burned.

'I wonder why Nell had the tunnel built in the first place?' she asked.

'The old Hall was still put to use, as home for the servants and an overflow for the guests,' Lawrence Payne answered. 'If she buried Alexander secretly in the old place, perhaps an old priest's hole or some such like, when the new Hall was built, the tunnel would have been the only way she could safely visit his grave.'

'Do you think Rufus knew his brother was buried there?'

'I doubt it, don't you?' Katherine opined.

'Should one of us open it?' she asked, trembling at the idea. But opened it would have to be.

'I rather think that's up to you,' Katherine responded quietly, still yet unable to disguise her own burning curiosity. But it was only fair. Bronwyn was the instigator, the one who'd fought Nell's corner.

Harry's eyes blazed with excitement. 'Go on, darling, open it please . . . '

Bronwyn gazed down at the casket. A silver box, encrusted with rubies and emeralds and sparkling in the light of the fire. Worth a fortune, she hazarded, and yet more concerned with what lay inside. She laid it carefully down on the table, positioning her thumbs under the lid to lift it up, surprised when it gave so easily. Excitement was too quickly replaced by disappointment. Inside were only papers, letters she assumed, by the looks of it, tied together with a faded red ribbon. She couldn't feasibly have expected anything else. Suddenly, surprisingly, her eyes were brimming with tears.

'Why don't we leave you alone a while?' Katherine suggested, exhibiting a surprising sensitivity. 'Find us when you're done. Come Lawrence, I'll show you the renovations now you're here.'

Clearly disappointed but doing his best to hide it, the cleric followed her out. Harry tarried, dropping a light kiss on his wife's cheek.

'Would you like me to stay?'

Bronwyn shook her head. 'I'd rather be alone. Would you mind?'

'Of course not.'

Smiling, he left her to get to grips with Nell's secret and feeling as if she'd been on a long and particularly eventful journey, destination unknown and arrived at only by accident. The evening was drawing in, the fading light pouring through the window and onto her bowed head, bent over the letters she lifted so tenderly from their resting place. With infinite care, she untied the ribbon which held the little cache together. A flowing script full of curls and scrolls, Nell's handwriting, a shadow of the past, made a living, breathing woman once more. 'Oh Nell,' she whispered softly, hoping desperately, that what she was about to read, would show at least Nell Loxley had found some measure of happiness in her life . . .

May 1645
My dearest Alexander, you must know, in your heart, why I'm writing. Know too, to say it is breaking my heart. Oh Alexander, last night was a moment of madness we must never allow to happen again. If only I hadn't unburdened myself of the unhappiness of my married life! Rufus loves my fortune, I know that now. Before God, I married him and, cold and distant as he is, I must tread this path alone . . .

June 1645
Dearest Alexander, I cannot bear it.

Hearing of your involvement with the Royalist forces storming the garrison at Leicester, Rufus has ordered the servants to bar you from the house. Just as your cause, you've pushed him too far. Please give this up and come home, if not for love of me, then love of your brother and the child I am to bear. Oh if only things could be other than they are! How can I confess all to my husband and drive a permanent wedge between the two of you? I care only for our unborn child and the love we bear each other. Hard as it is, I must live without you. Rufus will never forgive you and yet, how am I to let him assume the child is his? I pray to God to tell me what to do . . .

June 13th 1645

Alexander, I am uncertain if this letter will reach you. I only pray my man will find you, wherever you are and whatever danger you must be in. News is bad, the King at Naseby and made to accept battle or retreat . . .

The rest of this missive was obscured by a dark brown stain, Alexander's life-blood, Bronwyn realised, shocked by it. She curled her hand around the last letter of all . . .

June 20<sup>th</sup> 1645

Knowing, as I do, your dear eyes will never read this, my tears fall so thick and fast, I can barely see to write. My closest advisers have carried you here, the last hiding place of all and, together with my letters to you, returned to me by your servant, I shall bury this here with you. But where should you have flown, mortally injured but here, to me and Loxley?

Knowing nothing of the rabble at your heels, battering our doors, demanding I give you up.

As if I ever would! When Rufus hears of it, as he surely must when he returns from his business in London, I shall tell him crazed rumours caused the crowd to behave as they did.

Given the way things are between you, better he thinks you died on the battlefield, your poor bones consigned to some unknown grave . . .

This last was splattered with tears, seemingly as fresh as when they'd fallen. Bronwyn sat, long moments, staring into the fire, the scent of lavender, which had been growing with her, seeming now, to her heightened senses, to dwindle and die away. An inner quiet after great suffering and bringing with it serenity to her own heart too. Flames burst up the chimney back and suddenly, as if over a bridge stretching the years, she saw the face of a young woman, framed with flame-red hair, reaching out a hand towards her — a woman with frailties but a woman with uncommon courage too.

When Bronwyn looked again, the vision, if vision it had been, had quietly faded and a great peace stole over the room.

★　★　★

'She was a Royalist after all,' Katherine repeated, not for the first time that day and still clearly shocked by the news. They sat round the table after dinner. Lawrence Payne had long since returned home.

'She cast doubt on the family line,' Harry pointed out, bravely Bronwyn thought, surprised at Katherine's sanguine response. Her mother-in-law's gaze had fallen on Hettie and, in its usual way, softened instantly. 'She was still a Loxley,' she answered and appearing to have forgotten already how once she'd been so against her.

No-one could argue, Harry least of all, who quickly determined Alexander's remains should be buried, with ceremony, next to

Rufus and Nell in the village church. 'He's ours, Bron,' he said, as if he needed to explain. Bronwyn understood perfectly. A closure and, after all these long years, surely Rufus Hyssop would have found it in his heart to forgive the brother, once, he must have loved? Blood was thicker than water and no matter which way any of them cared to view it, it was Alexander Hyssop's blood and not his brother Rufus's which ran so strongly in the Loxley line.

★   ★   ★

Given Harry's improvement in health and the way renovations were well underway, life appeared, at long last and despite the war, to be returning to some kind of normality.

Katherine avowed if only they could get a move on, they could shortly remove back upstairs.

A few days before Christmas, leaving Hettie to the willing care of her grandmother and with a shopping list as long as her arm, Bronwyn and Lizzie, using some of their precious stock of petrol rations, drove into Derby.

'Sure you'll be alright on your own, miss?' Lizzie asked, lifting up little Bill, who'd sat the journey on Bronwyn's knee. She was taking him to see an aunt in Gerard Street.

'I will when I'm the other side of this shopping list!' Bronwyn chuckled. Since she'd discovered Nell's secret, she'd felt oddly light-hearted, as if, in some way, it had lifted a burden from her own shoulders too.

The two women parted and Bronwyn carried on past the cathedral and further into Irongate, spending an absorbing time in the shops there, ordering bedding, and curtain and carpet samples to be sent on to the Hall for Katherine's approval. Emerging from the haberdashery in Sadler Gate and bent on the purchase of a few small cakes for tea, she crossed the narrow street towards the baker's shop and joined the queue, watching idly as the man at the head of it dipped into his pocket for change to pay for his purchase, a loaf of bread which he tucked under his arm before turning to leave. Stern-faced, unshaven, cap pulled down well over his forehead, she'd still have recognised him anywhere. Suddenly, her heart was beating rapidly.

It was Reuben.

How she'd longed for this moment, dreamed she would find him again, if only to thank him for saving her life. He failed to see her, limping past, head bent and continuing on outside so, in her shock, Bronwyn's cry of greeting froze on her lips. But what was he doing here in Derby, hiding away from them all? Gathering her wits, she hurried after him, alarmed to see him so swallowed up by the crowds that she was in imminent danger of losing him.

Following rapidly, she saw him turn off into the Corn Market where he hastened through into the lock-up yard, disappearing into the public house there. Without a second thought, she followed him inside; ignoring the curious looks of the bar's few occupants, market holders to a man, musing over their pints, and just in time to see him head up a narrow flight of stairs.

She followed quickly, emerging onto a small landing just as he was putting a key into the lock of one of the two facing doors. He swung round, such a look of joy illuminating his face at the sight of her, Bronwyn couldn't help but feel her heartbeat quicken in response.

His smile froze, too quickly fading and replaced by an angry frown.

'You've followed me!' he accused.

'Reuben, please . . . I only want to talk!'

'You have no business here! Please go! Leave me alone.'

She moved towards him, laying a hand on his arm. 'Reuben, what are you doing here? Please come home. It's perfectly safe; the police know it wasn't you who started the fire.'

His gaze widened in astonishment. 'I

started the fire? But who would ever think I'd do such a thing?'

'But I thought that that was why you kept away!' Bronwyn frowned. There was something not right here. Why had he run away? It didn't make sense!

He shook her away, quickly opening the door to retreat inside, leaving her no alternative but to follow him, into a rude, bare room holding only a table and a bed and a set of drawers for his clothes. She couldn't bear to think of him living like this! He limped to the window, lifting a corner of the dingy curtain and staring moodily down into the courtyard below.

'Why Reuben? Why have you run away?' she persisted.

'Oh, but don't you see!' he cried, flinging away, all at once, startling her all the more. 'Of course I had to go!' he muttered wildly and seemingly out of his wits. 'I had to! Harry . . . What would Harry say?'

Harry? But what had Harry to do with this? He was making no sense, his face contorted with a passion he could no longer contain.

A great pity swelled up in Bronwyn's heart. 'Reuben, what's wrong? You must tell me. You know I'd do anything to help.'

Why wouldn't she give it up? Why must she

torment him so! Reuben threw himself down at the table to bury his head in his hands. At long and bitter last he looked up, despair etched on every line of his face, the words tearing from him to divulge the one secret he'd thought to keep from her forever. There was no doubting that he spoke the truth. A truth that rocked her world and still made no sense.

'Harry's my brother,' he said.

# 12

It was crazy to imagine Reuben was Harry's brother! The fire must have unhinged his mind. Bronwyn sank into the chair opposite, gazing at Reuben in dismay.

'I didn't mean to shock you,' he muttered.

'Please tell me,' she urged.

He lifted his head from his hands, staring at her helplessly.

'I wouldn't know where to start.'

'Somewhere, Reuben!'

Reuben rubbed the back of a hand across a mouth gone suddenly dry. She should have been told before now, he realised, appalled that it looked to be down to him.

'My mother was a maid employed in a big house in Oxfordshire where the family were well-to-do,' he began reluctantly. 'She met my father, George, when he stayed there on a shoot. He wasn't a Duke then, merely a Duke's son. Fresh from university, hating the thought he'd be tied to Loxley for the rest of his life. She was so pretty, Bron!'

'He fell in love with her?'

'She fell in love with him,' he answered quietly, leaving that unsaid she was sensitive enough to work out for herself.

'Oh Reuben . . .'

'When the week ended, he swore he'd be back to put things right.'

'Go on,' she coaxed, with an alarming conviction this had about it a ring of truth. He was eager now to tell her the rest, leaning forwards in his chair, his hands clasped together so tightly, his knuckles were white.

'When he returned home, it was only to find his parents pressing him into marriage with Katherine. They'd known her from a girl and thought she had the strength of character to make him settle down.'

'Your poor mother, Reuben!' she said.

He nodded unhappily. 'My father wasn't a bad man, Bronwyn, merely young and selfish. I doubt he even knew he'd left her pregnant. When it was discovered, her employers threw her out, though I guess she tried to hide it as long as she could. Out of her wits, no-one to turn to, she returned home to her parents in Oxford. Some would say it solved a problem she died in childbirth — never me, Bron, never me!'

His raw emotion hurt her. A sad tale and yet, was it so very unusual? 'I know you'd never think badly of her, Reuben,' she answered, longing to comfort him but her natural diffidence holding her back. There was more to this than she understood, or that he was letting on, and she couldn't yet make her mind up which.

'Her parents, my grandparents, fearing they were too old to rear me, took me to Loxley,' he continued doggedly. 'As chance would have it, they found Katherine at home alone and told her the whole sorry business.'

'But what must she have thought?' Bronwyn murmured, imagining the scene too well. Katherine betrayed; Reuben, a tiny baby knowing nothing of all he'd lost. Neither to blame and yet both hurt more than they'd had any right to be.

'I believe she never faltered,' he answered. 'When my father returned, she made him face his responsibilities . . . isn't that what they say? The outcome was, I was farmed out to a village couple. When I was old enough, I was apprenticed to the gamekeeper who was looking for a lad to train up.'

'And the Duke . . . your father?'

For the first time, the hint of a smile played on Reuben's lips. Whatever wrong his father had done, it appeared he'd long since been forgiven. 'The Duke made it his business to make a fuss of me,' he answered proudly. 'Much to Katherine's disapproval. A chip off the old block, he used to say! He was my father, Bronwyn and . . . I loved him just as I loved Harry. George told Harry about me but finding out we were brothers only seemed to cement our friendship.'

So Harry knew and had never said. Bronwyn pushed that little fact to one side to be considered later. 'It was none of your fault,' she broke in, quickly.

'It's not been easy, not just for me but for Katherine too. George was his own man and she didn't have the easiest of marriages,' he answered.

His sensitivity towards Katherine surprised her. He must be bitter as, but for a trick of fate, he should have inherited the estate. His tale had shocked her and yet, it explained so much. No wonder he'd grown reclusive, so much a man out of place. 'Reuben, please come home!' she burst out.

'I can't! You don't understand!'

She didn't, nor why he'd fled Loxley after the fire. Something had scared him off and it wasn't to do with his birth. Again the thought crossed her mind; there was so much more to this — and to Reuben — than appeared on the surface. 'But Harry's home. He'll be delighted to see you back!' she said, in desperation and not sure herself now why she so badly wanted him home, only that she did.

'You think I didn't make it my business to find out Harry was home safe?' he demanded, his gaze inexplicably sliding from hers — as if he couldn't bear to look at her! But she saw he was weakening and, taking heart from it, she tried one last time.

'Reuben, you know how we're fixed. We need every hand we can muster. Please come home. It's such a shame to think that after this long time, you'd ever let us down . . . ' It was emotional blackmail and unfair of her but to Bronwyn's great joy, she saw he'd do what she wanted. He had to go back and if for no other reason than to see if he could . . .

★　★　★

Finding Reuben had made her late and Lizzie would be waiting. Her mind a mass of contradicting thoughts, Bronwyn hurried through the darkening streets, past the bulk of the cathedral to the sanctuary of the car. Inside, she took little Bill on her knee, letting Lizzie's prattle wash harmlessly over her head, whilst she tried to make sense of all Reuben had told her. Back home, leaving Lizzie to drive on up to the stables, she returned inside, making straight for the downstairs room where Harry was spending the bulk of his days cataloguing the fire damage, a thankless, heartbreaking task he'd taken upon himself. He took too much upon himself and always had and now she was beginning to understand the reason why. Katherine was with him but Katherine would have to be faced sometime and better now, whilst they were together. Awkwardly at first, not knowing how to start other than to plunge straight in, she recounted how she'd found Reuben and what he'd told her. Katherine's intake of breath was audible.

'We'll talk about this later, Bron,' Harry said sharply, jumping quickly to his feet and darting a nervous glance towards his mother. Bronwyn saw this was not a subject for discussion between them and she was sorry for it. What a family they were for secrets when surely, problems were better aired?

They'd talk about it now, she determined. 'Katherine, I am sorry,' she said and for once ignoring her husband. 'I know this is none of my business. Reuben didn't mean to tell me. He sort of blurted it out.' She spoke earnestly, aware Katherine had always made the best of things and would hate to be confronted with this now.

Katherine stood long moments, the colour visibly draining from her face. 'I doubt you do understand, my dear,' she said at last and only the faint tremor in her voice giving away her emotional state. 'George wasn't a bad man, only a weak one. I loved him. What else could I do?'

She couldn't conceivably have done anything

else and Bronwyn understood exactly. This kind of thing happened in high born families all the time and, more normally, was swept under the carpet. 'You did the best you could!' she burst out and hastily crossing the room, impulsively threw her arms around her mother-in-law's stiff frame, a liberty she could never have imagined taking once upon a time. Wonderfully, she felt some of Katherine's tension relax.

'I . . . I sort of understand why you didn't tell me, Harry,' she told him later that evening whilst they were dressing for dinner. He was protecting his mother and she couldn't find it in her heart to blame him.

He stood behind her, fastening the buttons of her dress before turning her round to face him. 'The people concerned never wanted it aired and it seemed best to leave it that way,' he answered simply.

'But it concerned you too,' she urged, wondering what he'd thought during his growing up years. Reuben was his brother and yet not so in the eyes of society who turned a blind eye to such things.

'Father always thought much of Reuben.'

'There were . . . other affairs?' she probed.

He grimaced. 'He always had an eye for a pretty face.'

'Poor Katherine!' she burst out angrily and

wishing the wretched man was here so she could give him a piece of her mind.

'He hurt her so much . . . '

'He hurt Reuben and his mother, too,' she answered, heatedly. The consequences of his actions had been catastrophic.

'Life's not fair, Bron' he agreed. 'The war's taught me that much, if nothing else.' She leaned in against him, her cheek resting against the rough material of his jacket. This wasn't easy and there were no easy solutions. 'I still don't know why he told me, Harry. He must have been in shock still from the fire. It was almost as if . . . He wanted to stop me from thinking something else! But what exactly? You must talk to him, tell him Loxley is where he belongs and he must never disappear like that again . . . '

It was a week into the New Year and an evening following a quiet family meal before Bronwyn's wish for Reuben's return was granted. Harry was playing the piano, Schubert and Bach, his favourites. Bronwyn stood listening by the window, staring moodily into the dark outside and fretting over what the year would bring when it seemed the wretched war would go on forever . . .

'There's a light in Reuben's cottage!' she called excitedly.

Harry ceased playing and hurried to join her.

'He's back!' His voice was laced with relief.

It was a cloudless night, the moon, high and bright and he should have thought about the blackout, except they both knew Reuben was never troubled by niceties. They fetched their coats and made their way down the meadow towards the wood, reaching his cottage as his figure appeared at the window to draw the curtains.

He opened the door, emitting a shaft of yellow light to illuminate the darkness around. His troubled gaze rested on Harry's scar before he stood back to allow them entrance. He'd made himself at home already. Soup simmered on the stove. The table was set for one. They stood taking the warmth from the fire which flickered shadows onto the walls. An odd silence developed which none of them knew how to break. Brothers who scarcely acknowledged the fact and yet, now it was out in the open, Bronwyn determined it should make a difference to how they behaved in each other's company. Side by side, one so fair, the other so dark, there was little resemblance between the two men. A line of the cheek, a stubborn set to the mouth she'd been aware of in Reuben and only now saw in Harry. She couldn't think why she'd never noticed it before.

'I'm glad you're back,' Harry said, the first

to break the silence and with typical understatement.

'Aye, mebbe, but I still shouldn't be here,' he answered.

Harry frowned. 'Of course you should be here, man! Where else should you be? You saved Bron's life and I'll never forget it.'

He held out his hand and the two men shook hands warmly. It was a start and the most she was likely to get out of them, Bronwyn mused, grateful for this at least. 'But you knew of the secret passageway leading to Alexander Hyssop's grave?' she prompted, steering the conversation onto safer ground.

'I found it by accident when I was a lad,' he agreed. 'It tickled me to know of its existence and no-one else, though even I failed to guess I'd ever have such need of it.' His quiet smile released some of the lingering tension. That said, he crouched down by the fire, stirring it with the poker and staring meditatively into the flames which leapt up, casting his face in a ruddy glow. Thoughts of the fire and the likelihood they'd have been trapped if not for the secret passageway, sent shivers racing the length of Bronwyn's spine. Quickly, she filled him in on Nell's letters and all they'd revealed of Nell and Rufus, and Alexander, who Nell had really loved.

'She married the wrong brother,' he

muttered, looking pained.

Something was troubling him still. 'Reuben, you are pleased to be back?' she asked, unable to bear the thought he wasn't.

'Of course!' he'd answered quickly, too quickly for Bronwyn's liking, ever sensitive to his odd moods.

'He's unhappy about something,' she said later. They were making their way back to the Hall. Loxley loomed, a vast shape in the distance. Harry took her hand and she thrilled at the feel of his skin, warm against hers in the dark.

'You know Reuben,' he acknowledged ruefully.

But did anyone, really? 'Katherine will have to talk to him.' She frowned.

'To say what? Welcome home?' He sounded mildly amused.

Given the circumstances, that was too much but something, surely, acknowledging what he'd been through? Katherine made little comment on Reuben's return other than to quiz Bronwyn if he'd settled back into the cottage and resumed his duties. What was in Katherine's mind too sensitive to ask, Bronwyn could only guess. A few days later, she was fortunate enough to be party to their first encounter.

Slowly, the Hall was returning to normal and several of the downstairs rooms were already in use. Bronwyn had collected Hettie from the nursery and was crossing the hall just as Katherine emerged from the morning room, heading for the kitchen and breakfast, as Reuben came limping up the stairs with a basket of logs. Unexpectedly, they came face to face. Both gave an involuntary start of surprise.

'There you are,' Katherine murmured, the first to recover.

'So I am,' he muttered but glaring so fiercely, Katherine quailed.

Katherine Loxley was surprised to discover that she was pleased to see him and in such apparent rude health. George's son and she'd missed him about the place. How ambiguous were her feelings towards him and yet . . . Would she have minded if he really had been her son, the second son she'd always longed for?

The thought came out of the blue, shocking her but oddly pleasing her too, and in an entirely unexpected way. Quickly she recovered herself. 'You're well, I hope?'

He nodded briefly. 'And yourself?'

'Well, thank you, Reuben. We shall get through, never fear.'

'Aye, we must,' he muttered, going on his way and leaving her free to descend the stairs.

Smiling quietly to herself, Bronwyn exchanged greetings with him before following Katherine downstairs.

## May 1918

Cradling the flowers, marigolds and meadow vetchling she'd recently gathered from under the hedgerows outside the monastery walls, Ursula hovered by Freddie's bedside. He'd just been admitted and lay propped up against the pillows; his bad leg swathed in bandages and stretched out on top of the sheets.

To Ursula's relief, Matron said it was nothing too serious.

She put down the flowers and perched herself on the edge of the bed.

'First time I've known anyone be pleased to see a man in hospital!' he complained peevishly, his tone belying the way his face had lit up at her appearance. He'd been watching for her, eyes glued to the swing doors and aware at that moment, there wasn't a man in the ward who wouldn't have exchanged places with him.

The thought warmed him inside.

Even though it had been months since they'd seen each other, they'd corresponded regularly, mostly with regard to Ursula's plans after the war and Freddie's determination the only plan he'd put up with was that she should return home with him and settle down to life on the farm.

'Has Matron told you my war's over?' he demanded.

'Thank God for it and don't dare tell me otherwise, Freddie Hamilton!' she returned heatedly. 'You can't be sorry to be going home?'

His brows furrowed. 'There's part of me wants to be home, of course there is, but . . . Hang it Ursula, it makes me feel like a deserter!' he wailed.

'And how have you arrived at that idea? What happened anyway?'

If only it had been something other than the usual. 'The Bosch sent over a barrage,' he muttered. 'Shrapnel. You know how it is.'

She did know. The wrong place at the wrong time and he'd been left facing a trip to the nearest casualty clearing station with a wound liable to take months to heal. He turned away, struggling with an emotion years of fighting had left him too weak to conceal.

'Freddie, don't,' Ursula moaned. Aware that Matron was hovering nearby, casting frowsty glances their way, she moved her hand stealthily to his. He gripped it tightly, lifting it to his lips.

'I can't bear you'll leave me,' he muttered, pathetic on purpose, she suspected, so she'd do as he wanted. So hurt, so frustrated, so disbelieving she was knowingly being so hard. When he looked at her like that, it was hard to deny him anything.

'I'll never want anyone else,' she coaxed.

'Stay with me then,' he answered angrily.

She shook her head, part longing to do what he wanted and yet her actions ruled by her uncertainty. She did want to marry him. She didn't want to be a farmer's wife. She no idea what she wanted to do with the rest of her life. 'Freddie we've been over this countless times already,' she answered steadily. 'Wait until after the war. I'll give you my decision then, I promise . . . '

It was the most he was going to get out of her. Regardless of the wigging she'd get from Matron, she took his dear face, so unshaven and dirty and worn down, and, holding it tenderly between her two hands, sealed her words with a kiss.

## November 11 1918

The bells of Loxley's ancient church peeled out their message of peace, mingling with the cheers of the villagers who in their joy had rushed out of their cottages. Katherine turned from the window of the morning room, where she'd lingered with Harry over coffee, her face alive with hope.

'It's true. We really are at peace,' she murmured, hardly daring to utter the words, so much had she dreaded, even at this late hour, something would happen and the terrible fighting would go on forever. But following Wilhelm's abdication not two days before, Ludendorff had resigned and the German navy had mutinied. According to the papers, earlier this morning the leaders of both sides had been brought together to sign the armistice. 'I pray it's so,' Harry rejoined, dropping his napkin onto the table and joining her. The garden looked exactly the same as it had yesterday and the day before. Denuded of flowers, the leaves falling from the stark trees beyond, wind-blown into ragged heaps on the lawns for want of a gardener to rake them. A muscle twitched in his cheek. Katherine laid a gentle hand on his arm.

'I'm sorry. It must bring back so much.'

It did, and none of it good, even if he'd no intention of telling her so. He made an effort and forced a smile, stirred by an unexpected feeling. It was over. His eyes glinted with a dawning hope.

'We must do something, mother. Lay on food, drinks . . . '

Humour restored at this unexpected suggestion, Katherine smiled happily. 'Darling, what a perfectly wonderful idea . . . '

★   ★   ★

Lizzie was already unfastening Merry from his traces as Bronwyn climbed down from the gig. They were just back from taking a barrel of windfalls to Raith Hamilton's and, finding his son Freddie unexpectedly home from hospital, had spent longer there than intended. Bronwyn knew exactly how much she owed Freddie Hamilton and so did Harry. Both women thrilled to hear the bells ringing from their little village church, matched the length and breadth of the country.

'Thank God it really is over!' Bronwyn's cry was involuntary.

'So it is!' Lizzie buried her face in Merry's warm flank, her shoulders heaving with the emotion which would well up, no matter how she tried to stifle it, leaving her, momentarily, too weak to move. Bronwyn laid a gentle hand on her arm, struggling to know what to say when there was nothing she could do to bring Bill back, all Lizzie had ever wanted.

'You must miss him so,' she murmured helplessly.

Lizzie straightened up, of a mind there was no good giving in and, hard as it was, the day had still to be got through. 'At least my father will be home soon, miss,' she uttered fiercely and thinking it a miracle, against all odds, that doughty old Alf Walker had survived when many a younger man had been taken.

Her father or Bill, but how cruel she couldn't have both! Sorry she could do so little and unsure herself how to cope with whatever the day would bring, Bronwyn returned to the hall where she was amazed to find all in uproar, Soames polishing glasses, cook, red-faced and standing hands on ample hips, barking out orders to which the rest of the servants jumped. Harry had been despatched to the cellars for wine and Katherine, poised precariously up a ladder, was lifting down glasses from a Welsh dresser she'd picked up at auction several weeks since. Despite its half-finished state, it appeared the house was to be thrown open. Villagers, employees, friends and neighbours, all welcome. Invitations were even now winging their way.

'But we'll never be ready in time!' Bronwyn muttered, frowning at the strange feeling bubbling up inside; she was shocked to recognise for the happiness it certainly was.

'Most certainly we will,' Katherine decreed, descending to dump a pile of crockery on the table. Her mind was set, and what Katherine commanded, too quickly became hard fact. In as short a time as would have been believed possible, the table in the dining hall was laid and, if not groaning with food, bearing the most cook and a hastily-summoned Mary Compton could reasonably be expected to supply. Guests were already arriving, mostly villagers, some who'd yet to set foot in the hall since the fire and who stood round looking awkward, if happily dazed by the day's events.

'There you are.' Harry smiled. With some difficulty, he prised Bronwyn away from old Ned who was holding court by the fire, the rosiness of his cheeks denoting he'd been liberally helped to wine by Soames. By the looks of him, Soames hadn't been above helping himself either. Bronwyn allowed herself to be led through the gathering and into Harry's study where, from behind his desk where he'd secreted it, he handed her a large package wrapped in brown paper.

'Harry, it's not my birthday,' she laughed, taking it.

'Aren't I allowed to give my wife a present?' he teased. He leaned back against the desk, watching affectionately as she tore the paper away.

A warm swell of emotion flooded through her. Revealed to her delighted gaze was Nell's portrait and looking as good as new. He'd effected a miracle. She looked up questioningly, her eyes shining. 'But how?' she asked, confused.

'I'm afraid it's not the original,' he confessed. 'But there was enough left of the old portrait for the artist I engaged to come up with a replica. How appropriate it should arrive today, of all days! I do know what Nell means to you, darling . . . ' Even if he'd never quite understood it. Marriage, Harry Loxley was learning, brought with it a fresh perspective on most things in life.

Bronwyn was inordinately touched. 'It's the nicest thing anyone's ever done for me, Harry!' she enthused, trying, unsuccessfully to hide her emotion. The day, the end of the war . . . their survival . . . It was too much and she was horribly afraid she was going to break down and cry. 'I did it because I love you,' Harry said, if a little diffidently, happily speaking only the truth. First laying the portrait carefully on the desk, he took her into his arms.

Struggling with a stack of crockery, Lizzie fought her way through the press of bodies milling round the sitting room. Someone swung round, glass in hand and nearly sent her flying.

'Can I help?' Sam Tennant appeared from nowhere.

'I can manage, thank you,' she retorted, more sharply than she'd intended. But she had meant it as more than a rebuffal over his offer. Sam had been finding altogether too many excuses to come up to the stables of late, more often than not arriving with cakes and pastries from Mary, whom Lizzie strongly suspected of baking them for the purpose. She had to put a stop to it and now was as good a time as any.

'I only wanted to help,' he muttered, turning away but not before she saw the enthusiasm so briefly illuminating his face, cruelly extinguished.

Something about the defeated slump of his shoulders caught at Lizzie's heartstrings.

If this were a story in a book, she would happily fall in love with Sam Tennant, she mused. He'd be the doting dad little Bill so desperately needed and the company she longed for, if only she were honest enough with herself to admit it. She was lonely and she missed Bill and if only life didn't go on so!

This wasn't fiction but real life and surely that must make a difference . . . ?

'You can help with the washing up, if you like?' she called; shocked the moment the words left her mouth. Instantly, he spun round, a huge smile on his face, and a flash of the old Sam if only she'd known it. 'Only the washing up, mind,' she added belatedly, wondering then if that was really all she'd meant.

'What else could there be?' he replied, contritely, his smile deepening as he followed her out.

★　★　★

The afternoon was dwindling, the sun tumbling into a rapidly darkening sky. How wonderful it was to switch on the electricity in all the rooms so the Hall was aglow, the warm yellow light spilling out onto the lawns beyond. Bronwyn went through into the morning room, delighted as a child to see the gloom so gratifyingly illuminated.

The day's paper and an empty pipe rested on the arm of a chair, pulled up to the fire. Harry had been in here recently, she suspected, in search of some peace and quiet. She could understand why he'd felt in need of it. From the dining room came the sound of people taking delight in what they'd missed for so long, the chance to enjoy themselves. No-one would miss her. Pulling the door too, she crossed the room and sat down, wriggling round to make herself comfortable before closing her eyes. What a day it had been. How wonderful to think of a peaceful future untrammelled by the horrors of war . . .

She slept so deeply, she was blissfully unaware of Reuben, dressed in outdoor jacket and cap, a rough scarf wrapped around his neck, opening the door and stealing quietly into the room. He came to a halt in front of her, his hand reaching out towards her but just as quickly falling back to his side. He shouldn't wake her when there was no need.

368

A kind of death to go but go he must and better quietly fade away. She'd only try to stop him if she knew.

'My love,' he muttered, under his breath and wishing if only somehow, things could have been different. How happy he would have been! A wrongheaded decision to return and he'd known it from the moment she asked him. But then, he'd never been able to deny her. Somewhere, far away from here, a life, a happy life he hoped, lay waiting, but just this once he would allow . . . He stooped to gently kissed her cheek, his lips lingering as, wonderfully, she sighed and stirred as if, if only in her sleep, she was aware of the great burden of love he bore her.

Wishing with all his heart her every dream a good dream, he forced himself from the room. From Bronwyn and the house and Loxley and all it had ever been to him, leaving it far behind and glad in the heart of him there was no-one there to see him leave.

## A week later

The lights on Paddington Station pushed out against the darkness, illuminating the groups of shuffling Tommies, still unable to believe their luck they were back on home soil. The

369

overnight train to Derby waited nearby. Home was a breath away.

'We'll keep in touch?' Dodi muttered, as if there were any doubt of it.

'You bet,' Ursula replied. The two women embraced. They'd been through so much and it was hard to think from here they were going their separate ways. 'I'll write,' she promised, embarrassed to find her eyes stinging with tears.

'Don't forget,' Dodi returned, blinking rapidly. What a pair. Hoisting up her haversack, she walked away without a backward glance, into the gloom and the train for Norfolk where her father had arranged to meet her at the station.

Ursula slung her bag across her shoulder and boarded the train waiting on the platform behind, pushing through a carriageway heaving with bodies and nearly giving up before one of the men, a hardened Tommy, took pity and budged up, leaving her a seat by the window. Dirty, unshaven men, in ill-fitting uniforms, their pain at all they'd been through battling with their joy to be home, a thing they'd never thought would be. Pretty much how Ursula felt too.

The train pulled out. Smoke wisped past the windows. They were off, heading into the night. At Oxford Station, the boy in the seat across battled his way through onto the platform to fetch them tea which was hot and sweet and did her good. She smiled her thanks, feeling the liquid course through her veins, giving her strength, yet still relieved when they set off again, into the heart of the Midlands, a brooding countryside of muffled shapes and, here and there, a pinprick of light telling of women preparing for factory shifts, milking cows and driving automobiles and lorries, all the tasks they'd found they could do because it had been necessary that they should.

Home soil, if only a short visit for Ned and her parents' sake.

Freddie's face inserted itself neatly between herself and this sanitised view of the decision which still tormented her. But Freddie would understand! Freddie had been through the war too. He knew what war did. Why must he spoil the moment, transforming himself into the face of the boy opposite so Ursula wondered how she'd ever find strength to leave him?

Dawn arrived on Derby Station, bringing with it the connection which rattled its slow way onto Loxley. It was interminable but at last, unbelievably, she was jumping down onto the platform where a milky light revealed the craggy hills and valleys she'd missed more than she'd ever have believed possible. She shivered. There'd been a frost which clung to the roofs and low stone walls of the neat little gardens and stiffening the few bare plants within. A milk cart rattled down the road and it occurred to Ursula then, despite all they'd been through, it had done the same thing year upon year and nothing had changed. Curiously gladdened by it, she hoisted her bag onto her shoulder and set off through the village where already curtains were drawn and sleepy faces pressed to the windows looking out. A dog barked. She hurried on regardless, longing for Loxley and Freddie in equal parts. He would understand. He must understand!

Past the church, out of the village, she crossed the road and ran up the hill beyond it to the summit, arriving there out of breath so she crashed to a halt, full of a first fear of the fire and the damage it had caused. There was the ruin of the old Hall, next to the river and the bridge and there, rearing its yellow stone into the sky, was Loxley, giving her the strangest of feelings, that she was a stranger here and didn't belong! Her gaze shifted towards her home, just in time to see Ned, in his braces and shirt collar, shuffling out of the back door. Beyond the wood came the sound of a cow bellowing and then, causing her heart to leap, she heard a man's shout. It was Freddie, up early and moving the herd from their byre to the meadows, resuming the reins of his life already, the life he'd share with her if she would . . .

Instinctively, she turned away from home and, regaining the path, walked quickly up past the wood to jump the low stone wall into the fields beyond. Raith Hamilton's land and oddly, in some dim recesses of her memory, she was thinking of the young girl who'd so often run this way. Breathing heavily, she crashed to a halt to see, in the hollow below, a familiar figure, standing with his arms folded across the top of the gate through which he'd just herded the cows, the dejected slope of his shoulders telling her so much. Freddie and her heart melted at the sight of him.

Blast him! If you tore her in half wouldn't she bleed, Freddie Hamilton? She loved him and . . . and . . . he loved her too. What a simple fact and what a fool she was! Who was she to throw love away so blindly? Freddie loved her and needed her and if only she hadn't been too pig-headed and stubborn to see it . . .

Her heart swelled with a great flood of emotion and her every intention folded and dissolved. What a rum farmer's wife she'd make. How they'd fall out and how she'd try his patience demanding things be other than they were. She called his name, softly at first, then louder, and louder still, so he swung round in startled surprise to read the answer he'd so longed for, miraculously written on her face for all the world to see.

It was done, ended. She'd come home to Freddie. His lips formed her name though all she heard was the wind against her face as with an echoing cry of joy she ran pell-mell down the field and into his arms.

★ ★ ★

Seeing the two young people below, Bronwyn, Duchess of Loxley smiled quietly to herself. The men, those that were left, were returning home in drifts and drabs. But it was a shock Reuben had gone, his cottage cleared out, this time she sensed for good. She couldn't believe how much she missed seeing him limp about the place and she prayed one day he'd return to the home where he truly belonged.

She called to the two dogs, noses buried deep in the hedgerows. Loxley's day was already underway. Hettie would be causing uproar, Katherine calling the house to prayer and indignant the breakfast was getting cold, Harry trying unsuccessfully to calm things down. Some things were cast in stone and even Bronwyn, much as she saw needed doing about the place, would fight to the last it should still be so.

The sun was up, warming her through and dancing on the yellow stone of Loxley. A world to itself and for itself and all the people who lived out their existence there. And through it, a group of embattled women had come to understand, they'd strength and skills more than they'd ever have believed.

She'd be late and Harry would be fretting. Feeling the need of his two safe arms around her, she headed swiftly for home.

## May 1932

Leaving her companion trailing in her wake, a young girl ran up a grassy slope dotted with daisies and buttercups, a flash of yellow dress which clashed violently with her bright red hair, the bane of her life. At the top of the summit, she crashed to a halt, waiting impatiently as the boy, a handsome lad, laboured towards her.

'Hurry up, slowcoach!'

'We'll catch it,' he grumbled, out of breath, joining her just as the sun burst over the horizon, catching the windows of the great hall below with a crimson fire.

Hettie Loxley gasped out loud. 'Oh my, Bill! Look! But it's beautiful! Wasn't that worth getting out of bed for?' she cried, ecstatically.

It came to her then that all this would be hers, one day. Henrietta Arabella, Duchess of Loxley! She stood, hands on hips, her wild, sea green eyes flashing approval and appearing, at that moment, if only she'd known it, the spit of the portrait of Nell Loxley her mother so loved.

Bill was sheepishly aware he'd do anything Hettie ever asked of him. Why else creep out of a nice warm bed when his mother, his stepfather Sam, and his little brothers and sisters were still fast asleep? The view moved him not one jot. His hungry gaze fastened on Hettie's face and stuck there so, suddenly, despite his tender years, he understood the truth of it. She was beautiful and he loved her. And . . . and he always would no matter how the world might try to pull them apart.

Without conscious thought, he leaned forwards and planted a kiss on her lips. That done and appalled by his temerity, he sprang back, red-faced. 'Gosh Hettie,' he groaned. 'I . . . I don't know what came over me! What would anyone say if they'd seen?' What a milksop! Kissing her and then making out it had been a mistake! Hettie's eyes grew suddenly serious. Hidden depths swirled, rose to the surface. She liked him . . . she more than liked him, missing him whenever, as so often happened, the difference in their respective circumstances forced them apart.

She wasn't sure if she'd got to grips with growing up just yet. 'Think I care?' she goaded and aware she'd rather have died than tell him how she really felt.

Bill's steady brown eyes twinkled with good humour. Truly, he believed Hettie Loxley was scared of nothing and no-one. He'd never known anyone like her in all his young life. Already there was a stirring in the Hall below, figures scurrying to and fro, servants mostly, hurrying about their daily business. Her parents would soon be up and about, as would be her terrible grandmother whom she dearly loved and who would box her ears for certain if she knew they were out so early. Worse, Bill had kissed her so anyone might see!

She'd enjoyed it, she thought, defiantly. What's more, she didn't mind if he kissed her again — only sometime — when she was grown-up enough to enjoy such things.

'Catch me if you can!' she cried before spinning on her heels and running back down towards the Hall.

We do hope that you have enjoyed reading this large print book.

Did you know that all of our titles are available for purchase?

We publish a wide range of high quality large print books including:
**Romances, Mysteries, Classics**
**General Fiction**
**Non Fiction and Westerns**

Special interest titles available in large print are:
**The Little Oxford Dictionary**
**Music Book**
**Song Book**
**Hymn Book**
**Service Book**

Also available from us courtesy of Oxford University Press:
**Young Readers' Dictionary**
**(large print edition)**
**Young Readers' Thesaurus**
**(large print edition)**

For further information or a free brochure, please contact us at:
**Ulverscroft Large Print Books Ltd.,**
**The Green, Bradgate Road, Anstey,**
**Leicester, LE7 7FU, England.**
**Tel:** (00 44) 0116 236 4325
**Fax:** (00 44) 0116 234 0205

*Other titles published by*
*The House of Ulverscroft:*

## PLAYING FOR KEEPS

### Sally Wragg

Generations of the Vernon family have been involved with Rislington Rovers Football Club, otherwise known as the Rogues. But now the Rogues are not only faced with relegation but also an ongoing investigation into the club's financial affairs. The mayhem within the club is matched only by the turmoil of Vernon family life. Eleanor Vernon, wife of Rogues stalwart Landon, hates the influence the game has on her family, but things are about to get much worse. The Rogues are seeking a new chief executive and the shock appointment threatens the very core of Vernon family life . . .

# MAGGIE'S GIRL

## Sally Wragg

1938. Maggie Bates, widowed for nine years and unaware of the explosive family secret threatening to tear her family apart, has returned to her roots. In the Derbyshire town of Castle Maine, the industrialist Silas Bradshaw still casts his giant shadow. But Maggie determines to leave her past behind and forge a new life for herself and her two children, Holly and Harry. Fuelled by a looming threat from across the channel, family tensions rise to boiling point, and the tangled web of lies surrounding Maggie's true parentage is in grave danger of unravelling with shattering consequences . . .

# BARBARA'S WAR

## Fenella J. Miller

As war rages over Europe, Barbara Sinclair is desperate to escape from her unhappy home, which is a target of the German Luftwaffe. Caught up by the emotion of the moment, she agrees to marry John, her childhood friend, who is leaving to join the RAF — but a meeting with Simon Farley, the son of a local industrialist, and an encounter with Alex Everton, a Spitfire pilot, complicate matters. With rationing, bombing and the constant threat of death all around her, Barbara must unravel the complexities of her home life and the difficulties of her emotional relationships in this gripping coming-of-age wartime drama.

# AN HONOURABLE ESTATE

## Elizabeth Ashworth

England, 1315. Famine and unrest are spreading across the country, and when Sir William Bradshaigh joins Adam Banastre's rebellion against their overlord, the Earl of Lancaster, things do not go to plan. Sir William is lucky to escape with his life after a battle at Preston and, as a wanted man, he has no choice but to become an outlaw. Meanwhile, the lands at Haigh are forfeit to the king, who gives them to Sir Peter Lymesey for a year and a day . . . while Lady Mabel Bradshaigh must make a hard choice if she is to protect her children and herself.